"I just wanted to say I'm sorry."

Never would Lane have believed she'd hear those words from Roy's mouth. It threw her. Set her off her game for a moment.

"You really need to throw again?" The question was a stall. She knew he wouldn't be here asking if he didn't need to throw. But this conversation gave her a moment to regroup.

"It's the only thing I know how to do." He shrugged. "The only thing I'm good for."

In a weird way she found herself missing the old Roy. Which made no sense at all. But since nothing in her life made sense right now, Lane figured this little episode was par for the course.

She had no job. She had no life. She had a father and a sister, who, although they may have betrayed her, did seem to need her.

And Roy. She had Roy. Roy Walker needed her and that was just about the craziest thing she could imagine happening today.

"Okay. I'll do it. Let's go see if we can turn your arm back into a rifle."

Dear Reader,

It's hard to know where to start to explain why I wanted to write a book about baseball. The first reason is my love of baseball movies. *Bull Durham*, *Major League*, *For Love of the Game*, *Field of Dreams*... Okay, my love might be more about Kevin Costner than the sport. Still, I do love those movies and wanted to pay homage to them in this series, The Bakers of Baseball.

I also happen to love the game. As a former season ticket holder, I've spent some great summer nights watching my team, and I wanted to join my love of the game with my love of writing.

This series starts off with Roy Walker, a once great pitcher who has lost his fortune and needs to start over in the minors. The problem is to get back to form he needs the help of the one woman who never wants to see him again. Honestly, at the beginning of this book I think the only thing Lane and Roy have in common is their love of baseball. Whether they figure the rest of it out...well, you'll have to read the story to see.

I love to hear from readers, so if you enjoy this story or just want to chat about the Phillies contact me at stephaniedoyle.net or send a Tweet to @StephDoyleRW.

Happy reading!

Stephanie Doyle

STEPHANIE DOYLE

The Comeback of Roy Walker

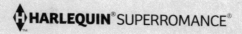

HARLEQUIN® SUPERROMANCE®

Recycling programs
for this product may
not exist in your area.

ISBN-13: 978-0-373-60900-0

The Comeback of Roy Walker

Copyright © 2015 by Stephanie Doyle

Printed in U.S.A.

Stephanie Doyle, a dedicated romance reader, began to pen her own romantic adventures at age sixteen. She began submitting to Harlequin at age eighteen and by twenty-six her first book was published. Fifteen years later she still loves what she does as each book is a new adventure. She lives in South Jersey with her cat, Hermione, the designated princess of the whole house. When Stephanie's not reading or writing, in the summer she is most likely watching a baseball game and eating a hot dog.

Books by Stephanie Doyle

HARLEQUIN SUPERROMANCE

The Way Back
One Final Step
An Act of Persuasion
For the First Time
Remembering That Night

SILHOUETTE ROMANTIC SUSPENSE

Suspect Lover
The Doctor's Deadly Affair

SILHOUETTE BOMBSHELL

Calculated Risk
The Contestant
Possessed

Visit the Author Profile page
at Harlequin.com for more titles

CHAPTER ONE

Five years ago

"GREAT PARTY, ROY!"

"Thanks," Roy said dismissively, nodding to some woman he didn't recognize.

Yes, it was a great party. Booze was flowing, food was plentiful. The music was loud and people were starting to dance. Any second now something would break and then he could call this party a true success. Not that he really cared one way or the other.

The invitation had come as surprise to many of his teammates. It was completely out of character for Roy to want to socialize with them outside of work let alone host a party with free booze and food. In fact, for many of the players this was the first time they had seen the inside of his apartment.

But everyone knew this was Roy Walker's last year on the team. It had been Roy's plan from the moment he stepped on the diamond to dictate when he stepped off for good. He always said he would go out on top and this season was it. His final farewell. And kicking it all off with a huge party before they got down to the grueling business of the one-hundred-and-sixty-two-game season seemed like the perfect idea. His colleagues no doubt thought that maybe, after all this time and with his career coming to an end, Roy Walker was finally starting to loosen up.

He wasn't.

"Roy, this is messed up!" Eddie Britton, the team's all-star second baseman, threw an arm around Roy's shoulder. This might be the first time a teammate had ever actually touched him outside of a fist bump or hand slap.

Roy was working on the assumption that *messed up* was a good thing. Mostly because Eddie was both drunk and smiling.

"I'm glad you're having a good time."

"Dude, free booze and food? Of course I'm having a good time. You should have done this years ago, man. People might have actually liked you." Eddie shook his head. "Now you're almost done."

Roy didn't take offense to the insinuations that no one liked him and that the only way he might have been liked was if he'd been supplying free food and alcohol to his teammates on a more regular basis. Eddie was probably right.

"Well, better late than never," Roy muttered. Not that this party was about making friends. There was only one objective for having all these people in his place.

"Speaking of friends, where is your girl? She's coming, right?"

His girl. Just the thought of those two words together made the muscles in his stomach go tight.

"I don't know who— I'm not dating anyone—"

"No, man. I mean, your *girl*! Or should I say, Danny's girl, who you wish was your girl." Eddie clearly thought that was hysterical.

Roy clenched his jaw. Had he been that obvious? So obvious that even the other guys on the team knew?

"I've got to check the beer supply," Roy said, rather than address that issue.

"That's cool," Eddie said, not upset by the brush-off. He stumbled away to take a dive into a couch where a bunch of baseball bunnies had congregated.

Danny's girl.

Maybe not for long, Roy thought. Not if everything went according to plan. This whole party was nothing more than a charade designed to do something he felt he needed to do. Before he retired.

Yes, after careful consideration Roy had made a decision about one person's need to know the truth. So he'd formulated a means to reveal it—a big social gathering to bring everything to light. It was meant to be a grand gesture.

This might not be a good idea.

He shook his head. It was too late. The wheels were already in motion. Both Lane and her husband, Danny, were on their way.

Only not together.

"Is this a bring-your-wife party?" Danny had asked.

"Are you kidding?" Roy snickered. "I want everyone to have fun. Bring whoever you like. But there will plenty of female fans in attendance…if you know what I mean."

Roy recalled the conversation with a heavy sense of dread in his stomach. What he was doing to Danny Worth was wrong. Maybe even cruel. Roy was deliberately setting him up and he was doing so for one reason and one reason only.

Lane Baker Worth deserved better. The daughter of the legendary Duff Baker, a Hall-of-Fame baseball player and manager, Lane was, to Roy, the princess of baseball. Yet, she'd married Danny Worth*less*. Roy would never understand what she'd been thinking. Maybe if he'd known her back then, he could have stopped it. Certainly her family should have stepped in to avoid the travesty of Lane and Danny's union.

Roy knew they had been young. Dating when they were nineteen, married at twenty-two. Hell, she was still young now at twenty-six, which was why Roy knew she didn't have to spend the rest of her life with Danny Worthless. If only she could see him for what he was, she could get out and start over with someone else.

Someone like Roy.

He didn't like to admit that was his end goal. It made the motivation for this party seem much less noble and infinitely more Machiavellian. He didn't kid himself to think that just because her marriage to Danny might end, she would suddenly see Roy standing in front of her with open arms.

Maybe because you hit on her the first time you met her.

Roy winced at the memory.

Even with her shiny new diamond engagement ring on her left hand she hadn't been safe from his come-on, although, to be fair, he hadn't been all that serious about it. Hitting on the other players' girls was something he did—Roy's personal vetting process for the women who dated his teammates, to see where their actual loyalties fell. Were they with the ballplayers because of who they were as men? Or were they baseball bunnies looking for fame and fortune and any player would suffice?

In a way, it was a matter of self-protection. Roy had been hit on by too many wives who wanted to climb the baseball hierarchy. Leaving their husbands to attach themselves to the next highest rung.

The best. Roy Walker.

Once he knew which category the women belonged to, he knew which ones to avoid.

So the come-on to Lane had been a test. In a bar filled with Washington Founders players, her fiancé included, Roy had asked her if she wanted to get together sometime. Just the two of them. To discuss…baseball.

A perfectly harmless invitation that Roy and Lane both knew wasn't harmless. Only by the time he asked the question he already knew Lane wasn't the type of woman who jumped from one player to the next. There was something too open about her to be that type. So when he made his pass he expected outrage and fury.

Instead she'd laughed at him. Actually laughed at him. Head back, full-on hysterical laughter.

"Seriously?" she'd said. "Are you kidding me? What are you trying to prove? That you're some badass who can have any woman he wants? From what I've seen so far you're sullen and brooding. Barely civil to your teammates. Hate to break it to you, Roy, but that doesn't make you badass and mysterious. It makes you sad and alone. I wonder if you know what love is. Even if I wasn't engaged, someone like you wouldn't get to have someone like me."

In a sort of crazy twist, in that moment when she'd been telling him how pathetic he was, he'd come to admire her. He could see how right she was—someone like him would never be worthy of someone as open and giving as her. He'd spent every day since then trying to establish…what?

He didn't know if it was a friendship between them. He didn't know if she took their small connection that seriously. And it was a small connection. A couple of words exchanged outside the locker room when she waited for Danny after a game. A hot dog or two at some out-of-the-way place he tracked down because he knew she loved them. Some mocking banter where she would call him out for being an ass.

That connection, of course, was fueled by the fact that he needed her. Desperately.

Lane Baker Worth was a miracle worker when it came to physical therapy. She called her specialty kinesiology, but Roy called it woo-woo medicine. Some magic she was able to perform with her hands and her fingers by applying pressure to certain spots of his body that allowed for greater blood flow and a decrease in inflammation.

It wasn't traditional, but it worked. Any athlete who wanted to avoid the drugs and sometimes even surgery sought out her services. She was the hardest appointment to get in DC. Athletes from all over the country would fly to see her for a couple of hours of work.

Danny Worthless had that gift every night if he wanted it. Danny Worthless had *her*. Her spirit, her smile, her love of the game.

It wasn't right. And Roy had finally decided it couldn't continue.

The doorbell rang and, despite the loud music, he heard it as if it was a special sound sent out over a frequency meant only for him.

Danny was on his way. Roy had gone so far as to text him that he had some girls here who really wanted to meet the Founders' shortstop. Danny texted back that he already had some company and would be there soon.

All Roy needed was the second actor in this play.

He opened the door and Lane smiled at him. Half sincere, half suspicious. It was always like that with her. As if she was afraid there was some prank he had set up that she'd step into or some joke he would make her the butt of.

Probably very smart of her.

"You came." Which made him irrationally happy. Crazy, considering what he planned for that night.

"You said I had to," she reminded him. "Or I would be, quote, 'the biggest loser who ever lived.'"

Roy smiled. "Clearly you have self-esteem issues if you thought you had to prove me wrong."

Of course she didn't. No one in the world knew who she was as well as Lanie did. That's what made her so damn compelling. She didn't play games. She didn't manipulate or strategize to get what she wanted. She was always simply who she was.

Unlike Roy, who frequently didn't have a clue

about himself outside of being someone who could throw a ball.

No, Lane definitely hadn't hunted down Danny as trophy-husband material the way so many of the other wives had. She hadn't pursued him like he was some prize to be won. Like baseball players were nothing beyond their gloves and hats and bats. And money. No, Danny had had to win Lane.

It's what made her different from the women currently in Roy's penthouse, drinking his liquor and shaking their well-toned, surgically enhanced bodies. Doing everything they could to attract attention. Hoping some player would notice them and set them up for life.

Roy saw nobody but Lane. Every damn time she was in the room.

"Well, Danny's not getting back in until tomorrow. Decided he needed one last golf game in Florida before the season starts next week. So I thought, what the hell."

A lie. Danny had been in town for two days. He was just spending his nights somewhere else. With *someone* else if his text was to be believed.

That should be enough, Roy thought. Enough to end it.

All Lane had to do was stay until Danny walked through the door with whomever on his arm. That alone should be enough to end their marriage. Lane wasn't a person to tolerate disloyalty.

Roy had no idea who the woman in question would be. Danny went through groupies like toilet paper. An easy thing to do when you were on the road for eighty-one nights of the season. It wasn't as if he even tried to hide his behavior from anyone. As if he expected everyone to understand that when they were home, Lane drove him to every game, watched every play of every inning and then took him home when it was over.

When Danny was on the road those tasks were done by some other woman.

Of course the guys didn't say anything. The locker-room bond was tight. It had to be to win championships. And this was a championship-caliber team, having already won two World Series and coming close again last year.

So no one talked. None of the players talked to their wives. Or if they did, none of the wives talked to Lane. They all sat back and observed. As if it was entertainment to watch a dumb-ass twenty-six-year-old kid, who happened to have been gifted with athletic talent, shit on the princess of baseball. Night in and night out.

Roy was done with it. When Lane had worked on his neck and shoulder recently he thought he could sense something in her. A sense that she wasn't happy, and rather...lonely.

Not that she would ever confide in Roy about her marriage. He was the man who didn't know what love was. How hard would it be for someone so proud to admit she was wrong about it, too?

Which is why he decided he had to help her. Save her, really. She didn't want to admit she'd picked the wrong guy. Understandable. No one wanted to admit their mistakes. Fine. He'd simply force her hand.

In front of the whole damn team.

"Uh, you going to invite me in?"

Roy realized she was still standing in the corridor. He thought of some of the women he'd invited. Thought of the other nonwives who had come with some of the married players.

Hell, he thought of the women he'd paid to be here. Backups to zero in on Danny if he didn't show up with someone else.

Lane would see it all. Instantly.

No. Suddenly, he didn't want to invite her in.

This is stupid. A mistake. She doesn't deserve this.

"Look, you can't change your mind now. I'm here, I'm thirsty and, if I have enough drinks, I might even dance."

Not waiting for his answer, she bounced around him and he had to move to let her in or risk her pushing him out of the way.

"At least let me walk you to where you can put your coat down," he said quickly, taking her arm. He needed to shield her from the party. They walked the long hallway from his oversize living room into a series of guest rooms. He didn't think. Just led her into his bedroom and closed the door.

Shit. You screwed this up. She is going to see all those guys not *with their wives. She is going to see Danny* not *with her. This is going to hurt her.*

Roy wanted to open her eyes to the truth. He wanted her to leave her worthless husband. He didn't want to destroy her faith. Not in love. Not when it was so damn pure.

"Lane, I screwed up."

Her eyes widened. "Wow. Did you just admit you did something wrong?"

He nodded.

"Because the Roy Walker I know doesn't do that."

"I get it. You think I'm an arrogant ass."

She smiled softly. "I don't think it, Roy. You *are*. But I realize it's a little, very little, part of your charm."

Damn, she was actually smiling at him. In fact, she'd been treating him differently since he'd helped her father by doing a charity stint at the Minotaur Falls Opening Day Fair. Danny had been away on another one of his "trips" and someone needed to raise money for the Youth Athletic League. Roy offered his services in exchange for a few therapy sessions.

A few hours in the dunk tank and suddenly Lane

had seen something in him that she hadn't seen before. Maybe it was that she'd learned it wasn't true that Roy didn't do any charity work ever—a reputation he had fostered along with his ass persona. He just didn't make a big show of his charitable work like so many of the other guys on the team. Which is why he never said anything about the equipment and uniforms he donated.

Only Duff had made a point of thanking him for the stuff in front of Lane.

Which meant his secret was out. He wasn't quite the selfish, arrogant ass he'd always presented himself as. It must have been difficult, after years of thinking he was a pathetic scumbag, for her to realize he was a better man than he let on.

The truth was he never really cared what other people thought. With Lanie, though, it mattered.

Only now he was about to prove her shiny new opinions wrong. Really, really wrong.

"Lane, I would like you to leave."

"What?"

"This party…I don't think…you're going to like it. It's getting a little out of hand. Not your kind of thing. I'm not sure what I was thinking asking you to come."

How far away was Danny? Hopefully twenty minutes. Maybe thirty. Roy should be able to get Lane away before Danny got here.

"What's the matter? Afraid I'm not hot enough to

compete with all the eye candy out there. I saw how some of those girls are dressed. The ones dancing on your coffee table. By the way, those heels will leave scratches. I know I don't compare."

She didn't compare. They were nothing. She was everything. But Lane Baker wasn't the type to worry about the other girls in the room. She was still smiling as if she found the whole thing funny.

She shucked her coat and he could see she wasn't totally unaware of what type of party he might throw. Dark, skinny jeans, high-heel boots up to her knees, a silver blouse that showed way too much cleavage, in his opinion, but was conservative in comparison to what the other women were wearing. Or not wearing.

"Look, Roy, I've been around enough baseball bunnies to hold my own. I've been cooped up all winter, mostly by myself, and I'm looking to… I just want to have a little fun. You know? I promise, if I see the other players getting a little handsy with the bunnies, I won't say a thing. I took a cab so I can get my drink on and unwind."

She walked toward him, but he still had his back to the door, shutting out the party. Shutting her in.

"Let's get out of here, then. I'll take you someplace else. You can get your drink on there and I'll make sure you get home safely."

She blinked at him. "You're going to leave your own party?"

"Yeah. Why not?"

She huffed, her hands on her hips, and shook her head like he'd exasperated her again. He did that to her a lot it seemed.

"Roy, I thought the whole point of this party was for you to make a new start with the team. Get to know them for a change. You said this might be your last season."

"It *is* my last season." There was no negotiating that. One more year, then he was done. Thirty-two years of age, the best in the game right now. This was how he was leaving baseball. On his terms.

"I figured you wanted to do something different. Get along with the guys."

"Why? I'm leaving. It's not like I've ever been friends with them before."

She rolled her eyes. "Then why throw this big party?"

He couldn't tell her truth. "As a going-away thing, I guess. But I don't expect anything to change in the locker room."

Where he had his bench, his locker, his privacy. No one bothered him beyond an occasional "Hey, man, you got an extra bar of soap?" It was his thing. Roy Walker, loner.

"Roy." She sighed. "You don't always have to be alone, you know. If you just let people in a little, you'll see we're not all bad."

"You want in?" he asked, his voice suddenly rough with truth. "I'll let *you* in."

He could see her expression change. Like she understood what he was offering. More than he'd ever offered any woman before. A good thing, then. Lane would get angry at the suggestion he wanted something more from her. She might slap him. Certainly she would storm out the front door in indignation.

How long until Danny got here? Ten minutes? Maybe he would blow off the party completely. Happy with the company he was with currently.

"You know it can't be me," she said tightly. She clasped her hands together. Didn't look at him. "I'm married."

And there it was. So obvious, so bald it almost made him gasp. She'd said the words like a death knell. Like she was trapped in a cage with no escape. It was his mission to save her.

"Get unmarried."

She jerked then, as if he'd hit her. When she looked at him, the tears in her eyes almost broke his heart.

"I can't. I can't fail. Duff wouldn't—"

"Duff would understand. He loves you. He would support you no matter what."

"You don't get it." She shook her head, her hair brushed her cheek. A cheek he so badly wanted to touch because it couldn't be as soft as he imagined. Nothing could, right?

"Then tell me."

"When Duff lost Mom he made us all promise we would try harder. That if we married, we wouldn't make the same mistakes he made. That we would find a way to be happy. Danny and I...we can be happy. Again. I have to believe that. I have to."

Roy pushed away from the door and advanced on her. He watched her, waiting to see what she would do, but she didn't move. Until he was close, so close their thighs were nearly touching.

"What if there is something else? Someone else."

She put her hand on his chest. She wasn't pushing him away, but it was her signal to stop. So he waited and just breathed her in.

"I can't..."

"I can." Without another word his head dropped and his mouth was on hers. And it was like no kiss he'd ever felt before. Not even his first. This was the thing he wanted. For so long and he hadn't even realized it. Now she was here, and he was kissing her and—

"No!" She backed up, almost stumbling to get away from him. "This is not who I am."

"Lanie, I know that." God, how he knew that. Her loyalty was unquestionable. But she had to see that with Danny, it was undeserved.

If she gave it to Roy, if he could have it, he would revere it and never betray it.

"Don't call me Lanie," she said. "You can't call me Lanie and you can't… I shouldn't have come. This was a mistake."

"Lane, I'm sorry." Roy ran a hand through his hair. This wasn't how it was supposed to play out. He was supposed to be saving her. Not taking her. "I didn't mean for this to happen. I know you would never do that to him. But you have to know though this wasn't some half-assed pass. Tell me you know that. At least give me that."

She stared at him and he hid nothing from her. She might as well see it. Might as well know what she meant to him. What all those conversations and outings together had meant to him.

Everything.

"I need to leave." She grabbed her coat and he didn't stop her. After all, wasn't this what he wanted. Her storming out before Danny got here?

Only it was too late.

She opened the door and on the other side was her husband. Who had a woman with long blond hair, wearing a halter dress and stiletto heels, pressed against the wall. His hand was on her breast, his tongue was in her mouth and he was grinding against her.

He stopped kissing the woman. "Dude, we're going to need your room for an hour."

Then Danny turned his head, saw his wife and the expletive that fell from his mouth was totally accurate.

"Lane, what the hell? Dude," Danny shouted at Roy, "you said no wives!"

As this weird buzzing noise filled his head, Roy tried to think through what was happening. The crazy thing was he really hadn't expected the plan to work so well. Here he was, this grown man, not some actor in a soap opera, who had devised a nefarious plot. It should have completely backfired.

Only nope. It had worked to absolute freaking perfection. Which, of course, meant that it really did backfire.

Lane faced Roy. Not her cheating husband. *Roy.* "You knew he was coming? You knew he was coming with someone?" Her voice had a raw, harsh quality he'd never heard from her before.

Since it was hard to form words while his head still buzzed, he simply nodded.

"You did this? To me? On purpose? I thought—I thought we were…friends."

Friends. She thought they were friends. She cared about him at least that much.

He'd had that and now he'd lost it. He could see it in her face.

"You bastard."

The word hit as if she'd stabbed him in the gut. Yes, he'd done this on purpose. He'd humiliated and inflicted pain upon the only woman he thought could ever really matter to him.

Roy held up his hands as if to remind her she knew what an ass he could be.

He could see her shake as she approached him and he kept his hands down, opened himself to whatever she would say next.

She slapped him. Hard, across his cheek. As punishment, it wasn't enough. Not nearly enough.

"I hate you for this. I hate you, Roy Walker."

Then she walked past Danny and his flavor of the moment without so much as a word.

ROY LATER LEARNED that Lane moved out of her home that night. She and Danny were divorced six months later. The Founders' season collapsed as the locker room never got over the pure hatred the star pitcher and shortstop felt for each other. And Lanie left her sports therapy business, putting the world of professional baseball behind her.

Roy heard she'd taken a job working at a veterans rehab facility. Helping soldiers with missing limbs adjust to their prosthetics. Sounded like something Lanie would choose to do.

At the start of his final game in baseball, Roy focused on doing what he'd promised himself he would. Go out on top.

And he did. Pitched a "no-no." No hits. Only one walk. It wasn't for the playoffs, or for the World

Series win. Just the end of a lousy season, but a great career.

In his heart Roy knew he did it for her. The princess of baseball deserved such a tribute. Even though he doubted she watched.

After, he changed out of his uniform, got into his car and drove away from the stadium and the game that had been his life since he was six years old.

It was time to start a new life. Maybe in this new life he could forget Lanie Baker ever existed. The way she had so obviously done with him. He'd written her a letter to try to explain why he'd done it and, more importantly, that he was sorry.

He never heard from her.

Yes, it was definitely time to move on and forget his princess. After all, everyone knew the villain didn't get the princess. Only the hero did. And Roy was never the hero.

CHAPTER TWO

A few months ago

"You're broke."

Roy looked at his accountant and blinked. Frank's face remained unchanged and entirely serious.

Roy knew the news would be bad. But not this bad. "That can't be right."

"You chose not to file for bankruptcy," Frank reminded him. "I told you to."

Stubbornly, Roy had refused. Bankruptcy had seemed like the coward's way out. He'd taken the products from his vendors in good faith and he was a man who paid his debts. All of them. This meeting today was to discuss what was left.

Apparently not much.

"Look, you still have a few assets you can sell to get you a little more liquid until you get back on your feet. Your father's house—"

"Not an option."

Frank sighed. "Right. Your town house, then."

"Great. I can sell that."

"That will take some time. It's November, not

the greatest season to move real estate. What about your ex-fiancée's thirty-thousand-dollar engagement ring?"

"Also not an option."

Frank shook his head. "In today's world it's custom to give the ring back, regardless of who broke it off."

Maybe, but Shannon hadn't offered and Roy couldn't ask for it. He'd met Shannon a few years into his new life and they had dated for nearly a year before deciding to get married. He'd tried, he really had, to make the long-term commitment work. But eventually he'd admitted to himself marriage wasn't in the cards so he ended it.

Six weeks before the wedding.

What he'd done to her—led her on, let her plan a big, public wedding—was wrong and if she took some consolation from an expensive ring, she was welcome to it.

But that decision seemed to kick off his entire life coming down on him like a ton of bricks. After he ended the engagement, his developers told him the coding logic in Roy's new high-tech gaming system, SportsNation, was faulty and would not be ready for their scheduled major launch. All the money they had poured into publicity, including print, radio and television, essentially gone as they had to push back the release date again and again.

By the time they got it working, there was

another—better—product on the market. Eventually Roy's company did launch the system, but it was too little too late. The company in which he'd invested every dime, every ounce of energy, for the past five years had failed.

Now he was broke.

He was thirty-seven, just beginning what was supposed to be the second half of his life. And it was over after five measly years.

Roy leaned back in his chair, looking at the stack of papers on the older man's desk. Roy's life had been reduced to overdue notices and collection letters. When all was said and done, there was nothing left but the loose change in his couch.

"What about advertising? You know, do a few commercials for some local auto dealer. They love that stuff. Or ESPN? You could become one of those baseball color commentators."

Roy knew Frank was trying to help, just like he'd given him sound advice about the bankruptcy option. But Roy didn't want to go back to any part of baseball. He sure as hell didn't have the personality for television. And given his nonrelationship with about everyone associated with MLB, he was fairly sure no one would be standing in line to do him any favors. The type of job offers players got after they retired were based on the connections they made while they were still playing.

Roy hadn't made any friends, let alone connections. He pitched. He pitched better than anyone. That's what he did.

Even if he could find a way to work up the enthusiasm to sell some product, advertisers wanted someone relevant. Roy hadn't been that in five years. Maybe after he was inducted into the Hall of Fame he would be, but not now.

"You could get a job. What kind of skills do you have?"

"I throw a mean sinking cutter."

"Look, you've got some cash. Maybe it's enough to get you through until you sell your house. If you've got some fancy watches or something…"

Roy shook his head. All of it, every last thing, had gone into the company. He drove a ten-year-old Jeep and his last investment in himself had been a five-dollar haircut. There was nothing to sell.

"What about some of your old baseball stuff? You hardly ever gave any of that away. I'll bet that might fetch you some bucks to hold you over."

Hold him over until what? The town house was in a nice area of Philadelphia, the city he'd chosen to establish his business, but it wouldn't set him up for life. It might provide some seed money to invest in a new company, but what kind of lenders would take a chance on him again?

He'd seen it in the faces around him at the end. From the people who worked for him and the people to whom he owed money. Roy Walker was a great pitcher but he didn't know much about building a successful company.

A vision of him selling used cars to men who shook his hand and said, "Hey, weren't you that pitcher?" flashed in front of his eyes.

"So what about it? You got a few gloves or something?"

Yes. He had gloves and jerseys and his Cy Young Award trophies. Next year was his first year of eligibility for Hall-of-Fame contention. Many considered him a first ballot shoo-in. He could see the headlines now: Roy Walker, HOF Pitcher, Now Failed Businessman, Desperate for Money, Sells His Gloves.

He was pathetic.

"Of course…there is the alternative. I mean, you're only thirty-seven. Who knows how many bullets you have left in that arm? You could go back to baseball, sign on with some team for a year, make a ridiculous amount of money and then start all over again."

Start all over again. Back to baseball. Those two things shouldn't be synonymous. There had to be other choices.

Because Roy was never going back to baseball.

Present day

ROY DROVE THROUGH the winding streets of the small town of Minotaur Falls, New York, with a sick feeling of dread in his stomach. The sick feeling had become fairly familiar to him. It had started when he'd learned he was broke and had pretty much continued ever since. All through November, when Frank had been proven right about the real-estate market being dead. All through December, when Roy had actually put together a résumé and started applying for jobs.

He'd been on three interviews. Two had been just baseball fans who wanted to the meet the legendary Roy Walker. Of course, since he didn't have any actual skills, he wasn't a fit for the company, but it sure was great to meet him. The third had been a nice older woman who knew nothing about baseball, but also told him that without a college degree or any real work experience he wasn't qualified for the position. Again.

Roy had tried to explain to her that he'd once been famous and a multimillionaire.

That hadn't swayed her.

He had considered going back to school. The money he could make from the sale of his town house would cover his tuition. But the idea of being a freshman at thirty-seven was even worse than the idea of baseball.

Which was what everything kept coming back to. Roy would look at his left arm and think if he could get back into shape, if he could get his velocity to

where it had been, all he might need was one season. One contract.

"Is there anything left in you?" he would ask
his arm.

Is there anything left in you? he imagined it asking him back.

Finally, he'd done the unthinkable and called his
former agent. Charlie Lynn had taken his call immediately, which made Roy feel marginally better.
Charlie loved the idea of a Roy Walker comeback.

Hell, Nolan Ryan pitched until he was forty-six.
Mariano Rivera pitched until he was forty-three.
It wasn't unthinkable. There was only one catch.

Can you still throw?

Of course Charlie had to ask the question. Roy
told him the truth. He didn't know. He hadn't put
his arm through any kind of workout since leaving
baseball. Which meant Roy was going to have to
find some minor-league team who might take him
on to see if he still had the goods.

Charlie started talking about bonus options if he
made the team and incentive clauses for a multiple-
year option.

All the familiar phrases and terms came back to
Roy like he hadn't been away for five years. Over
the course of his professional life he'd earned eighty
million dollars with Charlie as his agent.

Eighty million dollars gone. Because he'd put his
faith in some programmers who ultimately couldn't

deliver on what they promised and he'd been too stupid and stubborn to realize that until it was too late.

Charlie told Roy to find someone he could trust. A place he could go with baseball people who would give him a workout but who wouldn't be squawking to the sports reporters about what Roy was doing. They needed to establish if his arm still had the juice and what role he might play on a team. Maybe he couldn't be a starter, Charlie mused, but with Roy's sinking cutter, he might have closer potential. In baseball the only person who had the potential to make as much money as a starting pitcher was a lights-out closer.

One or two years playing, maybe an eight-million-dollar contract, and Roy could start over again.

Only this time he would do everything differently.

Roy shook his head. No, he couldn't see that far ahead. He'd already failed once, so he couldn't imagine having the confidence to try some other new business venture. Which meant he should stick to what he knew he could do. What he'd always done.

Throw a ball.

A ridiculous gift, really, that might set him up for life. Again.

Roy pulled up to the Minotaur Falls stadium,

home of the Triple-A minor-league team for the New England Rebels. Minotaur Falls was also the home of the legendary Duff Baker.

Duff Baker, the only person in baseball Roy thought he might be able to trust. Duff had won four World Series titles as the manager of three different teams. Two of them with Roy. It was a remarkable accomplishment because it meant he could reach the top with different groups of players. That was because Duff had a better eye for talent than anyone in the game.

He had walked away from managing professional teams about eight years ago, but he hadn't been able to leave the game entirely. Some might call being manager of a minor-league team a step down, but Duff just called it retirement.

Roy had phoned his former manager and asked if he could meet with him and if they could keep it private. Roy hadn't given him a reason or any information, really.

That the old man hadn't hesitated to say yes humbled Roy in so many ways.

Duff had been Roy's first manager when he'd made it to The Show. Roy had been as cocky then as he had been through the rest of his career. In hindsight he could see what a handful he must have been to his manager. He used to shrug off bunting advice from the old man like what he was selling was old news. Duff had had every right to punch the upstart Roy had been, but he never did. Instead Duff just kept proving how his way worked until eventually Roy figured it out.

He'd been sad when Duff left the team. It was the first time Roy had ever felt any emotions for one of his coaches.

Excluding his first, of course. His dad.

Roy got out of the Jeep, grabbed his equipment bag, which still smelled like his basement, and hiked it over his shoulder. He hesitated before taking that first step, though.

It wasn't the physical element of the game that bothered him. Either his arm could still do what it used to do or it couldn't. There wouldn't be much getting around that.

It was everything else.

Every failure out on full display, when he would have to tell Duff why he was here.

Well, not every failure. Roy didn't plan to discuss the time he humiliated and hurt Duff's daughter. That, Roy figured, he could keep in his pocket.

Lane Baker.

Hell, there would probably be a picture of her on Duff's desk. Roy would have to brace for that. Maybe even a new wedding photo. Five years since the divorce, it almost seemed likely she would have moved on with her life.

Damn, that was going to hurt.

Don't think about it. There was no backing down.

He'd turned his life into this heaping pile of dung on purpose and now it was time to face the music.

Roy made his way through the stadium entrance to the second level, where the team's offices were. Nothing fancy about minor-league security, so he was able to go wherever he wanted. He found a door labeled Private and Manager and knocked.

"Come in!"

It was a female voice who made the offer. For a second, Roy paused again. No, Lane couldn't be here. She was in Virginia Beach last he heard. Helping wounded soldiers. Doing everything right, while he'd been doing everything wrong.

Roy put his internal pity party on hold and opened the door.

The woman standing in the office did remind him of Lane. Long hair tied into a ponytail, face devoid of makeup, wearing a heavy plaid shirt that might have belonged to a man at one point.

She stared at him for a good second. "You're Roy Walker."

"Yep."

"My sister hates you."

Not that he needed further confirmation of who the woman was, but her statement gave her away. Scout was Lanie's younger sister. They also had an older sister, Samantha, who was known as one of the most cutthroat agents in the game, but everyone knew she and Duff weren't close.

Scout was the opposite of Samantha. Where Duff was, Scout was.

"Yep," Roy said again.

"You're here to see Duff?"

The Baker girls called their father Duff. It was something Lane had told him about once while working on his shoulder with her voodoo physical therapy. Their mother had claimed that, because he was gone for so much of the year, they couldn't legitimately call him a father. So they were to call him Duff.

Not hard to see why that marriage hadn't worked out.

Which was part of why Lane had been so devastated when hers had ended.

Do not go there. Back to baseball, okay. But not back to Lane Baker.

"I have an appointment," he said.

Scout tilted her head and eyed him as if he was a suspect in a criminal case. "He didn't tell me. He tells me everything."

"I asked him to keep this private."

She assessed him and he had a hard time trying not to think about Lane. Lane was prettier than Scout. Softer around the edges where Scout was all sharp lines. Cheeks and chin. Still, it was easy to see they were sisters. They both had the same honey-wheat-colored hair with green eyes. A similar shrewdness in those eyes.

And honesty, with no thought of pretense.

"You're here to see your first major-league manager. The man who led you to your first epic World Series win. You're carrying an equipment bag that smells a little moldy and you look like you're going to vomit if you breathe in that smell too deeply, which makes me think you're nervous."

"Hey, Sherlock, give it a rest. I need to talk to Duff."

"Damn, I'm good. Roy Walker is here for a tryout."

"It's not really a tryout," he mumbled. "More like an assessment. And I would appreciate it, if you didn't tell anyone—"

Scout held her hand up. "Please. My father wants it private, it stays private. But you have to let me tell Lane. She's going to die."

Please, please don't tell Lane. Don't let her know what a complete and total failure I turned out to be. In...everything.

"I doubt she would care," he said trying for nonchalance. "Like you said, she hates me."

"Yes, that's what she always said. All the time. 'Roy Walker, Roy Walker, how I hate Roy Walker.' Funny she never mentioned anyone she liked as much as she talked about hating you."

Roy really didn't know what to do with that.

"Let me go wake him up. He pretends he's watching scouting footage after lunch but he actually just puts a headset on and takes a nap."

Roy waited while Scout went into the inner office to wake her father. After a few minutes she came back wearing a grim expression but giving a solid nod. "He's ready for you."

"Thanks. Hey, you mean it, right? You won't tell anyone I'm here."

"I mean it."

Roy nodded. He didn't question her word.

"I won't even tell Lane. That is, if don't want me to. Do you want me to?"

He struggled to get the words out because he knew they would reveal too much about how he felt about Lane. But the consequences of Lane knowing how hard he had fallen were worse in his mind.

"I would prefer it if you didn't."

After all, what if he failed at this, too?

"Sure."

He summoned a smile and walked past her. Duff was slow getting to his feet and Roy's first thought was wow, Duff had aged. Thinner, his face drawn, his hair a bit wild around his head, probably from his afternoon nap.

"Duff, you're looking good."

The old man coughed up a laugh. "Ha. Liar. I look like shit. Which is appropriate because I feel like shit. That's what happens when you get to seventy-five. You only hope you feel as shitty as me when you get to my age."

Slowly Duff walked around the desk and Roy jumped to meet him halfway and shook his hand.

"Gotta tell you, you don't look so great yourself, Walker. You look…defeated, and that sure as hell is a look I never thought I would see on you."

Defeated.

"That about sums it up," Roy said, not hiding anything from Duff. "I sank all my money into a video gaming company that went under. I was too stubborn to file for bankruptcy so I paid everyone off and now I'm broke. Really broke. I don't have a college degree and the only thing I can put on my résumé is a failed start-up company. So I'm here hoping I have enough bullets in this arm to earn me enough money to try again."

Duff nodded like it was a story he heard every day. "Why me?"

"I've got to find out if I can still throw. Before Charlie can put it out there that I'm looking for a team. I needed someone I can trust. Both to tell me the truth and to not announce it to ESPN that I'm trying to make a comeback."

"How long has it been? Since you launched the rocket?"

"Five years. Since the no-no in San Diego."

Duff let out a small grunt. "What kind of shape are you in otherwise?"

"I still run. Twenty miles a week. Still work out with weights. Physically, I feel good. In fact, my arm feels great."

"Well, let's go change that."

ROY, DUFF AND SCOUT made their way to the field.

"You'll start with throwing on grass before you take the mound," Scout said, walking into the dugout and coming back with a ball, a catcher's glove and a mask.

"Okay, wait," Roy said, wondering if she actually expected him to throw to her. "It may have been five years, but my velocity still has to be pretty high."

"Relax, slugger, this isn't some scene from *Bull Durham*. I called Javier, who lives close by. He'll come and catch for you. Also he's a recent immigrant from El Salvador so he will have no idea who the heck you are and, even if he did, none of the sports reporters in town speak Spanish."

At that moment, a young man with a round face emerged from the dugout. Scout spoke to him in Spanish and he took the catcher's mitt and dropped to his haunches near home plate.

Roy stood in front of the mound on flat grass and gripped the ball in his hand. Like an old muscle memory waking up, he remembered the shape of the ball, the weight of it and how to hold it just so. There had been a time when the baseball had felt like a natural extension of his left arm. Like it had been grafted to his fingers with the thread of the seams.

He would hurl it as hard as he could, but those threads would retract and the ball would always come back.

When he threw it for the last time he told himself he would never pick up a baseball again. He used to tell himself that if he ever got married and had a kid he'd make sure his kid was into football or soccer. Anything but baseball. That's how much he'd wanted to move away from the game.

Funny, now it didn't seem so bad. He could admit, for the first time, that maybe he'd missed it. The grass on the field—although this field was mostly brown after a hard winter. The shape of the diamond. The sight of a masked man crouching sixty feet away waiting to catch whatever Roy threw at him.

"Keep it simple to start," Duff called out. "Fastball."

Roy nodded and he could see Scout had a radar gun pointed at him ready to record his velocity.

His throat tightened and his hand flexed around the ball. "Don't time me yet. Let me get a few in first."

Scout nodded and put the gun down.

Then Roy went through his motions—forward lean, left arm dangle, pull up, plant foot and fire.

He heard the snap of the ball hitting Javier's glove. It sounded pretty fast. Javier tossed back the ball and Roy did it again. After his third warm-up he nodded in Scout's direction. She held up the gun and he fired.

"Eighty-six!"

Roy held his glove up, asking for the ball. Eighty-six wasn't fast. His fastest had been ninety-two, ninety-three miles an hour. But eighty-six after not throwing for a few years was…workable.

"Try a curve," Duff suggested.

Roy changed the position of the ball in his hand and threw. It curved. It wasn't his killer curve, but, again, it was something to work with. He threw over and over. All of his old pitches, even the changeup, just to test that speed. Every fastball got a little faster, every curve a little curvier.

They worked him for an hour and when it was over, his body was covered in sweat and his arm hurt like hell. But he knew. He knew what they knew.

"You can still pitch, Roy Walker," Scout said, patting him on his right shoulder. Duff kept his hands in his jeans pockets and nodded his agreement.

"The New England Rebels are looking for pitching," Duff said. "Might be willing to offer you a minor-league deal to see if you can get your conditioning and timing up to speed. I'm thinking in a starting role, too, to build your stamina. It's a lot of ifs, but if we can get you back into form, if you don't blow out your arm while doing it, it might be perfect timing for the Rebels, heck, any team, looking to add to their rotation after the all-star break in July."

Roy nodded. "You really think the Rebels will give me a chance?"

"I don't," Scout told him bluntly. "No one will take a chance on what might be. You can still pitch, but you are nowhere near major-league ready. Plus you're old. Sorry to be so blunt but—"

"No, I appreciate it. I...need it."

Duff sighed. "They'll take a chance. They'll take a chance if I tell them to. Call Charlie, tell him to call Russell. He's the Rebels' new general manager. I'll let Russell know what's coming and what I saw. In the meantime, Roy Walker, you'll fill a hell of a lot of seats in this stadium and that's something that will make our owner very happy. I sure do like to make JoJo happy."

"You might want to start by not calling her JoJo," Scout said. "She hates it."

Duff scowled. "No, she loves it coming from me."

Roy tuned them out and focused only on what might be. The minors. Roy Walker, future Hall of Famer, was back in the minors.

Still, it was a start.

They walked off the field and Roy gave his

thanks to Javier. Something he might not have cared about before. But the guy had come on his own time to help Roy and the least he deserved was a thank-you.

"You good pitch."

Roy smiled. "Thanks. *Gracias*. See you around, maybe."

With that, Javier smiled and headed through the dugout to the door that would lead to the locker rooms. Roy put his mitt in his bag.

"You know, I've seen a lot of guys try this comeback," Duff said as they followed Javier to the locker room, where there was an elevator that would take them up to the second level.

Both Roy and Scout purposefully walked slowly to accommodate Duff's slow gait.

"The problem is the technique won't be there for a while, which means you could hurt yourself before you can get your arm into shape."

"Duff's right," Scout said. "Seen it a million times. You'll be almost there and then you'll tear something because you're not getting the right treatment. Treatment is the key."

"Okay. I'll try to find someone. You have any recommendations? A sports therapist you use for the team?"

Roy should have guessed by the look Duff and Scout shared but really, truly, he didn't see it coming.

"I do know someone," Scout said. "Maybe she can be persuaded to come home for a visit."

Duff chuckled before he started coughing. "Yep. Got the best in the business on my team. And I hear she works cheap."

Roy looked at Duff, then at Scout. They couldn't be serious. "She'll never do it. She hates me."

Scout and Duff both smiled back. "Yep," they said together.

CHAPTER THREE

"You need to come home."

Lane pressed her cell to her ear with her shoulder and opened the door to her apartment, two grocery bags hanging from her arms. "Hold on."

Once inside, she shut the door, made her way to the kitchen, put the bags—recyclable, of course—on the counter along with her phone and hit the speaker button.

"Okay, Scout, I'm here. What do you mean come home? I was just there."

"Months ago at Christmas. Things are different now."

Lane took a deep breath as she unpacked her frozen entrées and tried not to let Scout's anxiety get her freaked out as well.

"Has he been to a doctor?" Lane asked, knowing what Scout was worried about. This was about Duff. With Scout it was always about Duff. Or baseball.

"He won't go. He says he's fine, just old and tired—"

"Scout, he *is* seventy-five. I mean, he's allowed to be tired."

"It's not like that. It's not naps in the afternoon. It's not dozing after dinner. Something is wrong and you are the only one in this family who has any kind of medical knowledge. If you tell him to go to a doctor, he'll listen to you. With me he brushes it off as nagging."

Home.

The word blasted through Lane like a bullet into the gut. Suddenly the idea made so much sense to her when nothing seemed to make sense six days ago.

Six days? Had it been that long since the doctor told her Stephen had died? The eerie sense of lost time had Lane wondering what had happened during the past week. Most of that time had been spent on a couch staring at four walls. Until she got hungry enough to go to a grocery store to get something besides potato chips and peanut butter sandwiches to eat.

Now with Scout's worry about Duff, it suddenly felt like there was an answer. A place to go. A person to be. Not a physical therapist, but a daughter.

Because Lane was no longer a physical therapist.

Scout wasn't prone to exaggeration and she certainly wasn't the type to ask for help. Lane hadn't missed the fatigue Duff seemed to suffer from at Christmas. If he was getting worse, then he needed to see a doctor.

"Should we call Samantha?"

"The traitor sister? No."

Lane groaned. Sometimes family dynamics could be so draining. "Scout, you really need to get over it. Yes, she talks to our mother on a regular basis. That's normal behavior between a mother and a daughter. You should try it."

"Not going to happen. Besides, I'm not saying to not call Samantha because of her and Mom. I'm saying it because if all three of us gang up on him, he'll get stubborn. You know him. We need to make this look like it's a totally natural visit. Can you get the time off?"

The words got stuck in Lane's throat. As of three days ago she had all the time off she needed. Instead of admitting that, she just said yes.

"Good, I've set something up."

"What?"

"When Duff calls he's going to ask you for a favor. You will not want to do this favor, but you have no choice because you know your ulterior motive is to assess Duff's condition and get his butt to a doctor."

Lane tried to imagine what kind of favor Duff might ask for—one she wouldn't want to do. He was her father. She adored him. There wasn't anything she wouldn't do if he asked unless it was…

"Scout, is it about baseball? You know I'm done with the sport. Completely and irrevocably."

There was a pause. "I wouldn't use the word *irrevocably* so casually."

Lane gritted her teeth. "I'm not. I'm quite serious. I'm done with the game and, most importantly, I'm done with the players. If you need me in Minotaur Falls, fine, I'll come. But I'm not having anything to do with the game."

"Then he'll suspect something," Scout replied. "Look, I get it. You married a crappy guy and it eats at you every day that you couldn't make the marriage work. But I need you to suck it up and do this thing. For Duff."

Lane hated it when her younger sister was more right than she was. After all it had been five years since her marriage was exposed for the sham it had become. Maybe it was time to start letting some of the anger go. Anger that was mostly directed at herself. Something she rarely told anyone. Why would she when she had such an easy villain she could point to? Her cheating husband.

Her cheating husband *and* Roy Walker.

"Fine. I'll do it. Just out of curiosity, what is this favor? I mean, I assume you want me to treat someone. Some up-and-coming star with a muscle issue? Do I know him?"

Another pause. "Nah. Just another player. He signed a minor-league deal with the Rebels. Who knows if he'll even pan out? But Duff likes him, so he'll ask you to work with him. You'll say yes?"

"Was that actually a question?"

"I need you, Lane. I wouldn't call you if I didn't."

Once more the words felt like a physical blow to Lane. Scout really was serious. Which meant Duff was in trouble. When a parent reaches seventy-five a child had to start to thinking about things. Things like saying goodbye. Lane wasn't ready yet. She was barely surviving losing a patient she didn't know that well.

She couldn't even contemplate what losing Duff right now would mean.

Sometimes, though, life didn't give a person a choice. What worried Lane more than her own re-action was Scout and how she would cope with such a loss. "Hey, you know, kiddo, if there is something wrong—"

"Don't say it. I mean, I know where you are going and I know why you're going there, but don't say it. I can't hear it. Not yet."

Lane nodded and, really, there was no point in borrowing trouble. Not until they knew they had trouble on their hands. "Okay. I'll wait for Duff's call."

Scout hung up and Lane thought of all the things she would need to organize. Pack, of course. Maybe ask her neighbor to take in the mail. Then she re-alized there wasn't anything else that required or-ganizing.

It wasn't like she had a boyfriend she needed to

tell. Hell, she didn't have that many close friends who needed a heads-up. Everyone she knew in town worked at the veterans hospital. Since she'd resigned, a few of them had reached out to her, but no one had been able to talk her out of her decision.

Realistically, Stephen had been only a patient. Another soldier with a missing foot. Her job had been to get him back on his feet even though one of them would be prosthetic. She'd been so close, too. When anyone asked her about his progress, she always gave the same answer. The patient was doing great. He was ahead of schedule. She'd said it with pride. Because of her, he would be using his prosthesis faster than anyone else had before.

Yeah, she'd been doing a hell of job.

Until the twenty-four-year-old took a sharp razor to his wrists and killed himself.

Lane dropped onto the couch and looked around her apartment. It all seemed so empty. For the past five years she had put everything she had into a job as a way to escape her failure of a marriage and now that was gone.

Her supervisor had said it wasn't her fault. The doctor had said it wasn't her fault. She was a physical therapist, not a psychologist. She couldn't have known what was in Stephen's head. No one did, which is why the tragedy had happened.

Lane knew better. She should have sensed his reluctance to work with the prosthesis. She should have picked up on the fact that he wasn't ready to move forward with his life because he hadn't dealt with the loss of his limb. Or the explosion that had killed two of his friends. She'd worked for Veterans Affairs for five years. She'd seen amputations of every kind. She knew what it could do to the psyche.

Instead, she'd gotten caught up in getting a kid up on his feet only to have him take himself off them permanently.

The worst part was that, logically, she knew she couldn't blame herself. Unlike with some of her other patients, she and Stephen hadn't formed any kind of personal bond. He hadn't been overly talkative or particularly friendly. Still, he'd been a good patient—he had done everything she asked. A soldier through and through. Taking the orders she dished out without any back talk.

No, Stephen was no different than the hundreds who had come before him.

Only he was completely different because he was gone and she hadn't seen one sign. Not one signal that he was planning to take his own life.

She could tell herself that taking herself out of the work wasn't about punishing herself for her mistake. That quitting meant not being there for the next soldier. The next soldier who needed her help. She could tell herself that she had a responsibility to the hospital. Heck, she could even tell herself she needed a paycheck to live.

All good reasons to put this incident behind her and go back to work.

She'd tried. The day after she'd learned of Stephen's death, she had tried to go in like it was just another day. She'd walked into the therapy wing, had seen people working out in various capacities and instantly had known she couldn't do it.

The thought of being presented with another patient terrified her. Someone whose name she would learn. Someone whose life she would try to improve. Someone who might be hurting in ways she couldn't see because she only saw the physical.

What if Stephen happened again? What if she failed?

Lane couldn't do it. Not yet. Maybe not ever again. The easiest thing had been to resign and deal with the fallout later.

Home.

Yes, that made sense. It might seem like Lane was going home to help Scout, but really Scout was the one who had just offered Lane a lifeboat.

SCOUT PUT HER cell in her back pocket, chewed her bottom lip and wondered if she was doing the right thing. Her loyalty, after all, should be to her sister and no one knew better how much Lane hated Roy Walker than Scout did. Scout had been the first person Lane called when it all went down. The party, the irrefutable proof of what a scumbag Danny was, Roy's involvement in the whole thing. And when they had needed a coldhearted, ruthless lawyer, they had called their older sister, Samantha, to mete out the punishment.

Sam had eaten up Danny's lawyer and spit him out. But not for financial reasons. Lane hadn't wanted his money. She'd donated most of the settlement Samantha had won her to various different charities.

No, it was a lesson the Baker girls had wanted to enforce so Danny and anyone else in the game of baseball got the message.

You hurt us, we hurt you.

Scout remembered asking Lane what form of revenge she wanted them to inflict on Roy, but Lane hadn't wanted to even hear his name mentioned. It was as if the betrayal from him was somehow too big to deal with.

Bigger than her divorce from Danny.

Her sister's reaction always made Scout wonder about Lane and her feelings for Roy. And that speculation made her feel slightly less guilty about not telling her who Duff's favor was for. At the end of the day, it didn't really matter. Scout needed Lane to pressure Duff to get his health checked.

Lane was probably right. He was getting older and slowing down. Scout could accept that. Hell, it's not like she was going anywhere. She was here for him. Slow or not. She just needed some assurance there wasn't something else, something more serious with far greater reaching consequences, going on.

It was fair to say, Scout didn't like change. Very fair considering she'd lost the only man she ever loved because she wouldn't change.

That nervous niggle in her stomach reared its ugly head. The one she could forget about for hours until suddenly it was there again making her nauseous. She couldn't say why, but it sure felt like a whole lot of change was coming.

No, Scout definitely did not like change.

LANE PULLED UP to the stadium and thought about what it would feel like to walk through those doors. It had been five years since she'd done it. No matter how many times she had come home to visit, no matter how many times Duff had asked her to check out a game with him, she hadn't once set foot in this place. The home of the Minotaurs.

For that matter, she hadn't entered any other ballpark. Heck, she felt uncomfortable walking by a diamond in a park. She hadn't watched a single game on TV. She hadn't paid attention to any playoff runs or World Series.

She didn't even know if her ex-husband was

still on a team. Still playing. Still doing well. She didn't care.

Her love for baseball had died that night. No, it had been murdered, by her. She'd purposefully ejected it from her life. Went so far as to stop treating all professional athletes because she hadn't wanted to be remotely reminded of the lifestyle. She'd turned down a professional golfer's offer of ten thousand dollars for one hour of therapy without blinking.

She'd even stopped eating hot dogs.

She missed hot dogs.

It wasn't lost on Lane that after the failure of her marriage she'd turned her back on everything she loved except her immediate family. Her first major failure at her job, and she'd done the same thing to work.

Quitter.

The word sat ridiculously heavy on her shoulders. Was that what she was? Was that what she did? Did she quit when things got hard?

No, she told herself stubbornly. She made rational decisions to protect her mental well-being. It was not the same thing at all.

Besides she was here now, standing outside the stadium, wasn't she? Scout needed her and Lane wasn't going to let an old grudge get in the way of doing the right thing by her father. She would grant Duff's favor and he would, in turn, do her a favor by making appointment with a doctor. Just a normal checkup. Something any daughter might prod her aging father into doing.

She left her car, swallowed the crazy nervous thing that was in her throat and walked through the stadium doors like it was no big deal. It was early March and snow was still on the ground in upstate New York, although it was melting. Today the sun was out and there was a hint of spring in the air. Enough to give a person a sense of hope that warmer weather was coming. It was just a matter of time.

Spring used to be her favorite season. The start of everything new. New flowers, new grass, new life and, most importantly, a new baseball season. She thought about the date, and realized opening day for the minors was three weeks away.

There might be players around the ballpark. Those making a run for The Show would be down in spring training. But the cast of players who knew they would start in Triple-A would already be warming up. Hoping to prove themselves enough for some scout to see them and give them a chance.

Lane headed toward Duff's office, stopping just outside. She was supposed to meet the player Duff wanted her to work with. Like Scout, he'd played it off as no big deal. Just a pitcher who they wanted to gradually work up to full speed.

She figured he was someone coming off an injury.

A patient, she thought. That's how she would deal with him. Not a player, not an athlete, just a patient. If she could maintain that distance, then it wouldn't be like being involved in baseball at all.

Taking a deep breath, she knocked and opened the door. The outer office was empty and she could hear voices behind the inner door. Marching forward, she entered the office, ready to compartmentalize her task. She was here to assess her father's health. The other task was simply the means to an end.

"Hey, Duff," Lane said, seeing her father leaning back in his chair behind the desk. The player in question was sitting on the opposite side of the desk, his back to her. "Well, you got me back here. And I guess you're going to be my patient for the next few—"

The player stood and turned to face her.

"Roy Walker. Wow," she whispered. Because she really had nothing else to say.

Scout did this. Duff did this. They both did this to her. Yet another horrible betrayal by people she trusted. How could they force her to confront the one man she never wanted to see again?

The man who had ruined her marriage. Who had turned her into a failure.

It wasn't his fault. It was yours...

"Lanie," he whispered as if he, too, was not ready for the confrontation even though he'd at least had a heads-up it was coming. "You look…good. I mean, it's good to see you."

Lane shook her head. Roy was talking to her. Speaking actual words to her. She was in the same room as him. Unthinkable.

"I don't know what I'm supposed to say now."

"Lanie," Duff huffed. "Now, come on, girl. It's been five years. The man did you a favor and opened your eyes. He gave you your life back. Stop holding on to history and get over it. I need you to work with him."

"Oh, I can promise you *that* is not going to— Wait." Her gaze flew to Roy's face and she could actually see him brace himself for what came next. "What are you doing here?"

He swallowed a few times and she followed the movement of his Adam's apple. She started to take in things about him now that the shock of seeing him was fading. The gray mixed in with the dark hair at his temples. His body still looked strong, fit. Wide shoulders and long arms, which gave him extra zip when throwing a ball. She knew he was thirty-seven, but the person Duff had asked her to work with was a minor-league player.

Roy didn't play baseball anymore. He certainly didn't play minor-league ball.

"I needed a job. Duff helped me out."

"You *needed* a job? Yeah, right. You're a multimillionaire. What happened to your grand plan?

You said you were done with baseball. You said you wanted to leave on top and not hang around like all the other old-timers who didn't know when to walk away. You talked about it constantly. Almost bragging about how smart you were to leave while the leaving was good. Now, five years later, you want to pitch again?" She shook her head. "You're pathetic."

Her voice was sharp and she wasn't sure why. She didn't know if it was anger from seeing the man whom she considered her mortal enemy. Or anger that she'd believed all those things he said to her once. Because when he said them it had felt as though he hoped she would understand why he was making the decision to walk away so young. As though he wanted her approval.

Or maybe it was anger because she remembered all those times when he'd talked to her about his future and she had felt that damn...pull.

Damn. She hated Roy Walker.

"Lanie!" Duff shouted. "I didn't raise my girl to be a bitch. Maybe before you go spouting off on things you don't know about, you might want to check that attitude."

Lane looked at her father, who, she noticed, still hadn't gotten out of his chair, even though he was angry enough at her to raise his voice. Since she was still pissed at him for blindsiding her, that confrontation would have to wait.

"What? This isn't some attempt at a lame comeback? Let me guess, you couldn't stay away from the game," Lane said. "Is that it? The limelight. The rush. The glory. The fans, not that you had many of those. Had to have all that back?"

"No," Roy said stiffly. "What I said was true. I need a job. And this is all I know how to do."

It was the tone in his voice that stopped her. She knew Roy Walker. He was arrogant and smug on his worst days. A colossal ass on his best. He personified confidence and never let anyone forget that he knew to the dollar what his ability to throw a baseball was worth.

Now he stood in front of her with his head down. She didn't think she had ever seen him so...defeated. And she'd seen him after losing an NLCS game that, had he won, would have sent him to the World Series.

He was Roy Walker, for heaven's sake. A future first-ballot Hall of Famer. She wanted to slap him if for no other reason than to take that expression off his face.

"How can you need a job? What happened to all your money?"

He shook his head. "I lost it."

"Millions? Tens of millions?"

"Eighty million to be exact. I have the house I bought my father, which he still lives in, and a town house in Society Hill in Philadelphia that's up for sale. Other than that, it's gone."

Lane had a thousand questions about how that could happen, but quickly snapped her jaw shut. She wasn't supposed to care about that.

She wasn't supposed to care about anything when it came to Roy.

She hated Roy Walker.

"You seriously thought I would help you make this comeback?"

He smiled then, not his normal smile. Not the smile that said he knew more about everything than anyone else in the room. Not the smile that suggested he had secrets she might want to uncover.

No, this smile was completely self-deprecating and it didn't fit on his mouth.

"Hell, no, I didn't think you would help. I told them they were crazy to even ask, but Duff said—"

"I said she's my daughter and if she knows it's important to me, she'll do it." Duff leaned back in his chair, his eyes closed. As if he'd been napping during the tense confrontation unfolding in front of him.

"Why in the hell do you care about Roy Walker, Duff? You know what he did to me."

"Yeah, and I told you I'm grateful to him for it. You were hanging on to that loser with two hands and it didn't look like you were ever letting go. He was dragging you down, sweetie, like an anchor in an ocean."

"I was trying to save my marriage, which is what you always told us to do."

"Except you married the wrong guy!" Duff snapped. "When you marry the wrong guy, you walk away. Roy here forced you to do that. So, for that, he gets my help. However, my help will take him only so far. If he's going to make it all the way, he needs more."

Instinctively, her therapist brain started clicking in. Lane narrowed her gaze on Roy again. "How long has it been since you threw? I mean, before coming here?"

"Five years. The game in San Diego was the last time I picked up a ball."

Lane knew that game. It was officially the last game she'd ever watched. He'd pitched a no-hitter. She'd been in a bar near the hospital where she had just gotten hired. She was eating a hamburger and drinking a beer and doing everything she could not to look at the television screens filled with a bunch of different baseball games when suddenly they had turned all the TVs to the sports network covering one game in particular.

After all, it wasn't every day a pitching legend, during the last game of his historic career, didn't give up a single hit. Against her will, she'd been as captivated as everyone around her, waiting as he threw each pitch, as he racked up each out, as batter after batter went down in a frustrated huff. Until the ninth inning, when the noise from the crowd at the stadium was so loud, she couldn't imagine what someone standing on the mound in the center of it all might be hearing.

Three up, three down. Game over. His teammates had come in from the field, but no one charged him or lifted him off his feet as was typical with such an accomplishment. The catcher simply swatted him on the ass and handed Roy the ball. A few chin nods in his direction and that was it.

Because everyone knew his teammates didn't like him. It had been almost hard to watch as the television commentators tried to explain to the national audience why the team's celebration was so tepid. The best they said about Roy was that he was a loner. The worst they said was that he'd been known to be a cancer in the clubhouse, despite his great talent.

Lane swallowed the emotion the memory of that day caused her. In truth, she never really understood why she had left the bar to go home and cry her eyes out.

Letting that puzzle go, she focused on the present. "How hard are you throwing now?"

"I've got my fastball up to about eighty-eight."

"How does the arm feel?"

"Hurts like hell."

"And your shoulder?" Back in the day when he sought out her therapy services it had always been his shoulder that had bothered him. Sometimes the neck, too.

"Stiff."

Lane nodded. "You rush that arm too fast and you'll tear something."

"That's what I told him. That's why he needs you," Duff said.

Lane looked at her father and remembered what this was really all about. She was here to make sure her father was okay. Roy was nothing but a sideshow. A particularly attention-grabbing sideshow.

Lane turned to Roy. "If I do this, it doesn't mean I forgive you for what you did. You would be nothing but a body to me."

"Damn it, girl," Duff said. "How many times do I have to tell you you should be indebted to him, not angry with him?"

"You're wrong, Duff," Roy said. "You weren't there. What I did was crappy and I know it. I never got the chance to say it then. I don't know if you ever got my letter—"

"I tore it up and threw it out without opening it."

Which in hindsight, made her feel like a spiteful, immature girl. Setting her up had been wrong. There was no refuting that. She'd thought they were friends and by manipulating her into that position, he'd hurt her. Some of Danny's teammates actually had been laughing as she had to make her way out the door of Roy's place that night. That's when she'd figured out the other guys on the team had known. Everyone had known Danny was cheating on her.

She had to get tested for STDs because Danny couldn't remember all the women he'd been with and couldn't remember if he'd used a condom every time. The humiliation of that, of knowing how little she meant to him, had been crushing.

She would never be sure why Roy had done it, either. Why he hadn't just told her the truth rather than let her find out that way. But, at the end of the day, he hadn't forced Danny to bring that woman to the party. Hadn't forced Danny to cheat on her for who knew how much of their marriage. That was Danny's doing.

Worst of all, even though he'd initiated the kiss, that crazy kiss that had seemingly come out of the blue, she had been the one to respond. That was all on her. Five years ago it had been so easy to block out that part of the night and wallow in the pain and suffering of the divorce.

Danny cheated on her and Lane left him. That was a much simpler narrative than the truth. A truth she'd never told anyone. She had fallen out of love with Danny and had been struggling to hang on to something even while she was realizing she was attracted to another man. Yes, definitely much harder to wrap her brain around that.

"Anyway," Roy said. "I just wanted to say I'm sorry."

"You really need to throw again? This isn't some joke to you?"

"Lanie, standing here in front of you…this is definitely not a joke." He shrugged. "Pitching is the only thing I know how to do. The only thing I'm good for."

Again, the sense of defeat in his words startled her. This wasn't the Roy Walker she'd known five years ago. The ass whom she had always called out for his bullshit.

In a weird way she found herself missing that person—which made no sense to her at all. But since nothing in her life made sense right now, Lane figured this little episode was par for the course.

She had no job. She had no life. She had a father and a sister who, although they had betrayed her, did seem to need her.

And Roy. Roy Walker needed her and that was about the craziest thing she could imagine happening today.

"Fine. I'll do it. It's not like I have a choice, right? You've got my father involved. But don't call me Lanie again. You don't get to do that."

Duff clapped his hands together, startling Lane. This wasn't about Roy. She wouldn't let it be.

"Now we're talking," Duff said. "You two get to work and turn that arm of his into a weapon."

He pulled the brim of his hat over his eyes and settled in for what appeared to be his midday nap.

CHAPTER FOUR

"I can't believe you didn't tell me about Roy," Lane said to her sister as soon they were alone. Scout and Duff had just gotten home and he'd immediately sought his favorite chair in the living room.

As for Lane, following her confrontation with Roy, she had left the stadium and headed to Duff's house for some alone time. While she'd agreed to work on Roy's arm, she needed at least twenty-four hours to process seeing him again before she could work up the courage to actually touch him.

And yes, she would have to touch Roy Walker. The reality of that was hitting her.

After she'd left the stadium, Duff had apparently decided he wanted to make his famous burgers for dinner, which translated into Scout putting the ingredients together and making the raw patties, then Duff slapping them on the grill, adding cheese and calling it a cooking miracle.

It was a time-honored tradition in the Baker household.

"Shh, Duff's sleeping," Scout hissed as they unpacked groceries she and Duff had picked up.

It wasn't beyond Lane's notice that Duff slept a lot. As if that trip to the grocery store had expended all the energy he had so he needed to refuel for dinner. How the hell did he think he was going to manage the club this year? That was a conversation for tomorrow.

Scout not telling her about Roy was a like a slap in the face. Lane felt blindsided and more than a little betrayed. Which were not feelings she wanted from her family.

Her sisters were her core. Her sense of safety in the world, along with Duff. When she'd gone through her long and bitter divorce from Danny they had been her rocks. Sitting with her when she cried. Laughing with her when they knew she needed to be pulled out of a mood. Supporting her when she struggled with the pain of the breakup. True, she'd stopped loving Danny before the actual breakup, but that didn't mean separating their lives hadn't been hard.

The worst part of the divorce had been dealing with her own sense of failure. The acknowledgment that she couldn't make her marriage work. That she had been unable to see Danny for who he really was before she married him. That her love for him had been a fleeting thing at best.

Whether Danny had ever returned that love was hard to know. The awful truth was that his infidelities had started months after they were first married.

How could she have not known? That cluelessness alone had rocked her to her core until her sisters made her see that Danny's behavior wasn't about anything lacking in Lane. It was just who Danny was.

A character flaw Lane had failed to identify in her mission to find a person she could build a life with. How the hell could she screw it up so badly? How could she be totally unsuccessful at the one thing she'd been so committed to doing right?

That was why Lane hadn't once, in the five years since leaving Danny, ever considered taking the chance on love and long-term commitment again. Which didn't make dating easy. The one time she'd gotten remotely close to someone she had felt honor bound to tell him their relationship could never go anywhere. She wasn't getting married. Ever. She wasn't repeating that mistake. She didn't trust herself.

If she was to have kids someday, she would do it on her own.

The guy had said goodbye. And Lane realized that men in their late twenties and early thirties who were looking for a wife were not people she should be dating. Unfortunately, the other kind—who wanted no-strings-attached sex—usually turned her off completely because they reminded her too much of Danny.

Which meant she hadn't had sex in a really long time. Which meant seeing Roy Walker again, and having that same feeling creep over her body as the last time she'd seen him, made her want to throw something across the room.

She was going to have to touch him. His body. What in the hell was she thinking agreeing to that?

"You should have told me," Lane said again, having no problem taking out her annoyance on her little sister.

"I was afraid you wouldn't come."

"You honestly think I would let someone like Roy stop me from seeing my father if I was concerned about his health?"

Scout took a moment to consider the question. "Anyone else, no. Roy? He's different for you."

"He's not different. He's just someone I...I hate. That's all."

"Yep. Lane hates Roy. You really should get a tattoo of that so you can assure yourself you'll never forget it."

"What's that supposed to mean?"

Scout sighed and put down a head of broccoli that Lane knew their father wouldn't eat. She also knew Scout kept buying it and other vegetables in a vain attempt to keep him healthy. She looked long and hard at Lane.

"What really happened between you two the night of that party?"

Lane felt her whole body flush. "You mean other than finding my husband with his tongue down another woman's throat?"

"You know damn well I mean other than that. You were so mad at Roy over that whole episode—"

"He set me up! He purposefully staged an entire party to make me look like a fool in front of everyone I knew. Everyone who knew Danny was cheating on me!"

Just reliving that walk down the long hallway made her want to inflict physical damage on Roy. She'd never wanted an apology from him. Frankly, given the man he'd been then, so confident in his decisions, she'd never expected one. He probably thought the same as Duff had thought—that he'd done her a favor. That's why it had shocked her when he'd sent the letter. Maybe she hadn't read it because it was better to think about what he might have said than to know what he did.

"Why did he do that?" Scout mused. "I mean, seriously, you couldn't have been the first wife Roy knew was being cheated on. He'd been in the league for ten years before he met you. He probably knew every sordid story in the book. Yet he puts this plot together to expose Danny's cheating. That's a lot of effort from a man who you said never took much interest in the team or anyone else."

Lane didn't want to think about the events leading up to that party. She didn't want to think about the weird outings she and Roy took together. They both had a thing for hot dogs, so they would try new places around town, or new stands in the ballpark. Always in search of the perfect dog. It had been completely innocent, of course. Mostly they ate and argued about whatever the topic of the day was.

But what Lane had told him that night was true. She had considered them friends.

And as far as she knew, theirs was the only relationship Roy had.

Yes, he could be an ass. But as time had passed, there were things she'd learned about him that made him seem more human. Like when she discovered the reason for his isolation from the team. Or when she'd found out that his claim to not do charity really meant that he didn't do charity for show.

Because the one time Lane had asked him to help her out, he'd spent hours in a dunk tank making kids and adults happy.

"I don't know why he did it," Lane lied now. She couldn't admit the truth without remembering the moment he'd told her to get unmarried. When he'd leaned into her and kissed her.

When she'd kissed him back.

She couldn't imagine what Scout would say if she knew. All that fuss about breaking up with a cheating scumbag of a husband and the truth was, in her heart, Lane had also felt desire for someone other than the person to whom she was married.

The thought made her that much angrier at Roy.

"If you ask me, your story—the Roy-and-Lane story—is not done yet."

"There is no story. There is just me getting through these next few weeks. I'll get Duff to see a doctor. We'll make sure he's okay and then I'm gone. As far away from baseball as I can get."

"And the hospital was okay with letting you go for a few weeks?"

"Yep," Lane said quickly. Maybe too quickly because she could feel Scout's gaze on her. Regardless, Lane wasn't talking about that now. It was just too much to deal with. Stephen's death, leaving her job. Those things were behind her. Duff and Roy were in front of her. She needed to focus on that.

Scout had put away the last of the groceries and was leaning against the fridge. "What if we can't just make sure he's okay? What if something is wrong? Isn't that what you said we might need to get prepared for?"

"Well, I changed my mind." Lane said definitively. "We're not borrowing trouble. Duff's perfectly fine until a doctor says otherwise. You know what Duff always says—worrying about nothing gets us nothing."

Scout nodded but Lane could see the fear in her

sister's eyes, which coincidentally made Lane feel it in her heart.

"He's going to be fine," Lane said. "Everything is going to be fine."

She only wished she could believe it.

ROY FELT THE rush of adrenaline when he saw where the ball ended up. Exactly where he wanted it to, a little low and outside, but definitely a strike. Javier bounced up and tossed the ball to Roy.

After a week in the Falls, he was in shape enough to throw from the mound. A slightly elevated hill with a pitch to plant his feet. He wore cleats, work-out shorts and a long sleeved T-shirt, which helped to keep his arm warm. A standard bullpen session routine, and he could feel his body changing with each pitch he threw.

It was like there was all this dried-up, crusty stuff around his shoulder and arm, and with each throw it cracked a little more, and the dust blew away, taking time with it. When he'd left the game he'd promised himself he would never miss it and he'd kept that promise.

Until now.

Strange that he was becoming sentimental. Now that he was in a stadium again he missed the sounds of the crowds cheering and sometimes jeering. He missed the adrenaline rush of facing the best bat-ter in the league and watching as he swung helplessly at a ball that was sinking before it ever got across the plate.

He missed the feeling of winning. Of dominating. And now he had enough humility to know that he might not get back there. Yes, he could still throw. But could he still be Roy Walker?

That was an unknown.

What would it feel like to sit in the bullpen watching the game with a bunch of other guys, probably younger, waiting for the phone to ring so he could go out to the mound to pitch for just one inning. Hoping he didn't do any damage in that inning. Hoping he got the guys out he was supposed to get out.

Roy never used to hope. He just did. He'd always been a starter. He'd always been the first starter in the five-man rotation. For every season he'd played.

What he was going to be was anyone's guess. Duff had him slated to start in the minors, but that was to improve his arm strength. What he became in the majors, if he even made it that far, was a complete unknown.

As long as it came with a paycheck, he would have to accept it.

Trying to get out of his head, Roy got into his windup and threw again. The ball sailed over Javier's head and the catcher had to hop up and scramble to find it.

"Sorry, Javier!" Roy waved.

"*Juusssst* a little outside."

Roy turned and saw Lane walking toward him. She wore jeans with a T-shirt and cardigan, her hair loose around her shoulders. He was struck again by the awareness that he was seeing her again. When he thought he never would.

Damn, he'd missed her. He wondered what she would say if he told her that. Probably that he didn't get to say that, either.

"Quoting *Major League*. That's not a good sign," he said, smiling.

Lane knew *Major League* was one of Roy's all-time favorite baseball movies. The fact that she lumped him in with the Wild Thing didn't bode well for what she saw in his pitching.

She didn't return his smile.

"You should have been here earlier," he said. "I missed Javier by three feet on my first pitch. The ball hit the brick backstop, shot down into the dugout and ran all the way into the lockers. Not exactly where I wanted that pitch to go."

Lane crossed her arms under her breasts and looked toward the outfield.

"Look, I get it, Lane. You hate me and just because you're here doesn't mean you've forgiven me. Point made. But you are here and if we are going to work together, we have to at least talk to each other. We could always do that. Talk to each other."

She looked at him then as if his words had served

to remind her of what they had been. He couldn't tell if that made her angrier or if maybe she had missed him, too. Because the look on her face just then…it was wistful.

"Did I actually hear you apologize to Javier?"

Roy knew where she was going with the question. In his heyday he never would have considered apologizing to a catcher on a wild pitch. But those days were over and it seemed a man who was coming back to the game with his head between his knees could show a little humility now and then.

"Don't make too much of it. It's not like he understands a word I say."

"Session done?" Javier called out to the mound.

Roy nodded. "Session done. Thanks again, Javier."

"It's good. It's good." The catcher smiled, then jogged toward the dugout and the showers underneath the stadium.

"Does your father know you're here?" Lane asked.

It was another question Roy understood the reason why she asked. He really didn't want to talk about his father, but he had to take the fact that she was talking to him as a positive sign so he answered her.

"No." Roy wanted to avoid that conversation as long as he could. He could just imagine how it would go down. He would have to explain how he lost all his money. Instead of being worried about that or sorry it happened, his father would no doubt be thrilled to fly out and see him at his next game. His father would instantly revert to his old ways, thinking that he and Roy could be a team again.

When Roy left the game his relationship with his father had all but dried up. A lot of that distance had to do with losing his mother the year before. Once she was gone, he and his father realized the only thing that connected them was baseball. The reality of it after he'd left the game was even worse than he could imagine. It was as if his father didn't know how to speak to him anymore. Like all Roy had ever been to him was a star player instead of a son.

Now that he was back in the game his father would want to be in his life and the pain of that, knowing he would only take an interest because Roy was playing ball again, was something Roy really didn't want to deal with.

It was something he could have talked about with his mom. Six years gone and there wasn't a day he didn't wish he could pick up the phone and call her. Let her explain why Dad was the way he was and how baseball was his way of showing his affection. She had always made Roy feel better about himself, his dad and their relationship.

He should call his dad. He *would* call him. He just wasn't ready yet.

"How long do you think you can stay hidden?

The season starts in three weeks. You're going to be on the team—"

"You don't know that. It's not official."

"I saw the five pitches you threw before that last one. You're going to be on the team. The world will know Roy Walker is back."

There would be press, there were would be stories and assumptions and investigations. News of his colossal business implosion would be everywhere. Mike and Mike on ESPN radio would no doubt discuss it and his return for a solid week.

Forget the field day Roy would have with the local press, who would be jumping at the chance to beef up their distribution of newspapers with the story of Roy's return and being part of the Minotaurs. He'd met the owner of the team, Jocelyn Taft-Wright, who seemed ready to pounce on any publicity that Roy might generate that could translate into ticket sales. Considering she was married to a local sportswriter, Roy imagined she would have some influence over the volume of stories produced.

All of it would suck for someone who never craved the media spotlight. It wasn't as if Roy didn't love attention. But only when he was on the mound. There he craved it. Soaked it in like sun on a beach. He always wanted everyone to see what he could do.

Off the mound, he always felt like the less people knew about him, the better.

It would be something Lane might have teased him about when they were friends and say it was because he didn't want everyone to know what an ass he was. Maybe that was true. But he also didn't want everyone to realize how shallow he was.

What had he been other than a ballplayer? Nothing. Not husband or father. Not a person with interests or hobbies. Roy threw the ball. That's who he was. An interviewer could ask only so many questions about that. A player could give only so many answers.

Now those questions would be about whether he could still throw the ball.

The jury was still out. The throwing didn't feel like it used to feel. But he wasn't as bad as he might have thought after so long away.

"The plan is to hide for as long as possible," he eventually said. "When the storm shows up, I'll see how it goes. You know me and my love of the press."

"They used to call you One-Word-Answer Roy."

"They ask a question, I give them an answer. They don't like it, that's their problem."

"Right, but it was one of the things that fed in to your whole alter ego."

"*Alter ego?* I wasn't a superhero, Lane."

"No, Roy, you weren't. Hate to tell you but you were the bad guy."

It wasn't exactly news to Roy. He had always understood how he was perceived. He hadn't done it on purpose. He hadn't deliberately cultivated the image as the loner. The team villain. The guy who everyone wanted to hate but couldn't because he was too damn talented.

His reputation developed because of his nature and how he was brought up in the game. Maybe there had been a time when he thought about changing people's perception of him. Then he thought about taking time away from his regimented training schedule to do more interviews. Or spend more of his off time with his teammates. The extra effort it would take to show up at some swanky event just to get his face on camera.

The return on that effort hadn't seemed worth it. Only the pitching mattered to him.

Roy started his career with two, and only two, objectives: a World Series victory and the Hall of Fame. The level of commitment it took to achieve those goals was something that probably only twenty of the three hundred plus pitchers in the major leagues understood. The commitment—the work—was all he was. All he knew. And he'd accomplished one of his objectives.

His objectives this time around were even simpler. He needed money. A mercenary reason that didn't require him to be the best there was, because there was no way he could ever be better than his younger self. But he did have to be good enough.

Good enough. A heck of a lowly ambition for Roy Walker, but the best he could hope for.

"Maybe I'll try to do things a little differently this time," he said, thinking that his capitulation might gain him some goodwill with Lane.

"Don't do it on my account."

Or not.

"So you're going to tell the press the whole story?" she asked.

He laughed then. "There's no getting around what happened, Lane. I can't shake it, or dodge it, or pretend it didn't happen. So, I have to man up. I reached for something and missed and it cost me everything. All I can do is hope I have some gas left in the tank to give myself another shot."

"People love a good comeback story," Lane said. "And you'll be one hell of a comeback to baseball."

"Can I ask you something? Honestly."

"Have I ever been dishonest with you?"

Roy thought about that but didn't necessarily want to go to the past. The answer to that question wasn't as black-and-white as she wanted it to be. Maybe she hadn't been dishonest with him, but she'd damn sure lied to herself. It was the only reason her marriage to Danny lasted as long as it did.

"Do you really think I'm pathetic? A thirty-seven-year-old, has-been pitcher. Are they going to pity me?"

It felt like he was exposing himself. Like he'd ripped apart his T-shirt, shown her his bare chest and asked her if she wanted to take a stab at his heart. Except she was Lane Baker, and she used to be the princess of baseball. Before her breakup no one respected the game more, except maybe Roy, so he knew he could trust her to tell him the truth even if she did hate him.

Was he blowing up his reputation, his history in the game and everything he ever worked toward for a damn paycheck? Lane would understand, even through her anger, what it would do to him to shit on his own legacy.

She bit her lower lip. Five years ago that habit would have been enough to give him a hard-on and have him thinking about other places he wanted her lips.

But not now, in this moment. This was too real. Lane Baker had hated him for five years. Had walked away not just from her husband, but also from the game she loved because of what Roy had done to her. There was no reason to think she should give him anything other than a crushing, devastating blow.

He really hoped to hell she didn't.

"I shouldn't have said what I did. Yesterday. About you being pathetic. You were the last person I expected to see and I lashed out."

"You were being honest," he reminded her.

"I was angry. But I know what you're asking and I think it depends," she said. "Do you think you can do this? Do you really think you can throw again in The Show?"

Honesty. It's what he promised. "I don't know. Lanie—sorry, Lane. Help me."

Her arms closed around her body more tightly. "I already agreed to do your physical therapy. That's all I'm offering."

"No," he said, reaching for her upper arm, circling it with his left hand. It was strange to touch her again. Like suddenly she was even more tangible to him now than she had been standing in front of him with her arms crossed over her chest. "I need to find me again. Because right now I'm so lost I have no sense of what's up or down. And as crazy as it seems, you were one of the people who knew me best back then."

"You're asking *me*? For that kind of help? You don't think it was enough to ask for my skills, now you want more? That's a lot of nerve, Roy."

"I know it is. But I also know you were the most generous person around."

"Yeah, well, I'm not that person anymore," she said. "I don't *give* anymore, because I don't trust anymore. You did that to me. You and Danny."

To be lumped in with Danny Worthless felt like someone had shoved a knife through Roy's stomach and twisted it all around. But was she wrong? They had both betrayed her.

Roy dropped his hand and could feel that some heavy clouds had blocked out the sun. Cool air had rolled into the stadium and his arm felt all of it. Definitely the start of spring, where one minute it could be balmy and beautiful and the next minute a person could be shivering and cold.

His shoulder started to stiffen and he knew he needed to get to a hot shower fast if he was going keep it loose enough to take another session tomorrow.

"I gotta…" He pointed to his arm and Lane nodded, totally familiar with what was happening to his body in the cool air. That shared knowledge created a sense of intimacy between them. Just like it had back then when she used to work on him. There had been times when he believed she understood his body more than he did. It had always been an unsettling thought.

"Yeah. Right. Take your shower and then meet me in the therapy room. We'll get to work."

Therapy. *That* was more than he should have asked for. To ask for even more from her probably had been a dick move.

"Okay."

She walked away from him but then stopped a few feet away and turned back. "I don't know if it helps or not, but the Roy I knew back then had a lot of nerve, too."

Roy smiled at that. "Yes, he did."

Lane shrugged. "Maybe that's where you start looking for yourself again. See you in a few."

CHAPTER FIVE

LANE LOOKED DOWN at the lean body with the hairy chest and belly that was stretched out on the therapy table and listened as Roy let go with a particularly erotic-sounding groan. Her finger pressed against an artery, constricted because of the inflammation in his shoulder, and waited it out until the nerve relaxed and the blood started to flow. She could feel the pulse of it beneath her fingers, could feel Roy's muscles release the tightness. Then came the groaning.

Roy had always been a groaner. It wasn't as though he was her only client who would make noises during their therapy sessions. But for some reason that raw sound coming from him always did something funny to her insides.

And then there was his chest. With swirls of dark hair that always seemed intriguing, despite the fact that bodies were commonplace to her. Short ones, tall ones, fat ones, skinny ones. None of it mattered when someone was a patient on her table. They were like a big lump of clay that she needed to mold back into health.

The fact that Roy's chest fascinated her could have been borderline unethical. It wasn't as if she had ever given in to temptation and ran her fingers through those dark swirls of hair.

So she was fine. Mostly.

Danny had had a smooth chest. Something that had been so sexy to her when she had first started sleeping with him. Later, it became this big contrast between the way he and Roy looked. A contrast she never would have made had she been a happily married woman.

Roy's chest reminded her that when she'd still been married, there had been a part of her that saw Roy the man, not just the player.

"Jeezus, that feels good," he said, sounding like a man getting a blow job instead of physical therapy.

Damn it! Why had she even gone there in her head? This was work. This was a client. This man was her greatest enemy.

Except…he wanted her help. Because he was lost.

Despite what she told him, the hurt she'd tried to inflict, there was a part of her that wanted to give him that help. She couldn't lie to herself. Roy was different and she toyed with this idea that if she shook him hard enough, then the old Roy would return.

What a hypocrite that idea made her. Calling him pathetic, comparing him to Danny, telling everyone she hated him. If that was true, she should want to be as mentally and emotionally far from Roy Walker as a person could be.

Yet she was here, standing over his body, helping him to heal. If she'd wanted to, really wanted to, she could have walked away. She could have found a way to say no to Duff and still accomplish what Scout brought her home to do.

But instead she'd stayed and thrown words at him and reminded herself that he was the bad guy who hurt her.

It was the only way to hold on to the righteous hatred she had for him.

The hatred that deflected the blame for her failing marriage away from her. The hatred that kept her from looking too closely at her own mistakes. The hatred that, up close, didn't look at all like hate—not when her first instinct was to say yes to his plea for help.

"Can I ask a question?"

"Sure," Lane said, hoping that whatever he said would be a distraction from her thoughts. She slid her fingers deeper under his shoulder and started working there to get the inflammation to ease. His shoulder felt like it was on fire under her hands.

Just don't ask me about the past. My marriage. Or what my feelings were for you back then. Please don't ask that. Please don't ask about what I'm doing now because I quit my job and I'm as lost as you say you are.

Lane held her breath.

"Why did you really agree to come back here? Everything I heard about you said you walked away from the game. Didn't want anything to do with it anymore. You were helping veterans or something."

"I worked…work for the VA trying to get the amputees returning from Iraq and Afghanistan rehabilitated."

"Sounds important."

"Certainly more important than baseball."

"Then why are you here? Are you giving baseball a second chance, too?"

"No. Definitely not. I don't want anything to do with the game. I haven't even missed it."

That was such a lie. She'd allowed herself to forget how much she missed this. The stadium, the anticipation of the upcoming season. Hell, even the musty smell of the locker rooms. Soon the guys would be back and the locker room would be filled with jokes and nicknames and pranks.

The stadium would be overflowing with families eager to cheer on their local team. The games would start and then it would fill all her senses, reminding her of what she'd left behind.

For so long instead of seeing a pastime she loved, all she saw were men who knew what Danny was doing while on the road and never said a thing about it. How many of them were cheating on their wives, too?

Now it felt as though that raw pain had diminished. Maybe it was time for her self-imposed exile to be over. Time to start letting go of a lot of things. Yet, she couldn't help but wonder if she was running *back* to the thing she'd run away from before because she was running away from something else.

Quitter.

The word sat on her chest.

"Well, we both know you're not really here for me. That's a given. But even before you knew it was me, I can't see Duff talking you into something you were dead set against doing."

It was another silly instinct, but Lane had this urge to tell Roy everything. About Stephen, about how she hadn't seen a single warning sign of his depression. Not one damn thing that might have saved his life because she'd been so focused on his physical progress. She wanted to tell Roy she had no job anymore. That her future was as unsettled as his was.

The thought of letting all that out seemed like too much. As though all she had was this news inside her and, as long as she didn't tell anyone, then she could pretend she was dealing with it. If she started to talk about that news, it would be like all of the air whistling out of a balloon until there was nothing left but a floppy bit of rubbery nothing.

"I get it," he said when she'd remained silent. "No more talking. Not between us."

Talk, argue, banter, fight. He was right. They had always had that. And truth, she thought. At least, up until a certain point.

She'd missed that about him. It was something she never really had with any other man in her life.

Had she and Danny ever really been friends?

It was sad to admit it, but she didn't believe they were. And she certainly hadn't had a real friend since Roy. Just family. Because family was something you could trust. So could she do that? Could she open up to him again just that much? To be able to tell him the truth about what was happening and know that he might care and give her his honest opinion.

Maybe she couldn't tell him everything. Talking about Stephen seemed way too personal. Especially when she was supposed to hate Roy. But there was something he could know. A piece of the weight she carried that she could hand him and he might hold for her.

Didn't he owe her that?

"You have to promise not to say anything."

"Sure."

Lane didn't for a second doubt his word. Roy had done a lot of things to her, but as far as she knew, he'd never lied to her. "I'm worried about Duff.

Scout's *really* worried about Duff and she needs my support. That's why I'm here."

"He does sleep a lot, but he's seventy-five. Isn't that what they do?"

"He didn't a year ago. A year ago it seemed like he had more energy than a man ten years younger. Now it's changed pretty radically."

"And you're here to do what exactly?"

"Get him to see a doctor. Scout nags and nags, but it's too easy for Duff to brush her off. I'm here to see the stubborn old man listens."

"If that doesn't work?"

"We call in the big guns."

"Samantha? I think even I'm a little intimidated by Samantha."

Not surprising because Samantha was intimidating. She had to be as one of the few women to succeed in a mostly male business. She currently represented three of the top baseball players in America.

"With the way he sleeps, he's going to have a hard time making it through a game. Does the major-league club have thoughts about who they want to bring up to replace him?"

Lane slid her hands from under Roy's back slowly. No sudden motions that might tighten muscles she'd spent an hour trying to loosen. "Okay, sit up slowly. The blood flow—"

"Yeah, I know. It's intense," Roy said as he managed to sit upright. "Man, I forgot how good you make me feel when you do that stuff with your fingers."

Lane chose not to interpret that comment as anything sexual, but rather take it as a compliment on her professional skills.

Slowly Roy rotated his shoulder, testing how loose it was.

She shrugged. "I don't know who they are thinking about replacing Duff with. I think they assumed Duff would let them know when it was time. But when I see how much energy it takes out of him to do the simple things like grocery shopping, I can't imagine how he'll manage an entire game. Whoever that number two is should probably be on his way now."

"Age sucks."

"Yeah, but the alternative is worse. You know that time lost between a child and parent seems silly when you realize how precious time is."

Roy quirked his right eyebrow in a perfect arch. Lane had forgotten he could do that. It used to drive her insane because it was always his signal to her that he was seeing beyond her subtext. She'd never been able to get anything by him. Ever.

Now it made her smile. She hadn't been supersubtle.

"I get it. You're telling me to call my dad."

She shouldn't care about their relationship. She

shouldn't care about it because she was supposed to hate Roy. She shouldn't care about it because she had enough things to worry about on her plate. Confronted with the reality of an aging parent, though, she felt she couldn't not say something. Not when she knew up close what Roy and his father's relationship looked like.

"All I'm saying is he would want to know where you are. What you're doing. Don't forget, he's been alone, too, since your mom died."

"You don't understand."

No, Lane didn't. Because, as much as Roy had alluded to the difficult relationship he had with his father, he'd never discussed it openly.

There had been that one time she'd come across them at the stadium after a tough loss in the NLCS round. Roy had been shouting at his father, telling him that he wasn't going to reconsider retirement.

It's over next year, Dad, he'd said. *Better start dealing with that.*

Lane hadn't wanted to intrude so she remained in the tunnel, not letting them see her. Still, she'd been curious about their conversation. After all, it was Roy's career they were talking about. But she could sense from the frustration in his father's voice he was going to have a harder time dealing with the retirement than Roy.

She remembered asking him about it on one of their hot-dog lunches, but he wouldn't discuss it.

She'd told him he should at least talk about it with a friend.

Except Roy didn't have friends. Not back then. He'd had only her.

"Then tell me now," Lane said, sitting next to him on her table.

She looked at him and his eyebrow was arching again. Like he was startled he'd been invited to share something with her. Startled she had even bothered to ask. He opened his mouth and she knew he'd give some snarky reply about why should she care. At least that's what the old Roy would have said.

"Don't," she said, stopping him. "Don't ask why I care. Just…I'm curious, okay? Always have been about you and your dad. Back then you were always together. He was always around the clubhouse. All that time together, you should have been closer, but you weren't."

"Because Mike Walker wasn't my dad, he was my coach."

"Ouch."

"Yeah. I know it might sound like some angsty thing to say. 'Why was Roy like he was? Just ask him and he'll blame it all on his father.' But it's not like that. I don't blame him for anything. He made me what I was. He saw what I could become and never once let me back away from my potential. In many ways he was the greatest dad I could have had. It was when we both started to see the end of the journey that things fell apart. I think we both wondered what would happen to us. Our relationship. What would we talk about it if it wasn't my pitching? Then Mom died and it got worse."

"You were grieving. It's understandable."

"It was more than that. My mom had always been the buffer between us. Or, more accurately, the translator. Letting each of us know what the other was saying because we sure as hell didn't hear it the same way. I told him about my plan to retire. I could see how it affected him. This fear of losing what we had, it made him crazy. We started fighting about it and then finally there was nothing left to say. I was out of the game and the relationship we'd had since I was six years old and could throw a ball was over."

"You couldn't talk about it?"

"Have you met me? You know talking about my feelings isn't my strong point. A trait I inherited from him, by the way."

He was right. It wasn't. Still, she couldn't help but notice that what he'd just told her was probably the most intimate thing he'd shared with anyone. She didn't want to look too closely at why he had decided to share it with her.

"You're more than the game, Roy. Your father knows that."

"Does he? I'm not so sure. I remember when I

bought them their house. The pride in his expression as he opened the front door. It was like he knew how much of a role he'd played in getting me there. It was like he wasn't proud of me, but of himself for what he'd accomplished as a coach. I wasn't a son to him, I was his greatest accomplishment. He'll feel that again when I go into the Hall of Fame. If I don't tank my chances by making a comeback."

"No one can take away what you accomplished in this game, Roy."

"No, but if I turn into a subpar bullpen pitcher with a 4.72 ERA, it might put a damper on those first-time ballots."

"Well, then I guess you'll just have to work on being great again."

He looked at her and the sadness in his eyes pierced her heart.

"I'm thirty-seven years old. A failure in business, relationships… There's nothing great about me anymore. I think I'll settle for good enough. Thanks again for the shoulder work."

Lane watched as he hopped off the table. Feeling like she needed to say something, anything, that would restore a semblance of the confidence in the man she once knew.

"Roy. You said you wanted my help and I told you why I can't do that. But if you want me to, I can help you remember who you were."

He half smiled and the expression tore at her.

"You used to think I was an ass, remember? Maybe this humbler version of me will rub off on you."

"Roy…"

"Do you know my real name is Herb? Herbert Michael Walker. My mom named me after her dad, whom she adored. But my dad didn't think *Herb* was a baseball name. So he changed it to Roy. I just wanted you to know that. You see, Lane, I really am nothing more than the game."

Lane didn't say anything else. She couldn't. She only knew that he was wrong. Yes, she had called him an ass. And yes, she always called him on his bullshit. But he had been her friend. Because there was more to him. The old him was still in there somewhere. He had to be. If somehow the old Roy could mix and mingle with this new older and wiser Roy, well, then that might be one hell of a combo deal.

A man Lane might find herself liking a lot.

Which immediately scared the hell out of her.

ROY LET THE hot water rush over him. Not wanting to think about his father, or Lane, or the person he had once been, he just pushed everything out and focused on his body.

On his arm. It throbbed, but in a good way. Like it was reminding him it was still there, hanging off his body. Still useful to him.

He was five days into his cycle, which had to be

adjusted from what he'd done back in the majors when he'd pitched every fifth game. In the minors they would bring him out every seventh game until he got his stamina up. That meant day one of his training was long tossing, followed by three days of shorter-length throwing. Today's session was another ramp-up—full distance throwing from the mound. Tomorrow he would shut the arm down completely. Then on Monday it would start all over again.

It was definitely a risk to attempt the comeback so quickly, but so far, he hadn't done anything too stupid. Back when he was pitching in the majors he'd had the entire off-season to nurture his arm. Usually he'd shut down the arm for about six weeks after the season was over, then ever so slowly, bring it back to life. Reminding the arm with each pitch what its purpose was.

To throw.

By the time spring training rolled around he would move into his normal five-day rotation without a hitch.

What he was trying to do now was get in all his winter work along with his spring-training work in less than six weeks. But today had felt good. It had felt normal. After Lane's work with the magic fingers—he probably should tone down the moaning—he felt like a semblance of the pitcher he used to be.

Maybe she was right. Maybe he could do this. His agent hadn't called him to let him know the Rebels were making an offer, but a decision needed to be made soon or he might have to try out for some other team. Something he didn't want to do. Because of Duff. He liked the security of knowing his former manager was in his corner. Now that he knew Duff's health might be an issue, Roy liked the idea of being able to give something back.

Something like watching over Duff during a game. Roy would do that because of Lane.

Maybe it was crazy, but he felt protected here in Minotaur Falls, where the locals loved their team, embraced them, rooted for them and wished them well on their way to the majors. On another team he'd be some guy to gawk at or feel pity for.

Yes, a minor-league contract with the Rebels would be ideal. Probably something in the neighborhood of five hundred thousand dollars. Hell, some people never saw that kind of money in their lives and if it was all Roy could get, he'd take it in a heartbeat despite the fact that his last contract had been for fifteen million dollars a year over a ten-year period. He'd earned every penny of that contract, using the proceeds—minus his agent's commission and Roy's living expenses—to fund the ill-fated software company. That eighty million he was destined to lose.

With that perspective, yeah, five hundred thousand would be enough to get him on his feet. But if Roy could bring his arm all the way back, maybe work his way into the majors for a one-year sweetheart deal, that would set him up for life.

And this time he wouldn't make the same mistakes. No more investing in a business. No more risks. He'd by a buy an affordable place to live and a reasonable car. Then dump the bulk of the money into an account for his retirement and find some job to keep him busy.

Roy tried to predict what that future might look like. Maybe him wearing an orange apron walking down aisles and helping people find their hardware needs. Whatever it was, it would have to be enough. The game would be well and truly behind him. His thoughts of making it in the business world had already been crushed.

There wasn't any other dream he had. No future goal he was working toward. So yeah, if he was to become some aging, has-been pitcher who needed to take a job sweeping floors and pointing out which aisle the plungers were stocked in, then that's what he would be.

But any security he could set up for himself was all contingent on the arm.

Roy looked down at it like he often did. As if it was more like a conjoined twin than a part of his whole body. Like it had a soul and a purpose all its own. Lord knew he talked to the thing like it was a person. How many times, in how many games, had he muttered to the arm?

You're blowing it. Your release is off. Get with the program.

Oh, it burns? Well, suck it up. It's the ninth inning and I can pitch a shutout.

What? You can't throw anymore? It hurts too bad? This is a no-no I'm working here. We don't stop for anything. Now throw!

The pain was his arm's way of talking back. Of letting him know where he stood in the game and how much longer he could go. People probably didn't get that part. All they saw was the money and the fame and the glory. But the other side was the day-in, day-out struggle to force an arm to do a thing that ultimately caused it pain.

"One more year," Roy told his arm as he turned off the water and stepped out of the shower. "Two at the most. It's all I'll ever ask of you again."

"Holy shit! You're Roy Walker."

Roy took a towel and wrapped it around his waist. He looked at the twenty-year-old staring at him, his mouth wide open and his eyes a little buggy.

It wasn't the first time Roy had received this re-action. Hell, when he'd been playing on the Founders, every new kid who came into the majors did the same thing when he saw Roy for the first time.

Roy's reaction had always been the same. He'd shut the kid down cold. Ask him what he was staring at. Tell him to turn around and go back to the kids room. Let the guy know in no uncertain terms that Roy doubted he'd be able stay in the majors. That was a player's greatest fear—once they reached the pinnacle, all it took was a bad series of outings and the prize could be taken away in a blink. He could be sent down to the land of baseball oblivion.

Roy did everything and anything that screamed, *Don't talk to me again, kid. Don't try and get to know me. Don't think I will be your friend or that I will share my secrets.*

Roy delivered the same reaction every time, because his father had drilled it into him when he'd been growing up in Little League. From the time he was eleven everyone knew Roy was special. Knew that if he kept on the normal pace of playing and growing and improving, he had what it took to make it to majors.

Kids around him were in awe of him, jealous of him, and some of them thought he could help them along, too. If only he showed them how he gripped the ball on his curve. How he could make the ball sink on his slider.

At first he hadn't thought anything about it. If someone asked him a question, he answered it. He didn't understand that it wasn't just the grip and his arm motion that made his throws special. It was a thousand other intangible things that made what he could do with the ball different from all the other kids he played with.

When his father caught on to what the other kids were trying to get out of Roy, his father shut it down. Roy wasn't to talk to any of the other kids, period. Not about his game, not about anything.

"They are users, Roy," his dad had explained. "All they want is a piece of you. You give away all your pieces and you won't have enough left to take you where you want to go. I know it sounds harsh, but we're not doing this to make friends. We're not in this to have fun playing in Little League. Big picture, Roy. You need to think about the big picture."

Eleven years old and he'd been forbidden to make friends with anyone on his team. A habit he hadn't changed in the minors, and definitely not one he'd changed for the majors. To make it at that elite level he had to be even more hyperfocused. Less willing to give away any part of himself to his teammates.

Yes, he knew he was the exception. On teams across the country some of the players were friends. Some were enemies. Some were just coworkers. But few followed Roy's policy of isolationism.

It was just his way. It had always been his way.

"I'm Billy Madden. They just called me up from Double-A. You're like…you're, like, my hero, man. The best pitcher I ever saw. What are you doing here with the Minotaurs? You like a coach now or something? That would be awesome!"

The kid couldn't have been more than twenty-two. Maybe twenty-three. He had a little scruff around his jaw and the lean look of someone who was still filling into his body. He wore jeans and T-shirt promoting a band Roy had never heard of. Flip-flops on his feet and his equipment bag slung over his shoulder like a guitar case.

Five years ago he had probably been playing for his high school team hoping some day he could play in the big leagues like his hero, Roy Walker. Hell, he might even have had a Roy Walker baseball card.

Roy's first reaction was to walk away. But he didn't. Lane was right. If he made the team, he couldn't keep the secret about his return. But he sure as hell didn't want to explain what he was doing here to this scruffy young kid.

It was too humiliating.

Then he realized it didn't matter. The days of working to become something—someone—in this game were over. He was here to hopefully pick up enough cash to set up his retirement and that was all. Those pieces his father had always told him to hold on to just felt like extra weight at this point. He wanted to let them go, but he wasn't sure how.

In the end it was easier to resort to old habits.

"I'm not a coach," Roy said curtly, then spat at the kid's feet, just missing the kid's exposed skin to make his point. "I'm your competition. Think you can beat me?"

The kid's mouth opened even more. Then his face turned red and he tried to stutter a response but it only came out as so much noise.

"Yeah, that's what I thought." Roy walked away from the stuttering kid with a knot of something in his gut. Maybe guilt. Maybe resentment that he couldn't shake the teachings of his father from twenty years ago.

Either way he knew one thing for certain. Lane wouldn't be happy with him. He had a chance to make a friend on the team and he blew it.

CHAPTER SIX

"ROY, CAN YOU tell us what it feels like to be back in baseball?" Pete Wright called out from the crowd.

"Uh, good. I didn't realize how much I missed it. It will feel better when I'm actually pitching a game."

"What about the contract?" a reporter in the front row, someone from ESPN, called to him. "You were making fifteen million a year when you left, now you've just been signed to a minor-league deal. How is your ego handling that?"

"Ego? What ego?" Roy joked. "I'm happy to have a contract and I'll leave it at that."

Lane watched from the back of the press room and couldn't believe what she was hearing. Roy sat in front of a full-to-capacity crowd, who were asking him anything and everything. More surprising, he was…answering them.

Real answers. Honest answers. About his past, how he felt about his return. And the reporters, most of whom knew him before, were lapping it up like someone had handed them ice cream with hot fudge and whipped cream for dinner when they'd expected liver and broccoli.

"He really is a new man."

Lane turned to see Scout squeeze in beside her. They were tucked together in the back corner of the room. Their little own island away from the swarming crowd.

"I don't know what he is anymore," Lane said. "But they sure are embracing him."

"An honest athlete? Are you kidding? That's sports-reporting gold. They are never going to let him out of this room. Speaking of which, what brings you here?"

Lane shrugged. The answer wasn't an easy one. After a week of daily therapy sessions she thought she had done a good job keeping her emotional distance from him. She was polite. He was respectful of her boundaries. They could talk about pitching and his arm and his physicality, although nothing else.

This was what she wanted, of course. To stay firmly entrenched in her stance of hating him. Not that it was a stance—she did hate him. He had hurt her, humiliated her and, worse, broken her faith in their friendship. Made her less trustful of people in general. Of course she hated him.

It was just that, after a week of being with him, working on his arm, talking about the prospects of the other players on the team, she had come to an awful conclusion.

She had missed him.

She wasn't supposed to have missed him.

Once his minor-league deal had been finalized and it was confirmed that he would be on the team, she knew this day would come. Press day. And she'd had this crazy thought that if he was going to bare his soul to the media, someone should be there for him. A familiar face in the crowd. One he trusted, even if that person didn't trust him exactly.

"Why are *you* here?" Lane asked her sister in a weak attempt at deflection. She could tell by Scout's reaction that her motivation was obvious.

"Uh, I actually work for the Minotaurs. My boss, Jo—you know, the team's owner—wanted me to be here while our new star player gives a press conference. This is sort of something I should be part of. His physical therapist, not so much." Scout's reply was heavy on the sarcasm.

Why was it that sisters never let sisters get away with anything?

"I just wanted to see how he would react to the pressure. Okay? It's no big deal."

That also wasn't too far from the truth, Lane thought. She did want to see that as well. How a humbled Roy would answer questions. How he would handle the interrogation that would delve into personal information, most of which the reporters would already know about.

His raw honesty had been a shock to her. Probably to him, too. He'd told her he was going to try a different approach and he had.

"Roy, can you talk about how your arm feels after this short preseason? And will you be ready for the season opener in a few weeks?"

Another question from Pete Wright.

"Sore," Roy said as the media laughed with him at the obvious answer. "But it's getting better and stronger every day. I've had a lot of help with that. With the physical recovery after each bullpen session. I've been really lucky. So yeah, come opening day I'll be ready. In whatever role the team needs me."

"He's talking about you," Scout said, nudging Lane in the ribs. "The helper."

"Is that Pete Wright up front?" Lane asked. "The guy who's married to your boss?"

"Yep. They're, like, the oddest couple. She's ten years older and rich. He's still struggling to keep the paper going and won't take a dime of her money to help. But when you see them together you can just tell none of that matters. Like they found the real thing despite all the obstacles and bullshit."

Lane snorted. "There is no real thing. That's the bullshit."

"Says the bitter divorcée."

"Exactly."

Scout shook her head and Lane could feel the judgment coming. She should have kept her bitter mouth shut.

"When are you going to let it go? I mean, really, Lanie, it's been five years. You were young. You hadn't figured out what you wanted in life beyond knowing you wanted a husband who was as connected to the game as you were. So you made a mistake. It happens. I never thought you would be the one to hold a grudge against all men for the rest of your life. You never had that much anger in you."

Lane raised her eyebrow in what she hoped was a semblance of Roy's are-you-kidding-me? expression. "Really? You are going to lecture me about holding a grudge? When was the last time you talked to your sister?"

"I'm talking to you right now."

"You know that's not what I mean. When did you last call your mother?"

"Who?"

"Right," Lane said, knowing what the mention of their mother would do to Scout's disposition. "Now that's a grudge, Scout. Disowning the woman who gave birth to you and raised you is way worse than being jaded about true love."

"Gave birth to me, raised me, cheated on my father, broke his heart and abandoned all of us for another man. Yes, a model of motherhood."

It was an old argument. One Lane knew she wouldn't win so she wasn't sure why she bothered. At some point in Scout's life she was going to have to reconcile with her mother. Alice—formerly Baker, now Sullivan—wasn't a bad person. She'd simply made a mistake.

People weren't perfect, Lane thought uncomfortably.

At the time Lane had been devastated by the divorce. The idea of not living with her father and her mother seemed like the end of the world. Yes, Duff traveled a lot, but in the off-season when he was home it was always the best time for them as a family. He would dedicate himself to being with his girls.

Lane had been angry at her mother when Alice told them about the divorce. Then horrified when Alice announced she was remarrying once it was final, making it obvious to everyone that the relationship with Bob had started before her marriage to Duff was over.

Samantha had been in college at the time and had missed much of the drama. Lane had been sixteen and squarely in the middle of it. Pulled between two parents she adored. Conflicted because she knew what her mother had done was wrong, but Lane still loved her. It was easier to feel sadder for Duff, because he was the one left alone. Her mother already had someone else.

For Scout, at fourteen, their mother's betrayal had been very cut-and-dried. There had been no conflict, there had only been sides. Her side was Duff's. And because of that, she would have no relationship with her new stepfather and was so cold to her mother that eventually Alice agreed to let Scout live full-time with Duff.

Including traveling with him and a tutor rather than staying in school when the season started.

Lane ended up splitting the time between parents. When she was with Scout and Duff it was like that whole other part of her life didn't exist. Like the two of them welcomed her back from some unknown land they didn't acknowledge.

All Duff would ever say about Alice was that the failed marriage was his fault. That he had messed up what had been the best thing in his life. He implored his daughters to not make the same mistakes he had. He told them they had to fight for what they wanted. To never give up. To do everything they could to make their marriages work.

That was why Lane had held on as long as she had with Danny. Looking back, her father's advice was probably what made her so eager to get married young in the first place. She wanted to put all those ideas to work. She wanted to prove to Duff she had listened, she had taken his wise counsel and wouldn't make those mistakes. To prove to her mother that if you loved someone enough, you could make a marriage work.

Show them both how it was done and let them be proud of her instead of sad that their own marriage hadn't worked.

Yeah, that plan hadn't worked out so well for her.

"Okay, it looks like they are finally wrapping up," Scout said as the frequency of questions slowed. "Your boy did good."

Lane looked to the front of the room where Roy still sat behind a table appearing poised, steady and determined.

She was about to remind Scout that Roy wasn't her anything, but knew it wasn't worth the effort. It was crazy but she couldn't help feeling this swell of pride for him.

Which was odd. How could she possibly be proud of Roy Walker?

THE ROOM CLEARED and Roy breathed a sigh of relief. It was over. All his guts spilled on the floor. He knew there was no way around it. If he had held anything back, they would have only dug harder. So he'd offered them everything, hoping they might leave satisfied. Still, he felt as if he had gone through intensive therapy with a large group of reporters.

Pete, the local reporter, approached with a wry smile on his face.

"That was…different."

Roy shrugged. "Not what the press usually gets from me, I know."

"Not what the press usually gets from any star athlete. It took guts and we all know it. I can't wait to tell your story. The people of the Falls are going to love you, Roy."

"Only if I can deliver the goods. Jury is still out on that."

"They'll love you for the effort. Who doesn't love a good comeback story. Speaking of which, I don't know if you remember me…"

Roy absolutely remembered him. Five years ago. A stadium full of people. One pretty impressive kiss with the team's owner right there on the pitcher's mound while she had been throwing the ceremonial first pitch. It had been Roy's idea, oddly enough.

He and Pete had met as another favor to Duff. Pete was supposed to be interviewing Roy but all he could think about was the woman in his life who was trying to walk away from him. When Pete had gotten desperate enough to ask for advice, Roy had told him to make a big gesture. What woman didn't love that?

"The big gesture," Roy recalled. "You kissing her in front of all the fans. I watched it from the dugout. Not a bad move."

The man's expression seemed to say it all. "Anyway, I wanted to thank you. I married her because of that advice."

"Then I'm glad it worked out for one of us." Roy thought of the advice he'd taken himself. The big gesture that would finally reveal to Lane everything he'd wanted to tell her. A party. A setup. An unfaithful husband. And him. Instead of doing what he'd hoped, it had all come crashing down on him and she was lost to him forever.

Except she was standing in the back of the room now. Why was she here?

"You made your own big move?" Pete asked.

Roy could see Lane, standing with her arms crossed over her chest, studying him as though she wasn't sure what species he was. He'd caught her eye in the throng of reporters a few times during the conference and each time it had given him a jolt of courage. A sense of purpose behind what he was doing. Yes, he wanted to bare his soul in front of these reporters one time so hopefully he wouldn't have to do this again. But he also didn't want to look like an ass in front of her.

Five years, he thought, and that feeling that he could never shake when he was around her then was still there. Like he could be, and maybe should be, a better man for Lane. Because she deserved it. *Why had she come?*

"Crashed and burned." To say the least, Roy

thought. "Maybe next time I'll try a public display of affection."

Pete chuckled. "Look, I know the last person you might want to spend time with is a reporter, but I'm asking this as the husband of the team's owner. Why don't you come for dinner some night? I know Jo would love to meet her new star player. We're really excited about what having you on the team will mean for the town this year."

Roy's instinctive reaction was to say no, but there was something open about Pete. Something non-threatening despite the fact that he dug into other people's lives for a living. Roy had liked Pete five years ago, maybe because it was obvious how love-sick he was over a woman, and Roy could empathize. He liked Pete now because he had been the only reporter in the room to keep the questions solely about baseball.

"Sure. Why not?"

"I'll be in touch," Pete said. "And I mean it, Roy. This time if you manage your publicity right, the people will love you."

A concept Roy couldn't wrap his brain around—there was too big a gap between that behavior and the way fans and players had treated him before—but he didn't want to dishearten a man who appeared so optimistic.

Pete collected his stuff and left. Roy could see Lane push herself off the wall with her butt, unwilling, it seemed, to uncross those defensive arms. With the room almost empty, she probably had heard his conversation with Pete. No doubt mention of Pete's big gesture would make her angry again because Roy's attempt at a gesture to her had ended in pain.

The good ideas he could dole out to other guys apparently deserted Roy when he needed a gesture. Even his engagement to Shannon hadn't been the result of some elaborate proposal. Instead, they'd had a coolheaded conversation where Shannon asserted the near future would be a good time for them to get married. Roy hadn't been able to refute that logic. Not until he'd realized what a lifetime of being married to him would do to her.

It wouldn't have been fair. Bastard that he was, Roy did give himself credit for recognizing that disaster before the vows were exchanged.

He watched Lane walk toward him and, for the maybe the millionth time, he asked himself why her? Why had some twentysomething girl gotten to him then? Why he hadn't been able to shake her all these years since?

Someone like you wouldn't get to have someone like me...

She had been right. Where she was honest and open and friendly, he was aloof and cold and closed off. There was no reason why anyone like her would want to be with him. Especially because Lane didn't care about the trappings of his fame.

She only saw the man and, because of that, he wanted to be the best man he could be.

Still, he wasn't some damn romantic. He was a realist. The guy who always knew the score. Whatever chance he might have once had, he'd lost it with that stupid party.

A hundred times since his plans imploded, he asked why hadn't he simply told her about Danny? Why hadn't Roy taken her out, gotten her drunk, then told her that her husband was a cheat?

Because he'd been afraid. Afraid she wouldn't believe him. That fear had also made him certain that telling her would ruin everything they had. The party had seemed so much…simpler. Let her see for herself what Danny was. Let her discover it on her own. Then Roy wasn't the bad guy.

Only that's not how it all had played out and he'd become the bad guy anyway.

He'd wanted her. That was the truth. He'd both wanted her and wanted to be a person worthy of having her. Because when he was with her he didn't feel lonely.

Which probably made him mostly pathetic.

In a sudden burst of emotion, it also made him angry.

She'd walked away from him. Cut all ties. She hadn't even answered his damn letter—he'd spent days crafting that thing. How many times had he written that letter? A hundred, maybe more, trying to get every word, every sentence right.

So while he hadn't let her go entirely, he'd moved on, hadn't he? Tried to remake his life. She'd made it clear that whatever they had was over and he believed her.

But seeing her at the back of the room today had given him some kind of weird hope. Hope that didn't make sense given how she felt about him.

She hated him.

It wasn't fair of her.

He strode toward her even as she turned to leave the room, as if she had no intention of acknowledging she had come in the first place.

"Why did you come today?"

The question sounded more accusatory than he meant it to. He didn't want her to know he was angry. He didn't want her to know why.

She turned around slowly, like she was trying to think of an appropriate response. "I was curious about what you were going to say. That's all. Don't read anything into it."

Right. Nothing there to read into. "Except you knew I was going to tell the truth. It's all I have."

"That's not true. You could have spun things. All athletes spin. You didn't. I was…"

"What, Lane?" He jumped on her dangling words. "What were you?"

She ducked her head and shrugged her shoulders, which only made him angrier.

"Why did you come? Why are you helping me with my arm? Why did you want to know if I called my dad?"

"I told you—"

"No, that's spin," he said. "You hate me, remember? You haven't forgiven me for what I did. You don't want anything to do with me."

Her eyes got big, as though she couldn't fathom that she was the one under attack. "Hey, last week you were the one who asked me for help, remember?"

"I do. I also remember you telling me I had nerve. You're probably right. I mean, who the hell turns to someone who hates him for help? What are we doing? What is all this? You didn't read my damn letter five years ago. Do you want to hear what it said now? Do you want to know how sorry I was for the pain I caused you?"

"No," she said, her arms still crossed over her stomach. Only now it looked like she was being punched in the gut over and over again and was trying to protect herself.

Only Roy didn't stop. Wouldn't stop. When you had your enemy against the ropes you finished the job.

"I can't figure you out, Lane. You won't forgive me, yet you're here like you have some kind of investment in me."

"The only investment I have is in your arm."

He could see her face turn a deep shade of red. The way it always did when he pushed her. Five years ago he'd lived for these moments. When she would hang around the clubhouse waiting for Danny Worthless and he would find a way to engage her in a conversation. Sometimes it was about politics, sometimes it was about baseball, but always it was about pushing her buttons, engaging her in any way he could. Anything to build on that connection between them. A connection she had been part of.

They really had been friends and he could see that something was different about her now.

"You might not like to remember this but five years ago we knew each other pretty well, so don't think you can fool me. Something is going on with you. You're looking for something here."

"I told you, Duff needs me."

"Really? I find it hard to believe that's the only reason, given how you cut me and baseball out of your life completely. Now you're running back here—where both baseball and I happen to be— because Scout's worried?"

There it was. The flicker of hurt in her eyes. He'd hit a chord. Hit it because he could read her. Not anyone else. Just her.

She had other reasons for coming home than Duff. And if Roy had to guess what those reasons might be, he'd say she was running away from something. Because that's what Lane did when things got too tough for her to handle.

"What are you running from this time, Lane?"

There was more than just a flicker of something her eyes. This time her body actually jerked.

"What do you want to know, Roy?" she snapped, clearly having lost her temper.

"I want to know your truth."

"Fine. You want to hear my sad, horrible story about my patient who slit his wrists? A patient I was so damn proud of because of the amazing work *I* was doing to get him back on his feet. So focused on myself, I didn't once notice…"

Roy closed his eyes. "Lanie…I'm sorry."

"I quit." She said it like it was a challenge. Like she was waiting for him to criticize that decision. Something he wouldn't do. "I left my job and came back here. I was doing incredible work with men and women who had served this country, something way more important than getting your stupid arm up to bullet-shooting speed, and I walked away. Because I couldn't deal with failing again. There, does that make you happy? You think you're the only person who lost something, Roy? You're not."

"No, it doesn't make me happy," he said, hurting inside because she was hurting. "At least it's not bullshit, though. Just call it for what it is, Lanie.

You're lost. Like I am. Somehow fate put us here together. Maybe there is a reason for that."

"Oh, no. There is no reason for this. No purpose. Just bad luck. This isn't going to be some sweet reconciliation where I forgive what you did to me and we become besties forever."

The memory of that night at the party, which was so indelibly clear in his head, came to him. The way her lips felt on his. The way her tongue felt in his mouth. Suddenly he was tired of that, too. Of allowing her to heap all the blame on him. There had been two people in that room.

He moved toward her, but in traditional Lane fashion, she didn't retreat an inch. He loved it. He loved the way she never backed down from him. He was smiling when he pushed his face close to hers and it was the first time he'd really felt like himself since that night.

"Forgive what I did to you… Always the same refrain with you, isn't it? I will remind you that it wasn't me who had some baseball bunny against a wall with my tongue down her throat. That was your husband. You know how I know it wasn't me? Because my tongue was otherwise occupied. If I remember correctly, you were sucking on it. Hard.

"I know what I did that night was shitty. But if you stop being so damn insistent that you're the victim of that drama, you'll recall I tried to get you out of there. *Before* anything went down.

"As for our kiss…yes, I started it. But you didn't finish it. Not right away. And maybe, Lane, that is what you're really angry about. Maybe your outrage over the setup is smoke and mirrors for your guilt. Because in that moment, that brief little window, you wanted me, too. You know it and I know it. I'm the one witness to the horrible crime of Lanie Baker wanting a man other than her husband. Admit it. That's what I've been paying for these past five years."

Roy waited to see what she would do. Would she slap him? Would she rail at him? Would she kiss him again?

A tear fell down her right cheek. He tracked it all the way down her chin, her neck, until it finally disappeared into her shirt.

There, he thought—that was perfect for him. Hurting the thing he least wanted to cause pain.

"I'm sorry," he mumbled. "Just sorry."

Then he moved around her and left the room and wondered what the hell had happened to him to make him be this kind of man.

The kind of guy who made Lanie Baker cry.

CHAPTER SEVEN

"DAMN IT, DUFF! When are you going to stop pretending? I'm making the damn appointment and you're going to go! What if I hadn't just gotten home? What if you had fallen and broken something?"

Lane opened the door to her family home to hear Scout shouting at Duff.

"Because I tripped and stumbled back into the couch? You're making much ado about nothing, Scout. And, quite frankly, you've become a nag. I'm a grown man and if I think I need to see a doctor, I will."

Lane found the two of them squaring off in the living room. Duff towering over his youngest daughter by a few inches but, somehow, Scout still seemed the more powerful of the two.

"Tripped? You could barely pull yourself up."

"Nonsense. A man's entitled to lose a little strength when he starts looking at seventy-six. You think you've found some doctor who can turn back time? Trust me, they don't exist. Now forget about it and leave me alone."

Lane winced. She could only imagine the pain those words would cause Scout. Scout never left Duff *alone*.

"Duff…" The hurt in Scout's voice made Lane ache for her. Still, it was time for Scout to back off and there was only one good way to do that.

"Scout, give him a break," Lane said.

It had the intended consequence. Scout focused her fury and pain on her sister instead of their father.

"Tell me again why you came home?"

The question was rhetorical but suddenly Lane knew exactly why she had come home. She'd been lost. So lost. It was like waking up after a long sleep and while she felt sluggish and confused, at least she knew she was awake and not sleeping anymore.

"I mean it, Scout. Duff's right. You've become a nag. Go take a walk and clear your head. I'll start dinner."

For a moment, Lane didn't think Scout would listen. Her jaw jutted out and her eyes narrowed as though she was ready to go into full-on sister-battle mode. A place the three Baker girls had often found themselves over the years. A place where no one ever really won, but it was a place where they maintained their pride.

"Fine. I'm done. Duff, do you what you want. Lane, thanks for all your help." Scout marched toward Lane with speed and purpose, hitting her on the right shoulder just hard enough to send Lane skipping a few steps to the left. The brush-by was Scout's signature move. Lane could have avoided it if she had wanted to, but she let Scout get her shot in to save face.

As soon as she was gone, Lane watched her father slowly and carefully lower himself into his favorite chair, his arms supporting his weight until the very end when they started to shake and he dropped the last few inches as if in free fall.

Losing a little strength didn't quite describe that. "Want a drink?"

Duff sighed and leaned his head back. "Scotch. Neat. And, for Pete's sake, don't tell your sister."

Scout found the bottle in the cabinet over the fridge. She poured the first glass and thought if anybody needed a drink right now, it was her.

Because in that moment, that brief little window, you wanted me, too. You know it and I know it.

She hated how true that statement was. Hated that it had always been Roy who had the uncanny ability to look inside her and know exactly what she was thinking. Most of all, she hated that the smoke screen he'd talked about was now gone. No longer could she point to it, almost as if it was a tangible thing, and make sure he stayed on the other side of it.

Because he was right. If she looked too closely at

her righteous indignation, she might see how completely not righteous she'd been that night.

She'd caught her husband cheating. Had he opened the bedroom door first, wouldn't he have discovered the same thing?

"Oh, my God," Lane whispered, her hands shaking as she poured the drinks.

Roy had set her up. She had been humiliated. But the hate that she had always directed at him wasn't really for those things, was it?

She went into the living room and put Duff's hand around the glass, watching for a second to make sure he had a firm grip.

Then she sat on the ottoman in front of him and waited until he had his first sip.

"You have to go to the doctor's, Duff."

"Oh, not you, too…"

Lane put her hand on her father's knee to stop whatever defense he attempted to argue. It seemed today was a day for the truth.

"You can't protect her forever. I know you want to, but you can't."

Duff took another sip and eyed her warily as if deciding what he could trust her with, which only confirmed for Lane there were things he was hiding.

"Scout fusses."

"Scout is scared. She called me and asked me to

come home and she was right. Something is going on with you."

"You have a job, a life in Virginia. She shouldn't have done that."

Lane shook her head and took another sip. It was bitter and horrible and smoky and delicious all at once. Truth serum. "No, I don't. I quit the VA hospital."

"What? Lanie, you loved that job."

"I lost a patient. Suicide. They said it wasn't my fault, but I can't… I can't not feel some kind of blame. Like if I had been paying closer attention, I would have realized what was happening in his head, not just his body. So I quit. Like I quit my marriage."

"You know those aren't the same things at all, so I'm not going to sit here and even pretend to argue with you. You had a bad turn. You need time to heal. The hospital will understand when you go back."

"Go back to what?" Lane asked as if suddenly realizing it was a question she'd had for a long time. "Duff, there is nothing there. There was work and my pride in my work. Now that pride feels like so much ash in my mouth."

"Oh, Lanie…"

"Don't. Truly, I'm not here for any pity. I don't deserve it. I wasn't the one who was hurting so much. I am dealing with it, just in my own way.

I'm letting you know that Scout was scared enough to call me. You scare her anymore and she'll reach out to Samantha. Do you honestly want all three of your daughters underfoot?"

He smiled then. He and Sam weren't close. Something Lane knew bothered Duff, but it didn't diminish his love for his older daughter one ounce. No, his was the smile of a father who loved all his daughters more than anything in the world.

"Yes."

Lane smiled back. "I meant underfoot and nagging you."

"No," he said, quickly shaking his head. "Not now, certainly."

"Make the appointment. Your doctor will send you to the hospital and they will run every test imaginable. You'll grumble. You'll hate it, but then it will be done. If the diagnosis is old age, then Scout will lay off and you'll have a little more peace in your life. If not, then we need to deal with it."

Duff seemed to consider the offer for a while, but Lane couldn't tell if he was just getting a little loopy on the Scotch. Finally, he nodded. "Okay. I'll do that. If you'll do this for me. Start living your life again. Not this monastic existence you've resigned yourself to because you're afraid of getting hurt. People get hurt all the time in this world, Lane. It happens and it's no reason to stop living. When you get to my age you realize how short life really is."

"I'll try." Only she could see now the problem really wasn't about being afraid to get hurt. For five years she'd told herself she couldn't get married again because of the mistake she made in choosing Danny.

"Duff, can I ask you a question about Mom?"

"Anything."

"You've always said it was your fault that you couldn't make the marriage work, but she had to take some of the blame, didn't she? I mean, she cheated on you. That wasn't right. That had to make you feel awful. Betrayed."

"Of course it did. But I had to accept that her affair was a symptom of a bigger problem. I wasn't the kind of husband she needed, always on the road, always putting baseball first. Because of that she went looking for someone else. That's why I never wanted you to blame her. Scout, she was so intractable about it, but I think, in time, maybe she'll come to see people aren't all good or all bad. Including her mother."

Suddenly looking at her parents' situation through the eyes of an adult, Lane wondered if there wasn't more to the story. What if the real problem wasn't Duff's baseball schedule? What if Alice just never loved him enough? If that was the case, then nothing he might have done or tried would have held them together. Maybe that's why her mother went looking for someone else.

Danny certainly hadn't loved Lane enough and by the end of their marriage she hadn't loved him, either. She'd been so unhappy, she thought. For so long. Trying to hold on to something that was never really there.

She could see Duff was getting tired so she took the glass from his hand. He gave her a pat, then tipped his head back. Lane took their glasses into the kitchen and by the time she returned, he was asleep.

For a time she watched him, satisfied that she had gotten his capitulation and that he would be seeing a doctor. At least something good might come out of her return home.

She made her way up to her room. She sat on her bed, looked at the ceiling and came to the conclusion that there was no way around what Roy had told her.

This was the hardest thing she had ever had to admit to herself. Not only that she couldn't make her marriage work, not only that she had fallen out of love with her husband. All of that was bad enough.

She had also told herself that her lunches with Roy were innocent. She had told herself it was okay to have a friend when she'd been so lonely all the time. She had told herself that it was no big deal that he would sit in a dunk tank for charity when he'd never done anything like that before, just because she asked him to do it. She told herself so many things except the truth.

Roy hadn't been only her friend. There had been so much more to their relationship for her.

It was a hell of a thing to realize, but she owed Roy Walker an apology.

SCOUT WALKED AROUND the rear of the house to the woods beyond the backyard. A worn path through the dirt and trees would eventually lead to a lake she and Duff used to fish in during the off-season.

They never caught a fish. Not one measly minnow. But they would sit for hours and pretend they were doing something other than just being together. Because being together always was their favorite thing to do.

He wanted her to leave him alone? She was some nag, some irritant to him? When she was doing everything she could to keep anyone from finding out about how truly weak he'd gotten in the past year. No one knew how many decisions she made regarding the team. No one knew how often he slept during the day because she was able to hide it from everyone.

Hell, even the owner didn't even know who was truly running the team.

Because Scout was damn good at her job and more loyal than any daughter ever was.

She kicked the dirt in front of her hard and took

some satisfaction in the pain. Now Lane, who was supposed to be helping, was turning on her, too. Scout wanted to scream at her to go back to Virginia and she might have done that if she hadn't figured out that Lane was here for some other reason than Scout asking her to come home.

Lane needed home and Scout could appreciate that.

It was important for Scout to keep her anger focused. She was mad at Lane but she was furious with Duff.

She wanted to throttle him. She wanted to rail at him. She wanted to shake him until he could see what she could see. And she probably could do that because he was so damn weak.

But more than anything, she just wanted him to be like he used to be. Like he'd been ten years ago, five years ago. Last year.

Picking up a rock, she hurled it as hard as she could at a tree. She heard the sharp crack of bark splitting away. She might be a girl, but she didn't throw like one and that sound reminded her of who she was. Who she'd always been.

Duff Baker's daughter.

Who the hell would she be if she wasn't that anymore?

ROY WATCHED THE KID—Billy Madden—pitch and saw about three hundred things he was doing wrong. Harry, the Minotaurs' pitching coach—who was about as old as Duff—pointed out two of them. Maybe he couldn't see very well anymore.

"You're not extending enough on the release, kid," Harry shouted out. "And you're overcompensating."

Roy glanced at Harry, who stood beside him and snorted. "That's what you're giving him? Really?"

Billy was far enough away on the mound that he couldn't hear the discussion. But Roy could see the kid kept looking over at the two of them. No doubt wondering what his idol thought of his stuff.

It wasn't bad. It just wasn't good enough. Not for The Show.

"Kid's got a fragile ego. I'm trying to bring him along slowly."

"*A fragile ego?* Yeah, that will help him in the big leagues when he's getting rocked."

"You know what didn't help was your little pow-wow the other day," Harry grumbled. "You've got him so spooked he's seeing three catchers out there instead of one."

"You should tell him to throw to the one in the middle. It might help."

Billy wound up and threw again. Harry held up the radar gun and Roy took a quick peek.

Ninety-seven. Impressive. But speed without control would get him nowhere.

Roy could feel Harry's eyes on him, studying him instead of the kid.

"You know you could work with the kid. A coach can only show him so much. Sometimes hearing it from a peer makes a difference."

"Now, there's a new low point. Wild Bill out there on the mound is my peer?"

"Hey, Harry!"

Roy turned and saw Lane walking toward them. He had this crazy urge to run away. That made him as immature as Wild Bill. Maybe they were peers. He hadn't seen her in two days, since their blowup. For a time he'd wondered if she had gone back to Virginia, but then Duff mentioned her name and Roy doubted she would leave the old man anytime soon.

Now that he knew about Lane and Scout's worries, Roy found himself watching out for the old man. Noticing how often the brim of his hat dipped over his eyes when he thought no one was looking. How he sometimes struggled with those few steps from the dugout to the field.

Roy wanted to tell Lane about it, but he wasn't sure where they stood. If she'd hated him before, he imagined she hated him even more now.

Only she didn't look angry. If anything, she looked as nervous as he felt about seeing her again.

She nodded in his direction and he nodded back. They stood side by side to watch Billy.

"His windup isn't consistent," Lane noted.

"Tell me something I don't know," Roy said. "But Harry here doesn't want to tell him everything that's wrong at once. Fragile ego and all."

Lane shrugged. "I'm sorry—I thought the point of Triple-A ball was to get kids ready for the majors."

"Really? Well, I thought the point of a physical therapist was to do physical therapy," Harry snapped. Then he grumbled about backseat drivers and headed out to the mound.

"He's going to say something about his inconsistency," Roy said.

"Yep. Harry is a dinosaur, but he knows we're right."

"He wants me to help the kid." Roy wasn't sure why he'd admitted that. Especially when he knew she wouldn't be thrilled with his answer.

"He could use your advice," Lane said casually. "Learn from your discipline."

"Why would I want that? This kid is in my way from making it back. He's got a faster fastball, which makes for a better changeup. If he ever gets control over his arm, he's going to look way more tempting to the big-league clubs than an old has-been."

Roy kicked around some of the turf with his cleat and waited for Lane's it's-important-to-be-a-good-teammate-as-well-as-a-good-player speech. Hell, he almost wanted it. Five years ago she would have told him that it's not always about the competition. Sometimes it has to be about the team and what's good for it. A concept he'd never embraced since it seemed too far out of alignment with his own goal of being the greatest pitcher who ever lived.

Instead she put her hands in her jeans pockets and rocked a little on her feet.

"What?" He prodded her, trying to reach her core of outrage. Reminding her who he was. Wanting her to remind him of who he was. "You think I should help him? You think I should risk my future for the sake of this kid? Not going to happen."

She turned to him and he could feel the pressure of her stare. Wanting something from him. It was always like that when they were together. She wanted him to be a better teammate. A better leader in the clubhouse. She wanted him to be a better son.

A better man.

He'd made her cry the last time they were together, and yet here she was standing next to him as if she was ready for round two. Still waiting for him to be something more than who he was.

In every area of his life. Except baseball. That was why, back then, he'd made a conscious effort to be around her as much as he could. Because, while sometimes it made him feel inferior, he also knew he needed someone to push him. Someone he respected.

What a fortunate break she'd married a cheating scumbag husband who was away more than he was home, leaving her and Roy space to become friends. Because when Lane had been part of his life Roy wanted to be better than he was. He knew he'd never succeeded in being that for her. In the end, he'd been a complete failure. But he figured thinking about it was a step up from not thinking about it at all.

"I'm not going to tell you to help the kid."

Damn, she really has given up on me.

"Even though you should," Lane continued, "because *A*, it's the right thing to do for the team. *B*, it's the right thing to do for the kid, and *C*, I think it would be good for you to stop thinking about yourself for five minutes."

A little stab of happiness pierced him. He looked at her and saw the frown lines in her forehead. Lines he'd helped to cultivate five years ago by driving her a little crazy.

Back then he might have countered her logic with a stubborn refusal. This time, however, he wanted to show her that maybe he'd changed. Or, at least, that he had the potential to change.

"I'll think about it."

He could feel the shock his answer instigated in her as she jerked toward him. "You mean that?"

"I said I would consider it, Lanie," Roy said sternly, hearing the happy surprise in her voice. "I didn't say I would do it. Don't start expecting things from me."

"Heaven help me if I did. And don't call me Lanie."

There. That sounded more like them. She never liked him calling her Lanie, because that was what her family called her. It was the implied intimacy. A nickname that should have been reserved for her husband, except that he was a worthless, cheating scumbag who didn't deserve the honor.

And you do?

Roy conceded the point to his internal demons. He didn't deserve any part of Lane Baker. Not back when he'd been an ace pitcher with a thing for her. Certainly not now as a business wash-up clinging to some last gasp of hope that he could have a do-over.

"What are you doing here anyway? Shouldn't you be off somewhere seething with hatred for me?"

"You do make me so mad," she said, looking at her feet.

He could have taken back what he'd said about the party and the kiss. He could have let her off the hook by saying maybe it had been only his imagination that he felt her response. Or wishful thinking.

He didn't. Because maybe, just maybe, rather than trying to re-create whatever it was they had, he had a chance at creating something new. Something that wasn't based on either of them hiding anything from the other.

"But…I owe you an apology," Lane finally said.

"Lane, you don't."

"No, I do. I blamed you for something I did. I let you take the fall because I didn't want to look at my role in my failing marriage. I didn't want to read your letter because I didn't know what it would say. I was mad at Danny and you and the world. It just seemed easier to not deal with anything and—"

"Run away," he said bluntly.

She nodded. "And run away. But what you did to me… I can't let you off the hook for that. You have to know that really hurt. You've said you're sorry. That's fine, but why did you do it in the first place? If you were my friend, why didn't you just tell me—"

"What would have happened if I told you? What would have happened if I took you to some place and said, 'Lane, your husband is a cheater. No proof, no pictures, just take my word for it.'"

"I honestly don't know."

"I do," Roy said, because he'd played it out a million times in his head. "You would have told me to go to hell. You would have defended him with your last breath because he was your husband and you believed you owed him your loyalty, if not your love. You were my friend. My only friend. I couldn't risk it."

She shrugged. "But you risked everything anyway."

He had. Only it was five years later and she had asked him about his dad, and was working on his arm, and she had come to his press conference. She was still talking to him. Still standing next to him.

Silence set up camp between them as they watched the kid throw.

"How come you broke off your engagement?" Lane asked.

The question was like a backhanded slap, shaking loose all the other thoughts in his head. His engagement. Shit. He definitely did not want to talk about that.

Or maybe he did.

"I heard you were engaged. You were still in the media enough for it to make the papers when it ended. I was curious what happened. Why you couldn't make it work?"

Maybe now was the time to not hold back. He could tell her the truth about his broken engagement and see what she did with the information. Put all his cards on the table and see how she reacted.

A fear gripped his belly and suddenly it seemed like a little too much forthrightness. They had spent the past ten minutes talking to one another and so far neither had walked away either apologizing or crying. Roy considered it progress and it was not something he wanted to ruin.

On the heels of that thought he had to ask himself if he was sure he wanted progress with Lane. Was that hope a good thing?

He had thought he'd put whatever lingering feelings he'd had for her to bed a long time ago. Knew that there would be nothing more between them when he hadn't gotten a response to his letter.

Sure, he had acknowledged he would never forget her. His failed engagement was proof of that. But he'd stopped missing her every day. Stopped wanting her. Stopped thinking that something in the universe would change and give him another shot at her.

Yet, here they were. Standing next to each other on a ball field.

"Nope," he said eventually. "Not ready to tell you that story. Maybe someday, but not today. Ask me something else."

"Like what?"

Roy had no idea where the impulse came from, but the words were out of his mouth before he could stop himself. "Ask me if I've ever lied to you."

He watched her face scrunch up and he knew he'd hit a particularly raw nerve.

"It's not an answer I care about," she said, looking over his shoulder.

"Because you won't believe me."

"I'm sorry. I won't. Trust just isn't something I have a lot of."

"That's not true. You trust Scout, you trust Duff. You trust me to be an ass. Not everyone is a cheater and a liar, Lane. You got stuck with one, but it doesn't have to be that way again."

"There's not going to be an again, so it really doesn't matter."

"So, that's it? One bad relationship and it's game over?"

She held her hands up and shrugged as if to answer his question without having to say it out loud. But he wouldn't accept it.

"Ask me if I ever lied to you."

"It won't change anything, Roy."

"But don't you want to know? Aren't you curious? Don't you want to see if we're all liars?"

"Fine," she snapped. "Did you ever lie to me?"

"Yes."

He watched her face fall, then her body stiffened. "Right. My point exactly. Everyone lies to everyone else at some point."

"I hate hot dogs."

"What?"

"I hate them."

It had been their thing. Lane loved hot dogs. She told him she could spend her life eating nothing but hot dogs if she had to choose only one food. It had been stupid, really, but for some reason, it was something he thought they could share.

So he told her he loved them, too. A few times after a therapy session or when they weren't bickering about something, they would search for the best dog ever. Gourmet hot-dog places would open up around the stadium all the time. Or sometimes a new hot-dog stand opened in the stadium and they would always check it out together. Try all the various different options.

With onions, cheese, chili. With bacon and eggs. With jalapeños, pulled pork and coleslaw.

Watching Lane devour a hot dog was an event Roy could routinely get excited about even though it meant having to force the vile things into his mouth.

"But...you loved them... We always ate them—"

"Nope. Hated every bite. I spent my entire childhood eating nothing but dogs every day of the week. By the time I was twenty, I rebelled and said I would never eat another one again. Then, later, you came along and you loved them. So I would choke them down just so I could watch you eat and get excited about whatever combination of toppings was on it that day. I must have eaten...what? Like a hundred dogs with you. Hating every last one of them. But it was still the most fun I had back then."

Lane shook her head. "I don't know what to say."

"Nothing to say. Just know it was the only thing I ever lied to you about, Lane. I promise you that."

It was hard because he wanted to see in her face what the truth might mean to her, but part of him couldn't bear to watch it, either, so he turned away from her and walked toward the dugout, not once looking over his shoulder to see if she watched him.

He didn't have to look back. He could sense it.

Her eyes followed him all the way.

Roy didn't know what it meant. He only knew he liked the feeling.

CHAPTER EIGHT

"WELL, CHUCK, DID you ever think you would see this?"

"Do you mean Roy Walker pitching again or Roy Walker struggling so badly out there on the mound, Ed?"

"It will be interesting if this disastrous opening puts an end to his comeback."

"Let's talk about that, Chuck. What do you think this comeback is all about? A stunt? A way to fill more seats? It's not like the Minotaurs are lacking in support lately."

"He said it was about the money and I believed him. I just don't see it working out at this point. Or maybe that was a smoke screen for what he really missed—the spotlight."

"There is sure going to be a spotlight on him after this performance, only I don't think Roy's going to like it very much."

Lane took out the earpiece. She wasn't sure what was worse—listening to the various boos around her in the stands or listening to the local broadcasters dismiss Roy's comeback like it was some kind of gimmick. He'd been honest in his press conference. Everyone knew this was about him having no choice. It was not fair for them to question that.

But pitching the way he was today, it was hard to see how a comeback was possible.

Another swing of the bat, another hit. Roy had loaded the bases for the second time. The people in the stands grumbled. Even Scout couldn't suppress a huff of disappointment.

"Jeezus, he's sweating like it's a hundred degrees out there," Scout said.

Lane figured it probably felt that way for Roy. The sun blazing down on him, the energy of the fans who had started the day rooting for him, only to slowly turn on him as he gave up hit after hit. Roy didn't know what it was to fail like this. Not that he'd never had a bad day on the mound, but certainly never this catastrophic against Triple-A batters.

"Why isn't Duff taking him out of the game?" Lane asked.

Sometimes a manager would leave a pitcher on the mound as a way to test his fortitude. Could he continue to pitch in the face of adversity even when he was getting rocked? Could he keep his composure?

Roy wasn't some young pitcher who needed to be tested like that. Leaving him out there was borderline cruel.

"You're assuming Duff is awake."

Lane looked at Scout. They were sitting high up in the stands. Away from the concentration of crowds, no one within earshot. Still Lane took issue with Scout's sarcasm.

"You know he's still your father. A little respect, please."

"Hey, you're the one who asked why he was leaving Roy out there to get shelled. I'm just giving you the facts." Scout trained the binoculars on the dugout. She always had them at games to see the pitchers' movements up close. "He's got his sunglasses on and his arms across his chest. He either has no problem watching this train wreck or he's taking a catnap."

"Then why the hell isn't Harry doing anything?"

Harry had been slated as the temporary assistant coach. The permanent position had been left open until the Rebels made a decision about who they wanted to bring up to fill that role. No doubt the delay was because whoever it was going to be would most likely be the heir apparent to Duff. Which could mean he was a manager slated for the bigs someday. Much like the players, the coaching staff had to prove themselves in the minors before making it to the major leagues.

"You think Harry is going to challenge Duff? The guy worships him. Talk about respect."

"Well, this is just wrong. Someone needs to do something."

Scout laughed. "What are you thinking about doing? Going down on the field to get him yourself? That I would like to see."

"I might," Lane mumbled as she watched him struggle to get another ball over the plate.

Another crack of the bat echoed throughout the stadium. This time it was so loud there could be no doubt the ball was going out of the park. A grand slam. The score was now nine to one and it was only the top of the third.

"Get him out of there!"

Lane glared at the back of the man three rows in front of them as if he would sense her displeasure. It was pointless, though. She couldn't keep the entire stadium from expressing their frustration. Truly, she probably shouldn't care so much. She was here to make sure he didn't blow out his arm. There was nothing she could do about his pitching.

Except he'd had to tell her that he lied about liking hot dogs. Why had he done that? What man would do something like that just to spend time with her? Hell, she'd asked Danny to take a ballroom dancing class once and he'd flatly refused. Wouldn't even consider doing something he didn't want to do just to make her happy.

She'd watched Roy choke down hot dog after hot dog. For her.

"There he goes," Scout said. "Duff finally woke up."

Lane watched as Duff made his way slowly and deliberately out to the mound. Roy's jersey was soaked through with sweat and by the time Duff took the ball from him, Roy's head was so low it was as if it had been swallowed by his shoulders.

"You need to talk to him."

Lane didn't pretend to not know who Scout was talking about. "What am I supposed to say?"

"Whatever. He needs you. Remind him of who he is. He needs his swagger back, his mojo. Pitching is so much more than mechanics and you know that better than anyone. Or you used to before you turned your back on the game."

"You act like I betrayed baseball. I was the one betrayed, remember?"

"By a jackass of a husband, not the game of baseball. That guy out there has one chance to come back. *One.* You can help that cause or you can go back to your life in Virginia and put your head in the sand."

"I have no life in Virginia anymore. Okay?"

"What?"

It felt as if telling everyone all of her secrets made the reality of what had happened really sink in. There was no job waiting for her—not one that she was ready to take on again. And there was nothing else waiting for her in Virginia. What she really needed to do was start thinking about getting out of her lease and packing up her stuff. It just seemed like too much right now with everything else that was going on here. Eventually, though, Lane would have to make some hard decisions. Just not today.

"I had a patient. He killed himself."

"Jeez, Lane."

"I can't…do that work right now. I need to get my head around what happened. Otherwise I'm never going to feel right about working with these guys again."

"You can't know what's in a patient's head, Lane. Hell, sometimes even shrinks don't know that."

"I should have known," Lane snapped.

"Seriously? Who are you supposed to be now? Some kind of superhero?"

"I'm just saying that maybe the problem is with me. I didn't see Danny for what he was until too late. I don't see that I have a patient who is suffering until it's too late. How can I not take responsibility for that?"

Scout threw up her hands. "It's not going to matter what I say, so I'll shut up about it. But, Lane, let me remind you that you were a nationally known physical therapist. Athletes all over the country killed for your services. The work you did for those soldiers, that was important stuff. Really important.

You can't not do that anymore because you think you have to be perfect at everything you touch. It's not fair to the people who need you. More than that, it's too much a part of who you are."

"I just need a break," Lane said, trying to not feel the guilt Scout was inflicting. "It's not the end of the world, okay? I have some savings to hold me over until I find another job. Eventually, I'll decide what's next."

She didn't want to turn quitting her job into a big deal. But walking away from the work forced her to evaluate everything. She had an apartment, not a house. She had patients, not friends. And her family lived in another state.

Really, what had she been doing in Virginia, so far away? Why had she been doing it?

Running.

"Where will that be?"

"Huh?"

"Where are you going to get a new job?"

That, Lane thought, was a very good question. One she wasn't absolutely sure she had an answer to yet.

"Well, you let me know when you figure it out," Scout said. "Because I sort of care about the answer."

ROY HUNG ONTO the showerhead with his right hand like it was the only thing preventing him from falling into a deep and endless well. Hot water poured over his head and all he could hope was that it burned out the memories of today.

He looked at his left arm, now hanging uselessly from his body.

"Traitor," he muttered.

His first outing of the season and it had been a complete and total disaster. He tried to tell himself that he'd pushed it. Came back too fast. Duff had given him carte blanche to make his own schedule for return, but having the contract meant taking a place on the roster. A place some other young kid wasn't getting a chance at because Roy had messed up his life.

So he'd fought to come back as fast as he could. Maybe the arm just wasn't ready. Like he told it, it had betrayed him.

"Horseshit." Roy sighed. The problem wasn't in his arm, although his shoulder had hurt like hell toward the end.

Really, the problem was the space between his ears.

Space that used to be filled with a bone-deep confidence in himself and his abilities was suddenly empty. Each batter at the plate felt like every creditor to whom he'd owed money after he'd failed to deliver his product.

Finally, Roy had to concede that a shower wasn't going to cure him. He wasn't sure anything could.

As he stepped out, he saw he wasn't alone. Billy stood there and tossed him a towel. The game was still going on but Billy, not being available to pitch today because he pitched yesterday, could leave the bench if he wanted to.

His expression looked pained. Must be hard for a kid to watch his idol crash and burn. Which, fortunately, made Roy angry enough to salvage some of his pride.

"What the hell are you looking at?"

"Look, man, I know it was rough out there. I just want to let you know those kinds of days…we all have them."

Roy didn't. Roy had never had that happen. He'd never not believed he could strike a batter out. Today he'd lost that faith after the second batter and he never got it back.

"Are you giving me a pep talk, kid? Because let me tell you where you can stick that."

Billy held up his hands as if in defense. "Hey, I just wanted to say it's okay. What happened. You'll get them next time."

"Kid, if you don't get out of my face in five seconds, so help me, God, I will find a bat and take it to your head. My left arm doesn't work, but my right arm still does."

The threat registered enough that he actually took a step back. "What's your problem anyway? I'm trying to be a decent person here. A good teammate."

"Haven't you heard about me? I don't give a shit about my teammates."

"Yeah, well, you keep pitching like you did today and you won't have to worry about having them much longer."

The blow was brutal and right to the core of Roy's vulnerability. Billy's jaw dropped as if he couldn't believe the insult had come out of his own mouth.

"Nice shot, kid. That's how you hurt an asshole like me."

"I didn't mean… I mean…I'm not like you—"

"Yeah, I know. Do yourself a favor and stay that way."

Roy walked around him and the kid did the sensible thing by not following him.

After the game Roy waited for his teammates to come down the tunnel. He'd gotten dressed and had to sit in the locker room as the innings played out. He'd come close to leaving before the end. The thought of just walking away, getting into his Jeep and pretending this whole comeback idea had been one big mistake was tempting.

He was being paid under a contract and he still had enough sense to know he needed the money. He also had enough respect for Duff that he wouldn't blatantly show up his manager by doing something so disobedient as leaving before the end of a game.

As everyone came in and started getting undressed, no one said much to him. Duff made his way over eventually and Roy squirmed a bit under the scrutiny.

"Never seen you do that."

"Because I've never done that."

"Hmm. Arm okay?"

This was it. An easy way out. He could say he wasn't ready and maybe take his next few starts off. Anything to not have to face going out there again. Not until he got his head straight.

"The arm is fine."

Duff nodded. "Thought so. You got six days before the next start. Better figure something out."

Roy nodded. "Can I go?"

"Sure. Go get drunk and forget today ever happened. Just be ready to go again by next Thursday."

Roy slung his bag over his right shoulder and left the locker room and the guys behind him. The thought of getting drunk right now sounded ridiculously appealing. He thought about the Maverick at the end of Main Street, the most popular bar and restaurant in town, and immediately crossed it off his list.

He didn't need to see anyone tonight. Especially any of the locals who had been at the game.

And especially not her. The woman who waited for him outside the stadium, sitting on the hood of his Jeep. Why he thought he had the kind of luck where Lane would have decided not to see his first outing of the year, he didn't know. Luck wasn't something Roy ever believed in. Never needed to when he'd been given so much talent.

"Rough day?"

"Yep. You know Billy actually tried to give me a pep talk."

"Ouch," Lane said. "Does he still have his head?"

"If I was going to do permanent damage to anything, it would be his right arm." Roy leaned against the Jeep next to her. "You going to try and cheer me up? Tell me it wasn't as bad as I think it was."

"Oh, hell no. It was every bit as bad as you thought it was."

Roy nodded. "Thanks."

"Do you want that? For me to coddle you?"

He didn't, of course. It was always important for any athlete to appreciate the truth about his performance. For a second, though, he thought about Lane opening her arms and letting him rest his head against her soft breasts while she rubbed his neck and murmured that everything was going to be okay.

He'd seen her do it once. When he'd been on the Founders. The first year after she married Danny, when she was still so filled with love and hope. It was Danny's second season as a full-time starter. They had a tough game that went into extra innings only to lose in the eleventh. When they had left the locker room all the wives who hung around were lined up waiting for their men. Lane was always the first face the guys saw. A pretty face it was, too, with her sparkling green eyes. She had wrapped her arms around Danny and rubbed his back and told him how proud she was of him for fighting so hard.

Roy had watched that interaction and felt a deep-seated need to have that kind of comfort. The kind he hadn't gotten since he was a boy. It made him miss his mother and want Lane all in the same instant, which had been odd and strange.

He should have told her then. That the man who was sucking up all her comfort had been banging some redhead in the hotel room next to Roy's on their last away trip. Of course, he hadn't. He had called his mother, though, when he got home.

"What happened, Roy?"

He shook his head, trying to bring himself back to the present and reality. A place where Lane wasn't here to welcome him into her arms. In truth, he wasn't certain why she was waiting for him. Lately, though, he hadn't been certain of why she did anything related to him.

In the past few weeks they hadn't talked about much beyond the shape of his arm. She seemed to be still digesting the truths he kept dropping on her head like bombs and he wasn't certain where that left them. But unlike Billy, he didn't feel compelled to send her away.

"I don't know. I couldn't get my head straight. I would throw a bad ball and get pissed, then I would throw a strike without thinking about where I was putting it. Hit after hit. It felt like they all had five-inch-wide bats. That anything I got over the plate was coming back the other way."

"What did Duff say?"

"To get drunk and forget about it."

"Okay."

Roy looked at her. "Okay what?"

"Let's get drunk. I'm guessing you don't want to come back to the house. Scout will be there and she'll break down all the things that were wrong with your mechanics. I'm also guessing you don't want to be amongst the townsfolk. They are not exactly pleased with you right now so it'll have to be your place."

"You would do that?"

"I said I would."

"Why? You hate me, remember?"

"You know, as pathetic as you are right now, I'm willing to overlook that."

She smiled at him and he couldn't not smile back.

"Okay. Drunk it is. At my place."

"WHAT'S GOING TO be your poison?" Roy asked as they entered the kitchen. He'd dropped his things by the door and held it open for Lane to follow. In a way it was all rather surreal. Like they had been transported to some other place and time where they didn't have all this horrible history between them.

Back to a time when they'd been friends.

"What do you have?"

"Pretty much everything, but I figure if we're going to go down, we might as well do it like men and drink whiskey."

Lane smiled. "Bring it."

Together they set the scene. Roy put some classic rock on the radio. He sat on the couch while Lane sat on the floor, facing him over the coffee table. She found a deck of cards and started dealing. The whiskey bottle sat between them and Roy poured out a few shots into short glasses.

"Gin?" she offered, holding up the cards.

"Sure. Goes with whiskey."

For a time they fell into a sort of numb silence. Cards going back and forth hitting the table with thumps. Lane kept adding up points on a pad she found, all the while cackling to herself and telling him she was winning. It was odd but it was the closest he'd felt to anyone in a long time. Certainly closer than he'd been to his fiancée.

He didn't want to think about what that meant and because he didn't want to think about it, he took a few more sips. Eventually his head started to mellow and, for a moment, he could forget what happened earlier that evening.

"You know this is a pretty nice place." Lane looked around, ready to deal another round of losing cards to him.

"I'm renting. The owners are letting me go month to month. I figured that was best since, at any moment, I might be called up by the bigs. Now I'm thinking I'll be lucky if I'm still with the team in another month."

"Duff isn't going to give up on you after one bad start. This is a process, Roy, and you know it. You probably should have set your expectations a little lower."

"Lower than giving up nine runs in three innings of work? Trust me there is nothing that low."

"I meant about the mental aspect of the game. You turned it off like a switch when you walked away. You probably thought you could just turn it on again. You forget it took you years to get ready for The Show. From the time you were in Little League, through high school and the time you spent in the minors. It wasn't a switch. Your dad had been preparing you for years."

"My dad." He groaned and reached for the bottle. "He's going to hear about this."

"You didn't tell him what you were doing?"

He could hear the censure in her tone. "Don't get on my case, Lanie. I was going to tell him. I meant to tell him. I just…didn't. I'll call him tomorrow. Hard to know if he'll be thrilled to know I'm back or horrified after today's start."

"Why do you do that?"

"Do what?"

"You call me Lanie. I tell you not to, but you still do it. All the time."

She looked at him so intently and, even through the beginning haze of alcohol oblivion, he knew the direction of their conversation had changed. His defenses down, he considered getting up and walking away. He could call her a cab and send her on her way without getting into it. Because right now he felt vulnerable. Exposed to his very core.

Instead of doing any of that he answered her.

"It's how I think of you," he said simply. Honestly. "Like you're someone who is close to me even though you haven't been in a long time. Sitting here now it doesn't seem we had that five-year break. With every day that passes it feels like how it used to be back then. Between us. Is that crazy?"

"Maybe a little. And you lied about hot dogs, which is just flat-out weird."

He chuckled. "I would have eaten a hundred more hot dogs if it meant spending time with you."

"What about your shoulder…did you lie about that, too? So I would work on you?"

"No. Anytime I asked for help, that was real. I wouldn't mess with you like that, not with your work. Your gift."

Lane shook her head. "The first time I ever met you, you hit on me even though you knew I was engaged."

"Yes, and you laughed in my face and told me I

was pathetic. 'Even if I wasn't engaged, someone like you couldn't have someone like me.' I've never forgotten it."

Lane winced. "I said that? Ouch."

"You did and you were right." Roy took another slug of his drink. "I was a brooding ass and you seemed to be the only one who would call me on it. It's why I wanted to spend as much time as I could with you. I needed you then, Lane, to keep me in line."

She nodded slowly. "Can I ask you something? And this is really hard. But I have to know the truth. Did I do anything to encourage you, you know… that night at the party. Did I make you think that what happened was going to happen?"

"Oh, hell no. Don't get me wrong. I knew things weren't great with you and Danny. It was on your face every time I saw you. You were sad and… lonely. But you're one of the most loyal people I've ever met. You never would have done anything if I hadn't pushed you. You should also know it wasn't even entirely about wanting you for myself. I just knew I wanted something better for you. Someone better than him. I can't believe I'm saying all this. Must be some pretty damn strong whiskey."

Lane instantly leaned over and poured him some more. He laughed and watched her fill up her own glass. "You sure you know what you're doing?"

She shrugged. "Maybe it's time we just got it out there."

"Maybe. I always did like talking with you."

"Talking? What about all the fighting we did? When we weren't eating the hot dogs you hated."

"Interpretation." He shrugged. "You called it fighting, I called it sparring. I liked watching you get all fired up about whatever the topic was. I loved listening to you talk about the game. The way you loved it like I did. Then I would see you with him, and know what he was doing to you behind your back and it would drive me a little crazy."

"Crazy enough to have a party," she said, shaking her head in bafflement.

"It was my big gesture. When it came to relationships I had no idea how I would be. What I could offer. You're right, I didn't trust people enough to let them in. I thought I was saving you and that was all I was doing. Then in that moment before I kissed you, I knew. I knew you weren't in love with him anymore."

Lane uncurled her legs and stood. She hesitated for a second as if to make certain she wouldn't topple over, and then she sat next to him on the couch, but she wouldn't look at him.

"It's sort of my biggest secret," she whispered. "Actually my second biggest secret."

"I won't tell anyone. I swear."

"I knew after the first year with Danny that he

wasn't… That I needed more. I knew something was wrong. We looked happy. I made us look happy, but we weren't actually happy. I didn't know he was cheating, but I had this sense we were growing apart when we should have been growing together."

"That sucks."

Lane nodded. "It did. You have to know when my mom left Duff it almost destroyed him. I had a front-row seat for all of it. He kept talking about how it was his fault. His fault for being away so much. His fault for not giving my mom what she needed. His fault she found it from someone else. He made us say over and over again that relationships were worth fighting for. They were the *only* thing worth fighting for. So I fought and I fought harder. But the harder I fought, the harder it was to have the energy to keep fighting. During that time you and I were becoming friends, I thought it was all so perfectly innocent. Until you kissed me and I couldn't pretend anymore."

"That's what upset you the most that night. I was right about that, wasn't I?"

"I cheated, Roy. I cheated on my husband…with you. You weren't just my friend."

Roy sighed. "What's your biggest secret, Lanie? I want to hear you say it."

She looked at him then. "I don't hate Roy Walker."

CHAPTER NINE

LANE SAT STILL, not exactly sure what was supposed to happen next. She'd finally said the words out loud to the one person she thought she would never tell.

"It was so easy to play the victim," she admitted. "I'd been lied to and cheated on. Yet the whole time I knew I had stopped loving Danny long before that. Then when you kissed me… I felt something. I did. I couldn't pretend we were just friends. I couldn't pretend you hadn't meant something to me. I guess I wasn't ready to deal with that so I poured all of that confusion into being mad at you for betraying me. It was so easy to blame you for what happened. To hate you instead of me."

Roy was quiet as he brushed his fingers along her chin. Touching her, but not moving in on her.

"I cheated and I have to deal with that," Lane said.

"You're human like anyone else. Some relationships just don't work out. No matter how hard you want them to."

"Is that what happened with you and your fiancée? I think I've shared enough secrets with you by now to hear that story."

Lane wasn't sure why it mattered so much, but it did. In acknowledging that she had feelings for Roy, it was easier now to see there had been that little pang of jealousy when she'd heard he'd gotten engaged to someone else. She'd also been a little sad.

Like the credits had rolled on their movie and it was officially over. No happy ending in sight.

Then she'd heard the engagement had been called off and it wasn't as though the news made her happy. It just made her feel like Roy wasn't going to get his happy ending, either. She shouldn't have cared, but she did.

"I didn't love her," he said softly. "Not all the way. I liked her too much to let her be stuck with me for the rest of her life. She always thought there was some ghost in my past. Some traumatic event that wouldn't let me truly commit to anyone. For a while she thought I hadn't gotten over the loss of my mother. I never told her about you."

Lane whooshed out a breath. "Wow."

"Yeah. Wow."

It was strange because as they sat on the couch with their legs pressed together and the lingering feel of his fingers against her cheek, Lane thought there might be more anticipation. That moment when the truth was out there between two people who had been as honest as they could be with each other.

Now it was time to move on to the next part.

Only Lane wasn't entirely sure what that next part was. She wasn't even sure she was ready for it. Five years of denying her feelings, five years of holding him to blame for everything, five years of holding on to the emotion as strong as hating him. All of those things didn't just go away because they'd swapped secrets.

She assumed the logical next part involved kissing Roy. Something she very much wanted to try again to see if it had all been real. The flutter in her stomach. The desperate need she had to return his kiss. That sudden physical connection to a person she was already mentally connected to.

He didn't lean into her. He didn't press her back into the couch. He didn't touch her other than with his rough fingertips, so hardened by holding and throwing a seamed ball. His hand on top of hers, smothering it. Until he moved his hand away and stared at the floor instead.

"I'm not sure what's supposed to happen next," she said, vocalizing the turmoil inside her head.

"Me, either."

Yet another thing that had changed in Roy. That night at the party he hadn't hesitated in telling her what he wanted. Hadn't stopped until he kissed her.

Now he looked like a man frozen in indecision.

"You don't want me anymore," she stated. It was a crushing conclusion but there was a certain sense to it. She'd fallen out of love, she'd cheated—at least emotionally—on another man. The whole time she told herself she would never risk getting married again because she would never trust herself to choose the right person. That decision, made with eyes that weren't clouded with denial, could have also been made because she didn't trust herself to be the right person for someone else.

Although as soon as she said it, he tossed his head back and laughed.

"Wrong guess. I've got over a thousand fantasies revolving around you, Lane Baker, stored away. I could spend every last waking moment trying to execute them all and I would still die unsatisfied that I hadn't gotten enough of you. All of you."

That sounded promising. "Then isn't this part when we kiss?"

He stood, walked away and she thought that probably wasn't a good sign.

"I guess not," she muttered.

He'd picked up the whiskey bottle between his fingers, took a slug and leaned on the wall as far across the room as he could get from her.

"I don't deserve you. I sure as hell am not any more deserving than Danny Worthless right now. I'm a mess. What in the world would you want with me? I lost all my money. I'm making a desperate attempt to do something I haven't done in five years to get some of it back. Hell, if tonight's any indication, I can't even do that anymore. Look at me, Lane. Look at me, now. Not at the man I was ten years ago when you met me, or five years ago when maybe, for a hairbreadth of time, you wanted me."

Roy stretched his arms wide, then turned in a slow circle so she could see all of him.

"That man is gone. So no, I don't know what happens next."

Lane did look at him. She remembered the jerk who had hit on her to test her loyalty to her fiancé. She remembered the cocky son of bitch who would guarantee wins and always delivered. The horrible teammate. The reclusive loner. The grieving son.

She remembered the man who stood on a mound and, for his farewell performance to the game, pitched a no-hitter. His last love letter to baseball.

The guy who wouldn't do charity events publicly, but who would quietly fund the Youth Athletic League for a year without anyone knowing.

He needs you.

Scout had said it, but until right now, Lane hadn't really understood what that meant. She'd worked with enough vets who had lost pieces of themselves, literal pieces, to know how hard the journey back to being whole could be.

Roy hadn't lost his arm. Just some money. So there was no real tragedy for him. But he'd lost something else—his confidence, his swagger—and it was time for him to get it back.

Lane stood and rubbed her hands on her jeans like there was a big project in front of her and she had procrastinated long enough. It was time to get to work.

"You're right. You don't deserve me."

She wasn't exactly sure she deserved him, either, but she would hold off on those thoughts for now. This wasn't about what she was capable of giving to him, it was about showing Roy how to be the man he used to be, at least on the mound.

"I guess that means if you want a shot at fulfilling all those fantasies, then you're going to have to earn me."

His eyebrows arched and then his smile seemed to grow out of some deep part of him. "Really?"

"Sure. I mean, you want me. You better do something to impress me. That is what men are hardwired to do, aren't they? You're going to have to bang on your chest a few times and see if I take notice."

Roy undid the first few buttons of his shirt. "You know, I've always thought you had a thing for my chest."

Lane walked toward him, putting her hands over his to still them. When he dropped his hands she buttoned him up again. This moment between them hadn't ended the way she thought it would, but it felt right. Like maybe neither of them was ready for what came next.

"Not so easy, stud. I was speaking metaphorically. As impressive as your chest is, I'm going to want more."

"Like what?"

Lane shrugged. "I guess that's what you'll have to figure out. I'm going to call a cab. Try not to get too drunk. You'll have a day off tomorrow but you should probably watch some footage so you can figure out what you were doing out there today and fix it."

"Will that impress you? If I pitch better?"

"I'm a baseball girl. It can't hurt." She opened the door, her cell phone in her hand. "Oh, and Roy, you know what else impresses me?"

"What?"

"Being a good teammate. Total turn-on."

TEAM. MATE. THE next morning Roy showed up at the stadium to find the footage one of the crew had taken so he could see just how bad his outing had been. Following Lane's advice, he hadn't gotten too drunk, just drunk enough to make the pain of embarrassment go away. Although it really hadn't required any more whiskey to make that happen. Not when all he could think about was Lane.

Did they seriously have that conversation? More importantly, did he seriously have a chance?

You're going to have to earn me.

More than anything in the world he wanted to

do that. He'd wanted her for years. From the moment she'd called him out for the fraud he was, he'd known she was special. He'd taken every opportunity to get to know her. Every chance to spend time with her. Making the most supreme sacrifices when it came to her. Including eating hot dogs.

Then he'd blown it and had figured that part of his life was over. Even when he'd called off the wedding with Shannon, he hadn't done so with any hope that someday he might find Lane again. He'd just known deep in his soul he didn't feel about Shannon the way he'd once felt about Lane. He'd thought that unfair to both of them. Him for perpetuating the lie. Shannon for having to live it.

Now his whole world had suddenly gone through this crazy shift. Up was down and down was up. Lane didn't hate him. Lane wanted him to impress her.

Lane wanted him to be a better teammate.

Team: a group of athletes working toward the common goal of winning. Mates: friends.

Roy could understand the first concept. It was the second one he was a little hazy on.

Instead of tracking down the footage, he made his way through the lockers and down the hallway leading to the dugout. Stepping outside onto the field, he could see Wild Bill working a bullpen session with Javier.

The kid was all over the place and once again

Harry was keeping the coaching a little too simple. Coddling the kid wasn't going to get him anywhere. Certainly not to The Show. Roy thought about what the kid had braved yesterday. Coming down to the showers to be what Roy had never been: a good teammate.

For his efforts Billy had gotten his head bit off.

Maybe that's what Lane really wanted him to be. A better man. The type of man who wouldn't chew up and spit out someone fourteen years younger just because he could. Because he'd had a bad day.

Roy walked up to Harry. "Hey."

"Hey. I got the footage in my office. Keep in mind it's not what you're used to. This is the minors."

"Yeah, I know. I'll be on the bus with everyone else tomorrow for our road trip to Scranton."

Harry cackled. "No private jets in our league. Better get used to slumming it."

Given that Roy had no other choice he kept his mouth shut. "I was thinking maybe I should talk to the kid."

"You've talked enough to the kid," Harry said abruptly.

"No, I mean, I want to— I'm thinking I could… help…him."

The words didn't come out easy, but he'd said them. Which meant he'd already made the decision. He was going to try to win Lane Baker. Going to attempt to be that better man he'd always wanted to be for her, but had never managed to fully pull off.

Harry looked at him and Roy could feel the skepticism in his gaze.

"I'm serious," Roy said. "You want this kid to have a shot, give him to me. He needs discipline. Not to mention another pitch."

"He doesn't need to have his soul crushed."

Roy thought about the conversation he'd had with his father last night. Of course his father had found out about his outing. It was all over the sports news.

Roy hadn't known what to expect, but the hurt in his father's voice was something Roy hadn't been prepared for. Not because Roy had lost the money. The press conference he'd given apparently had been reaired. Not because Roy had pitched so poorly in his first outing. Just because his father hadn't known where he was or what he was doing.

Hadn't known where Roy was currently living.

"Do you need something from me, son?" he'd asked. "I don't need this big fancy house you bought me. I can sell it. You can use that money, get a new start."

The words, so quickly said after Roy explained what happened to his company, were like a punch to the gut. That house was the symbol of everything his father had achieved through Roy. That his father had not only recognized Roy's talent, but he'd also refined it. Improved it. Protected it. So that Roy might achieve greatness.

And he had. It should have been the end of the story.

Now suddenly that story was starting all over again and his father's first instinct was to sacrifice what he'd rightly earned to help his son. For a long time Roy had wondered if he'd ever been anything else but a ballplayer to his father.

Now he knew it wasn't that simple.

Mom, I think I'm starting to hear him.

He told his father that he didn't need to sell the house. That even the minor-league contract he'd signed would be enough to get him back on his feet. That he was working toward maybe another one- or two-year deal, which would take care of his retirement.

His father thought it a good plan but then asked the question Roy wasn't sure he knew how to answer.

Do you still have it, son?

The question still lingered in Roy's mind. So did his answer.

Absolutely.

He wasn't sure if it was actual confidence or more like an attempt to fake it until he started pitching better, but Roy thought it was a good sign. There was a sense of rightness in saying it. A hint of how he used to feel about his talent.

The kid throwing the ball in front of him needed some of that confidence, too.

"I'm not going to crush his soul, but I'll need to beat on it a little. To harden it some if he's going to stand a chance."

Harry gave him a slight nod and Roy held out his hand. Harry took a ball from his jacket and tossed it in the air. Roy caught it and made his way over to where the kid was standing and waiting for Javier to give him his next signal.

"Wild Bill, a minute."

Roy could see the kid stiffen. It was an off day for the team before they left tomorrow for their road trip, so the stadium was empty except for the skeleton coaching crew working with the pitchers. Wild Bill's throwing session was the first of the morning so it wasn't like there was an audience.

"What?"

Attitude sat pretty well perched on the kid's shoulder, something Roy had encouraged.

"You throw a wicked fastball."

The kid jerked as if he'd been expecting a punch and instead was rewarded with a hug.

"But if you don't figure out how to consistently deliver it, you're going to spend your baseball career on a bus heading toward Scranton and that's as good as it's ever going to get."

Billy jutted his chin out. "Really? After yesterday you think you're going to give me tips?"

"Yeah. You want me to get my World Series rings and put them on first? Or maybe I should get my Cy Young Awards? You want to see those?"

The kid shifted on his feet.

"It's your consistency," Roy said. "Every single time your follow through has to be the same. You do it for the first pitch, then the second. By the third you're wavering. By the fourth I don't know what the hell you're doing."

"I'm feeling the moment," he said, as if that meant anything.

"What?"

"You know. You have to feel each moment. Be in the present."

"Who in the hell taught you that?"

"My psychic counselor."

Roy grimaced. "What the hell is a *psychic counselor*?"

"She reads my auras. Checks my signs. Let's me know when a streak might be coming, that kind of thing. She says I need to feel the moment. Be in the present, otherwise I might miss the signs."

Roy's face must have expressed his disgust because, if it was possible, the kid delivered even more attitude.

"It's a real thing," Billy snapped. "And she's got me this far."

"Kid, come here." Roy waited while the kid took a step forward before Roy cuffed him on the side of the head. Hard enough, hopefully, for Billy to see stars. "Get that shit out of your head. You want to stay in the minors or do you want to get to The Show? Because The Show doesn't care about chakras and auras and shit. The Show cares about mechanics. Day-in and day-out mechanics that you must master completely. Feel the moment? Please! Start focusing on what the hell your body is doing, not your head. The head will come, but you are not even close to tackling that."

"Why should I listen to you? You said you were my competition. Maybe you're saying all this just to mess me up."

It was a reasonable suspicion. Roy figured he needed a good answer. Something the kid would both understand and believe. Roy saying he had a change of heart sounded as lame as a psychic counselor.

"I'm doing it for a girl."

"Huh?"

"I'm helping you because I want to get laid and she thinks I need to be a better teammate so that's what I'm going to do. You get that?"

Billy seemed to think it over. "She hot?"

Roy laughed. "Yeah, she's hot. She's Lane Baker."

"Oh, man. You got no shot. She's totally major league."

"You been checking out my girl?" And why the words *my girl* felt so right to him, he couldn't say.

Roy smiled just thinking about Lane's reaction if she knew how he had referred to her.

My girl. My girl, Lanie Baker.

"No, she's, like, too old. But I'm thinking I might have a shot with her sister."

"Kid, your only shot with Scout is if you develop a solid curveball."

"Yeah," Bill said, looking a little more smug than he had a few minutes ago. "Well, maybe your only shot with Lane is if you help me develop that curveball."

Roy considered the offer. His intention hadn't been to work so closely with the kid. Roy had thought he'd give him some hard, real feedback, maybe give him a few pointers. Nothing to the extent of what Billy was asking for. But... Help the kid, win over Lane. A chance. A real honest chance to have something with Lane Baker. He would have been scared out of his mind if he wasn't so damn happy about it.

"Deal."

"You mean it?"

Roy nodded. "You listen to everything I say. You do everything I tell you. I find any funny crystals in your locker and the deal is off."

"I'm telling you, Madame LaRange is legit. This is baseball, man. Every dude in that locker room is superstitious as all get-out."

"I mean it," Roy said. "From here on out it's about the body. Not the soul."

Roy left the kid to return to his session and went in search of his own footage. Scout was waiting for him in the dugout with a DVD in her hand.

"I would watch it with one eye closed," she told him.

"Good advice."

"What were you saying to Wild Bill?"

"I'm going to help him develop a curveball."

"Really?" Scout asked, surprise evident in her tone.

"Yeah. If you wouldn't mind, could you let your sister know?"

Scout smiled. "Sure."

Roy returned her smile, took the DVD and headed through the lockers. He had this odd feeling in his stomach like suddenly he was hungry when he hadn't been a moment ago.

Odder still, he sort of felt like having a hot dog.

CHAPTER TEN

LANE ROLLED OVER in bed and thought for a second about what had woken her up. Not her alarm. She didn't have to go to work today. She didn't have to go work any day because she'd left her job.

Temporarily, she told herself to quell the panic that hit her. She'd only left her job temporarily. She would go back when she was ready. If she was ever ready again for that kind of work.

A conscious thought tried to make its way up from the depth of her slightly whiskey-addled brain. Something about today being different than yesterday, but it was quickly cut off with a reminder of what had woken her up.

"You have got to be kidding me!"

The sound of Scout screeching. In many ways her sister was what most would consider a tomboy. She could catch, throw and hit a ball better than most grown men. However, her one girlish weakness was that when she was upset her voice rose about five octaves until she sounded like a howler monkey.

It was her girliest quality.

Assuming her sister was about to engage in

another battle with their father, Lane pushed herself out of bed. She'd already made a doctor's appointment for him for next week. There was no point nagging him anymore.

She made her way down the hall to the shared bathroom, where she planned to smother her toothbrush with extra paste to forever wipe the dry, stale taste of whiskey from her mouth. Her minty breath restored, she headed downstairs to referee. Lane stopped at the sight of her sister standing in the kitchen with tears running down her face. For a second it nearly took the wind out of Lane.

She hadn't seen Scout cry since the day their parents announced they were getting a divorce. Getting a divorce and Scout having to live with her mother. That's what had actually brought on the tears.

Not one tear since then. Not that Scout didn't cry. Lane could think of a few cry-worthy events in her sister's life, but she never did it in public or even with her family. Until now.

"I didn't think you would be this upset," Duff said quietly.

"How could you not think… How could you even let this happen?"

"It's not entirely in my control, you know."

Lane felt her gut tighten as she entered the kitchen. The doctor's appointment wasn't until next week. There was nothing anyone could know now.

"What? What are we talking about?"

They turned toward her and Lane could see that whatever they were talking about was serious. Serious enough to make Scout cry in front of Duff. Although now that Lane was also in the room, Scout was scrambling to wipe the tears from her cheeks.

"Tell her!" Scout screeched. "Bad enough you made her come back to face Roy Walker, now you're turning around and doing this to me. What the hell, Duff? Is this some kind of revenge plot because I asked you to go see a damn doctor?"

"Now, you calm down, Scout. I told you. I didn't have a choice. They are looking to bring him up as my replacement. Possibly as the potential future manager of the Rebels. This is coming from upstairs and I can't stop it."

"I'll talk to Pete," Scout said, as if she was already running potential solutions. "He can talk to Jocelyn. If the owner of the club doesn't want him here—"

"Who?" Lane asked. "Who are we talking about?"

It was as if neither Scout nor Duff wanted to say the name. Silence hung as Lane tried to put pieces together.

"I can't think of anyone being more upset than me having to face Roy. Who could possibly be worse than that for Scout to be so upset— Oh."

"Yeah," her sister said tightly. "Oh."

"Jayson," Lane murmured. The only man who

had the slightest chance of meaning more to Scout than Duff. Until Scout had cut him loose.

"He's been managing a Double-A club in Texas," Duff explained. "The Rebels just hired him to be the new assistant manager here. The kid has got a way of cultivating talent. A real player's manager, which seems to be in vogue these days."

"I won't let this happen. Jocelyn can stop this."

"For what purpose?" Duff asked, throwing his arms up in the air. "To not have the best manager she can have for her ball club? Really, Scout, I don't get it. The way you're acting, you'd think he was the one who broke up with you and not the other way around."

"He left me!"

Lane winced. Complete howler-monkey mode.

"No. He took a job. He asked you to go with him and you didn't. There is a difference. Now all this ruckus has worn me out. I'm going to rest for a while and when I wake up we can talk about this calmly and sensibly."

Duff rose and slowly climbed the stairs. He was supposed to be leaving tomorrow for a three-game road trip. How the hell was he going to manage that if he needed a nap before noon?

Maybe Lane could drive him so he wouldn't have to take the bus with the team. Then she could get a hotel room where the team was staying—where Roy would be staying—to keep an eye on Duff.

Was it wrong to be thinking about her father and Roy at the same time? Lane decided she needed some coffee before tackling such philosophical problems.

"Can you believe it? I mean, that he would even consent to it is unbelievable."

And there was also her sister to consider. Scout had been with Lane through every bad moment of her divorce. But when Jayson left, it was as if no one was supposed to talk about it. That Jayson had all but begged Scout to go with him wasn't to be mentioned. That everyone, including Duff, thought she was making the biggest mistake of her life by not following him was also not a topic open for conversation.

Outwardly, Scout hadn't seemed the least bit fazed. She acted as though it was a normal breakup of a casual relationship that didn't stand up against the pressures of distance. Scout's behavior told Lane how much she hurt inside. The more Scout pretended she was fine, the more Lane knew it was eating her up.

Yet Scout wouldn't talk about it, with anyone. Basically for three months after he left she stopped talking about anything that wasn't baseball.

Come to think of it, Lane realized, not much had changed in the past four years.

"It didn't sound like Duff had much of a choice," Lane said gently. "If the decision is coming from the Rebels' front office, you know how that works. They have the final say over all personnel decisions. Players and support staff included."

"He's Duff Baker. He's still got some sway. If he wanted to object, they would listen. I mean, he's a Hall of Famer for crying out loud. He could tell them Jayson's not ready and they would believe it."

"Wow," Lane muttered.

"What?"

"You would go that far? You would actually derail his career just because you can't handle seeing him?"

Scout's eyes narrowed and her mouth became a straight, tight line. "There are other teams. Other ball clubs. Why does he have to come here?"

"Scout, you know better than anyone that timing is everything. The right opportunity at the right time. Sometimes it's the only way to get ahead. You can't be angry with him for leaping at this job. Truthfully, the sooner he gets here, the better it will be for Duff. Maybe if he thinks he's left this team in good hands, he can finally retire. Maybe the thing really wearing him down is trying to manage the club. It's not exactly a nine-to-five kind of a job."

Lane could see the glimmer of hope in Scout's eyes and she wasn't sure if it was wrong to give her that. Then it seemed to fade as quickly as it had come.

"So Duff gets to nap whenever he wants and I have to find a new job."

"New job? What are you talking about?"

"You think Jayson is going to keep me on staff once Duff steps down? Don't be naive. He won't want to see me anymore than I want to see him." Scout paced around the room as though she needed to expend energy. "I can't believe all this is happening now. Can't you feel it? Can't you just feel everything slipping out of control?"

She was right. Lane felt it, too, in so many different ways. Her work, her life, her family…Roy.

Lane wanted to ask Scout about how the relationship between her and Jayson really ended. How much of a fight Jayson had put up when Scout refused to leave Duff? A big one? Or had Jayson recognized the futility of competing with her dad? The few times Lane had met Jayson, she'd thought he was such a nice guy. Maybe too nice for Scout.

Because the guy who successfully separated Scout from her father would probably have to fight a little dirty.

Although, depending on what the medical tests revealed, the separation between daughter and father might be happening for a different reason altogether.

Too much to think about without coffee.

"You want me to talk to Duff for you?"

Scout's laugh was harsh and brittle. "Just make

sure he keeps his appointment next week, okay?"
She made to leave, but then stopped. "Oh, and I was
at the stadium earlier this morning. Roy says to tell
you he's going to show Wild Bill how to throw a
curve. Got the impression there was a reason for
that. Am I wrong?"

Lane shrugged.

"Great!" Scout threw her hands up in the air.
"Just great. You and Roy will start making eyes at
each other and I have to deal with the fact Jayson
is coming back. I really don't think things can get
any better for me!"

With that, she left the house, making sure to slam
the door on the way out. Probably not caring if it
woke up Duff or not. Her small bit of revenge for
her father scaring the crap out of her and Lane now
caught up in a…what? She had no idea what she
was doing with Roy.

If anything, what she was doing could be cruel.
Using herself as some kind of bait to lure him out
of his malaise. What would happen if it worked?
What would happen if he made it back to himself
and the prize he found standing before him was
Lane Baker? This woman he idealized who had
blamed him instead of herself when she cheated.
Who ran away from things when they got too hard.
Who quit jobs where people needed her.

He'd reminded her of that night at the bar when
he hit on her. She hadn't remembered her exact

words to him, but she had remembered feeling so smug. Like she had figured out all the answers because she was twenty and in love and about to be married. And poor Roy Walker would never understand what that kind of happiness meant.

Now he was a man pulling himself up from a hole so deep he could barely see daylight. And despite all that, he was trying to do what she wanted—helping a teammate improve his game.

He thought he didn't deserve her? The truth was she didn't deserve him.

She wondered exactly when he was going to figure that out and what it would do to her when he did.

"You got to grip it like this," Roy said, showing Billy how his fingers circled the ball. The two of them were sitting together on the bus on the way to Scranton. The scenery along Interstate 81 passed by them in a blur of trees that were just starting to fill out with spring growth. "Your middle finger right there. Not a centimeter off. Your thumb right here. See that? See that?"

Billy studied the position of the ball in Roy's hand and nodded. Roy tossed the ball to him and Billy played with it idly before holding it in the exact way Roy had shown him.

"See. Good. Curveball." Javier was sitting behind them and seemed to be encouraging the knowledge exchange between the two pitchers.

"What are you two doing?" Max asked. The Minotaurs' first baseman, who was sitting next to Javier, leaned over the seat and shouldered his way between Roy and Billy.

"He's showing me some stuff. What's it to you?" Billy asked as Roy reached over and changed Billy's grip on the ball ever so slightly.

"What the hell, Walker? I thought you were the antiteammate."

Roy shrugged. "Yeah, well, maybe I'm not anymore."

"He's trying to get laid," Billy said as if that was the most logical reason for anyone to undergo such a transformation.

"Can you maybe not share that?" Roy sighed. "That was supposed to be private."

"What? You said you wanted to be a better teammate. Teammates talk about getting laid all the time. The other night I had this girl, man, she was so hot—"

Roy slapped him upside the head. "I don't want to hear about you nailing some baseball bunny. Save that for your boys when you're out drinking at the bar. You want to be a professional baseball player, you act like a professional when you're on the job."

"But we're on the bus?" Billy pointed out.

"Going to the job. This is part of the business."

"Laid." Javier chuckled, nodding his head in total concert.

So much for trying to be an example. These kids would never learn. Which, in turn, made Roy feel like an incredibly old man.

"So who is she?" Max asked.

"Lane Baker," Billy said.

Max shook his head. "Dude, you got no shot. She's an ex-baseball wife. They hate all baseball players by default because they've had the life. One and done, you hear what I'm saying? They take that money and they find some nice houseboy who won't even blink without checking in with them first."

Not what Lane had done at all. Instead, she'd buried herself in work when she probably had enough money from the divorce to never have to work again. Roy thought about Lane taking some big million-dollar payoff, but the image wouldn't come. Revenge money? Blowing it all on fast cars and expensive shoes? Boy toys?

It didn't fit. Especially when he considered that she drove a relatively sedate two-door car. And as far as he could remember, flip-flops had always been her favorite shoes.

Still, there had to be some money. Samantha had represented her in the divorce and there was no way Samantha would have left a penny on the table out of sheer hatred for her ex-brother-in-law.

Roy wanted to ask Lane about it. He wanted to ask her about everything that had happened in the past five years. He wanted to know every moment of every day because then maybe he wouldn't feel like he'd lost something vitally important to his happiness. Something he'd lost because he'd been so stupid as to throw that party.

If he'd only kept his mouth shut and let Lane's marriage play out. How much longer would it have been before Danny got caught? Then Roy could have stepped in with a sympathetic ear. Someone she could lean on. They could have turned their friendship into something deeper and then who knew where it might have gone from there.

Maybe if Lane, with her practical intelligence, had been in his life, she might have seen the proverbial writing on the wall of his gaming company way before he did. Helped him get out before it crashed down around him. Lane would have never held back her opinion.

Shannon hadn't cared about the company all that much. Only their relationship mattered to her. Roy's job was just the thing he did so he never felt compelled to share any of the problems with her. And because he didn't share, he didn't get another perspective about the company's situation.

If only. The two worst words in the English language as far as Roy was concerned. Because there was no going back in time and changing any of it. His decision that night of the party might have impacted every day of these past five years and there was not one damn thing he could do about it.

Only now it seemed like that story was over. Behind them. Lane didn't hate him. That was some kind of miracle in and of itself. More than that, it felt as though she wanted something from him. Which meant he had a chance. A real chance to have something—some*one*—he never thought he could.

His chest tightened at the thought. For that matter, so did his balls.

"Well, I'm going to give it a shot. She wants me to be a better teammate, so that's what I'm doing. See this here, what we're doing, talking and everything? This is me trying."

"Not bad," Max said. "I mean, for a start, but if you really want to be a better teammate, tell us about how you made it to The Show. How do we get from this smelly bus heading to Scranton to our own private plane?"

"I'm telling you, Madame LaGrange says—"

Roy hit Billy upside the back of the head hard enough to make him stop talking.

"Stop doing that, man," Billy moaned. "You're going to give me, like, a concussion."

"Or knock some of the idiocy out of you. It's a toss-up to see which one happens first."

"Come on, Walker, tell us what we need to do," Max prompted.

"You want to know the trick?" Roy asked. "The secret no one tells you?"

Billy, Javier and Max pressed closer, waiting for Roy's words as if they were about to hear the password that would allow them to enter the magic kingdom.

"Yeah, but don't feed us some bullshit like we have to want it more," Max groused. "Every guy on this bus wants it more."

"Don't tell us we have to work for it, either," Billy said. "I've heard that freaking cliché from every pitching coach I've ever had."

Javier nodded, pointing to his chest. "Me. Already work hard."

Roy nodded. "Yeah, that's the stuff they feed us because they think they need to motivate us, right? If we really want it, if we really work for it, if we strive for it with everything we have... It's all bullshit. We're here. We already know what we want. To be the best there ever was. To be part of a game that's been our nation's pastime for well over a hundred years. But there is one way and one way only to make it to The Show and that is to be better than the next guy. The sad fact, friends, is that's not something you can control."

Roy turned and saw their faces. Knew deep down they felt the truth of his words. You could work the hardest, you could want it the most and still, it didn't make a difference. Not if the other guy playing your position had more talent.

The men quieted and settled in their seats. Roy rested his head and closed his eyes, thinking a power nap might be in order. Maybe Duff had the right idea all along with his little naps. Because suddenly Roy felt exhausted. Whether it was from the jostling of the bus, the weight of his thoughts about Lane, the sheer panic over his future...all of it seemed to be taking its toll.

After all, the last time he'd ridden the bus to Scranton he'd been in his early twenties.

Back then he'd never had to ask for advice on how to get to the majors. Never had to ask because he knew he belonged there. That he was destined for it. This time around the uncertainty was nearly paralyzing and he found himself empathizing with Billy, Max and Javier.

Empathy. That was definitely a new feeling for him. The question was, did it make him a better man?

CHAPTER ELEVEN

LANE PULLED IN behind the bus and parked the car. "Duff, we're here."

She looked at her father sitting in the passenger seat, apparently sound asleep, and reached over to gently shake his arm.

"Hmm," he muttered as he jerked awake, blinking a few times as if trying to remember where he was.

"We're stopping for lunch."

The restaurant was part of a chain and the cost would fall within the budget of the players' food stipend provided by the team. She thought of the forty-seven dollars Roy had been given for food for the day and wondered how painful a reminder it was of his new station in baseball life.

A far stretch from the days of endless, high-quality food provided for free, of having any whim granted. Danny had always insisted there be Diet Dr Pepper with lime in the clubhouse at all times.

Lane should have known then that their marriage was doomed. Forget his cheating, he was also a major prima donna when it came to stuff like that. His shower flip-flops could only be worn three times before they had to be replaced. He always had to have scrambled eggs on game day. Three whole eggs and one egg white.

Looking back, she realized what a jerk that behavior made him. Roy never pulled any of that crap. Maybe that's why he was able to face riding the bus now.

Because the crazy part about all of it was he seemed to be taking the changes well. Humility wasn't something she would have imagined sitting well on Roy's shoulders, but he managed to carry it gracefully.

"You know, honey, I'm not that hungry. Why don't you go in and order something to go for me. A milk shake sounds great."

Such a simple statement. In many ways totally innocuous. Sure. Why wouldn't he want to stay in the car, where he was comfortable and resting? She could bring him a strawberry milk shake, his favorite, which would be cool and soothing for the rest of the drive.

Only it was one more reminder that Duff Baker wasn't the same man today as he'd been a year ago. When a trip to a restaurant that offered essentially any fried-food item known to man would not be passed up.

Lane used to joke that he had the digestion of a man a quarter of his age. Like a steel drum, Duff's stomach could handle not only fried food, but also his truly favorite delicacy, fried food covered in hot sauce.

Now he wanted to stay in the car and get a milk shake to go.

"Duff, you need to eat," Lane said, quietly uncertain as to how to handle the situation. She could see the players piling off the bus and heading inside, some looking at her expectantly to see if Duff would get out of the car so they could take the opportunity to walk inside with him. Maybe have a chance to sit with him.

That was the one thing that hadn't changed in the past year. The players still adored Duff. He was a legend and, like any legend, he was filled with stories he loved to share and players loved to hear. Beyond the laughs, those tales usually made the players feel connected to something bigger. A part of the history of the game. And maybe, just maybe, one day in the not-so-distant future, Duff Baker would tell stories about them, too.

Duff didn't make a move to get out of the car.

Lane felt frozen with indecision. When she'd told Scout she planned to drive Duff, Scout had shrugged and said it was probably a good idea. Duff and Scout hadn't spoken to each other since the announcement that Jayson was coming to New York. Though Lane knew their mutual silence had to do with more than an ex-boyfriend's return.

Still, Lane couldn't help but feel a little guilty. After all, Scout had been the one to keep Duff's fatigue from the team and the other coaches. She'd been there for him day in and day out while Lane had been burying herself in her work in Virginia. It felt a little sacrilegious stepping into her sister's shoes at this late date. But no good would come from Duff and Scout being in the same car together for hours on end.

The two of them were at a stalemate. Scout seemed to be done asking questions and Duff seemed to be done giving any answers. Given their equally stubborn personalities, this freeze-out could last for days.

As each day passed, as each change in his normal patterns emerged, it was getting harder for Lane not to get to the place where Scout already was—thinking and fearing the worst.

Next week. The doctor's appointment was on Tuesday. They couldn't know anything until then.

But attempting to calm her panic gave her no insight into how to deal with this Duff, the one sitting in her car still half-asleep.

The thought, when it came, was so ugly, yet Lane didn't look away from it.

Maybe I should leave.

If she went to Virginia and negotiated to get her job back, she wouldn't have to see what was happening to Duff. Maybe if she were a few states away, she wouldn't have to know he wasn't eating fried food anymore.

She'd already run away from her work because something bad had happened. If she was going to run away from her family next, then that would officially confirm her as not only a quitter, but also a coward.

Why did she do that? Why was her first thought always to run when things got hard?

It's what Mom did. And, after all, aren't I just like her? A cheater?

"You go in, Lanie. I'm just going to check out the eyelids a little more."

Right, not a nap. Not acknowledging the fact he'd already been sleeping for two hours. No, this was perfectly harmless. He was only ever checking out his eyelids.

"I think some food might give you a little more... energy. The game is at five o'clock."

It was already noon. They would eat then head directly for the stadium. Figure more than two hours for the game and Duff would be weak from hunger if nothing else. She hadn't seen him eat anything more substantial today than a few bites of a bagel for breakfast.

She looked at him and could see him watching her as if weighing some decision in his mind.

"Okay, Lanie. Maybe some French fries would taste good."

"With American cheese melted on them," Lane added, smiling, feeling as if she'd been given a gift.

"Now you're talking." He winked at her and she knew the effort, whatever it cost him, was for her. So she might be a little less afraid for another day.

He swung open the door and slowly started to pull himself out of the car.

Then he stopped.

"What's the matter?" *Please don't let him have changed his mind.*

"Just giving the legs a second or two to wake up."

Lane was a physical therapist. She knew about blood flow and what it did to muscles. She got out of the car and walked to the passenger side, waiting as Duff rubbed his legs.

She moved closer to help him stand. "Here, Duff, let me—"

"Lanie, I love you, but can you back off for two seconds?"

Feeling like she'd been scolded, Lane stepped back and collided with something solid. Roy's chest.

"Hey," he said as he caught her arms and held her steady.

"Hi." She turned and attempted a smile.

Roy was looking over her shoulder and it seemed with that one glance he'd figured out the situation. He reached out his hand and Duff took it. All it took was a simple tug, a flex of Roy's arm, and Duff was on his feet. Lane had worked with enough men twice her size to know that she would have been able to accomplish the same task, but not as seamlessly and with as little fuss as Roy had.

Duff took a few careful steps and then seemed to have his ground underneath him.

"Much obliged, Roy. You ready to throw tomorrow?"

"As ready as I'll ever be."

Duff chuckled and patted his shoulder a few times. "You'll be fine. You'll see. And do me a favor, tell Lanie to get that worried look off her face. It will give her premature wrinkles."

Lane crossed her arms over her chest and watched as Duff caught up with the players. Anyone looking at him chatting easily wouldn't suspect he'd slept the entire drive and had contemplated sleeping through lunch, as well. Now he looked like a manager in command of his team. Heading into a restaurant for some power food before he took his men into battle.

Lane had never appreciated how good an actor her father was.

"You okay?"

Lane looked at Roy and shook her head. "It's an act," she said, hoping he would understand.

"I know. It's his act. Let him have his pride. Sometimes it's all that keeps a man up in this world. I know because I hardly have any of it left myself."

"I don't know what to do with him. Why didn't

he see someone sooner? Why didn't he take care of this?"

"He's not stupid, Lane. And he's not a child. You have to stop treating him like one."

Lane wanted to rail at Roy that he couldn't possibly know what this was like. Then she remembered his mother. He had known exactly what this was like. To see the slow decline of a beloved parent and be helpless to stop it.

"Between the constant sleeping and the not eating, I don't know how he manages to make it through a game. I get paranoid about extra innings. What if one day he collapses as he's going out to get the pitcher off the mound?"

And then something strange happened. Roy reached out and put his arms around her, pulling her into his body. The expression on his face seemed to say he couldn't believe he was doing it.

"Are you hugging me?"

"I think so. This is supposed to be how it works, right? I don't have much experience with it."

"You didn't hug your fiancée?"

"She really wasn't much of a hugger, no. Or maybe it was me. Who knows? So, is this working? Am I providing you any comfort?"

Lane looked into his eyes. He was serious. He wanted to help keep the fear away a little longer and make her not be so sad. It was the most unselfish thing she had ever known him to do. And as awkward as he looked doing it, he was rather adorable.

"Okay, wait a minute. If we're going to do this, we should do it right."

Lane moved closer to him and wrapped her arms around his back. Then she rested her cheek against his chest. A chest with a swirl of dark hair that she had long wanted to run her fingers through. God, it felt good to admit that to herself.

She listened to his heartbeat, felt the steady in-and-out of his breath. Yes, this was working. With his arms circling her and holding her just tight enough that she felt like no one could break them apart, she felt the fear subside.

You don't deserve this. Lane heard the inner voice, but she was tired and sad and didn't want to listen to it.

"Mmm."

"Is that a good sound?"

It was the best sound. She couldn't remember the last time she'd felt this connected to someone. To someone not her family. After Danny she'd cut herself off from allowing that type of connection. Now she was home and staring down the possibility of maybe trying again—with Roy Walker, of all people—and suddenly she was terrified.

Immediately she put at least an arm's length between them.

"I guess that's a no."

She could see the disappointment in his eyes, but she didn't know what to say. How do you tell someone you not only don't trust him, but you also don't trust yourself? It sucked because, with that hug, that one strong wrapping of his arms around her, he was able to take away the fear and the sadness for a few moments.

"You're a good hugger, Roy. I'm just…"

"Freaking out?" He lifted his eyebrow in that way she knew so well. She was reminded of how well he could see through her.

Which meant there was no point in lying to him. "Yep."

"Good. Because I am, too."

"Really?" For whatever reason his confession made Lane feel better about the situation.

"Hey! Roy! You going to hug Lane all day or are you going to eat? We got a game, you know."

Lane and Roy turned their heads toward the doorway of the restaurant. Billy stood there with his hands on his hips looking slightly put out.

"I think someone is jealous," Lane told Roy.

"Yeah, he's my new BFF," Roy muttered. "Kid, tell her I've been helping you with your curveball."

They didn't have to be near him to know that Billy was rolling his eyes. The gesture was evident in his body language.

"Yes, he is a real good teammate. Now, come on,

man, we want to hear more stories about the bigs. Everybody at our table is waiting for you."

Lane laughed as Billy walked inside the restaurant. "You're really doing it? You're making an effort with the guys? I mean, they saved you a seat. That's never happened to you before."

"I know. I'm talking to them and they seem to like it. Does this mean I can get laid later?"

Since she knew he was being deliberately crude to egg her on, she folded her arms over her chest like a woman who intended to keep her good parts under wraps and gave him a severe frown. There was no reason he had to know that the idea of having sex with him, of opening herself to that kind of relationship again, scared her infinitely more than his hug.

"I'll take that as a no. Fine. Since we're both freaking out and sex is obviously off the table for now, let's try a date."

"A date?"

"Yeah, you know, where I pick you up. We eat a meal together. I have an invite from Pete Wright to have dinner with him and his wife when we get back. Considering she's the boss, it's not like I can refuse."

A dinner. With another couple. The idea seemed safer than a date with just the two of them. A perfect dry run to see what a night together with Roy in a semiromantic setting might look like.

"Okay. But this doesn't let you off the hook. You

still have to try to impress me. That means Billy's curveball should actually curve the next time I see it."

"I promise. And Lanie—yes, I did call you Lanie—everything is going to be all right with Duff. You'll see."

Sadly, Lane didn't see that possibility at all, but now wasn't the time to say it. Roy had done his part and had lifted her mood. Her part was to make sure her father got some nutrition in him before the game.

Then after this road trip, it appeared she would go on her first date with Roy Walker.

Who the hell would have seen that one coming?

SCOUT TURNED OFF the radio that had always held a central spot on the kitchen table. This was where she listened to the games. Not in the living room, but in the kitchen, where there were more windows. The sunlight could stream into the room, making her feel as though she was outside. A part of the game even though the guys were away.

They were down three in the top of the ninth with two outs. She was fairly certain she could count the game as a loss and, frankly, she didn't want to hear the final out called.

Duff hated to lose. More than anything. And despite his age, despite his health, despite anything else that might be going on with him, she knew when that last batter went down, there would be a little jolt in his stomach. A sick feeling as if he'd let the guys down by not doing enough to put them in a winning situation. Which was ridiculous because as much as managers could contribute to the winning and the losing, the players still had to play.

A sharp knock at the back door startled her. She turned and saw Pete give a wave through the glass.

Now it was her stomach's turn to sink. She knew why he'd come. She could probably avoid the conversation they were about to have with a firm "no comment," but it would only be a stalling tactic. The fact that he'd come to the house instead of trying to catch her at the office meant he was considering her privacy, which she respected.

Still, he was a reporter. Reporters needed stories to fill the pages. Even the pages of a local gazette.

Opening the door to him, she attempted a smile. "Hey, Pete."

"Hey, Scout. I figured I would catch you alone here. I know there is not much to do at the stadium when the team is traveling."

"Nope."

"I was hoping we could talk."

"On the record or off the record?"

Pete shrugged. "I'll do either. Whatever you want. I'm not just here as a reporter, you know. You are my friend."

He was, Scout realized. A good friend, come to

think of it. A good friend who hadn't written one negative story about Duff even though everyone could see what was happening. It was as though they all agreed to turn their heads and let her try to cover for him.

"I take it you heard about Jayson coming back." Just saying his name hurt her physically. Like the name scraped along her vocal cords, a reminder that her world was about to implode any day now. How long would it be until the knock at the back door was Jayson coming to say hello?

Because he was that kind of guy. The kind of guy who would want to be gracious about their previous relationship. Because his relationship with Duff was important and he wouldn't want to do anything to mess that up. Jayson would arrive with a smile and a suggestion they be friendly, if not friends. Letting the past go, moving on with the future. All that garbage.

Hell, Jayson was the kind of guy that if he had a new girlfriend, he would want her to be Scout's friend, too.

Oh, my God, what if he comes back with a girl-friend?

Scout was pretty certain there was no wife. A girlfriend might fly under the radar, but someone connected to the game would have let her know if he got married. Baseball was, for the most part, a small, tight community.

"Yeah. I wanted to see how you felt about that. Both professionally and personally."

"I'm fine with it," she said tightly.

"He's been gone, what? Four years now?"

Four years, three months and two days.

"About right."

"I remember because you brought him to my wedding. When I saw you two together I thought he was the one. Then a couple of months later he was heading to Dallas."

"Yup. Guess not everyone is as good at keeping a relationship together as you and Jo."

Pete laughed and took a seat, comfortable in the Baker kitchen. "Are you kidding me? You remember that time she tried to cancel the wedding."

Scout sat next to him and put her feet up on another chair. She did remember. Scout had been devastated because that wedding was going to be her first night with Jayson as a girl instead of as a colleague. Jo had asked Vera Wang to design Scout this killer dress and Scout had bought high-heeled shoes to match. She'd made an appointment to get her hair and nails done.

She'd even gone so far as to buy perfume, though, after she got home, she'd decided against smelling like a fake lilac.

Then Jo got cold feet and all of Scout's careful planning had been almost ruined. Because what Pete and Jo didn't realize was that their wedding wasn't really about them. It was about Jayson finally seeing Scout as the seductive woman she could be.

The good news was that Pete had the tenacity of bulldog and wouldn't let Jo off the hook that easily.

Pete carrying Jo down the aisle over his shoulder had been the most memorable scene. Jo had laughed the whole time.

"You figured it out."

"Because we love each other," Pete said. "Before I met her, if someone had told me how hard it would be, I don't know that I would have believed them. Maybe I was naive or didn't think about it that much, but I always thought love would be so easy. You love her, she loves you, what's to figure out? Life has this way of making what should be simple complicated. We've been married for more than four years and it still isn't always easy."

Scout knew that. Over the course of their marriage she'd gotten closer to Jo and Pete. She knew they were still debating over the kids issue and that was taking a toll on their relationship. Jo was forty-five and couldn't have children herself, but they were discussing adoption or possibly a surrogate. The crazy thing was Scout wasn't sure if either of them knew what the other really wanted. Or if they were just trying to give each other something they thought they wanted.

Her closeness to Jo was one of the things that had weighed on Scout. They would go out for drinks and Jo would tell her all this stuff about her life. Yet Scout could never share anything about hers. Her life was the team and Duff.

Scout certainly couldn't tell Jo about what was happening with Duff. Considering Jo was her boss, too, made it even more awkward. Hiding things from her employer wasn't the best way to establish job security. Yet Scout couldn't share what was going on in her life. It would feel like too much of a betrayal to Duff.

Besides Jo seemed more concerned with the ballpark and the commitment to the community rather than the team activities. Duff's performance as a team manager hadn't been a major issue for her.

Only now Pete knew that Jayson was coming. That was why he was here as a reporter, as well as a friend.

"I've got to ask the question on the record, Scout."

"Shouldn't you be asking Duff?"

"I'm asking a member of the staff who might have inside information about why the Rebels are bringing up Jayson to assist Duff. Is Duff planning to retire at the end of this season?"

Retire. It sounded like such a soft word. A nice fluffy pillow of ease and comfort. No, Scout didn't think he was planning to retire. It wasn't in his nature. He used to joke about how he planned to die at a baseball stadium. Scout didn't think that joke was funny anymore.

"Duff hasn't told me what his plans are. And you would have to ask the Rebels' GM about his decision to bring Jayson up for the remainder of the season."

"I did. He thinks Jayson can learn a lot from Duff. Which could make Jayson major-league-manager material."

It really shouldn't be there but Scout couldn't quell the burst of pride she felt at hearing those words. Because Jayson hadn't learned only from Duff. He'd learned from her, too. They were both always too realistic to think that baseball was ready for a female manager. Scout had ranted and railed at the injustice for maybe ten minutes. Then she had accepted the fact and turned her attention to what really mattered. Passing on everything she knew about the game to someone who could make her team better when he was on the field.

She'd given Jayson everything that mattered to her.

And he still left.

Now, because of what she'd given him, he might one day be a manager in The Show. His dream realized because of her. She wondered if he would ever give her that credit. Ever acknowledge that, for a time, when they had been working together, they had been a team.

"Then we're grateful to have him on our team.

The Minotaurs could use all the help they can get right now."

"Yeah, tough loss today."

A loss. Definitive. No magical ninth-inning rally. She'd known that when she turned off the game. But that was the thing about baseball—as long as there was still one out left, one swing of the bat, there was always hope.

"Yep."

"How is Roy coming along?"

"He pitches tomorrow. We'll see then, won't we?"

Pete stood and Scout looked at him. She could see he wanted to ask another question. In truth, she couldn't believe he'd held back as long as he had. Pete wasn't a reporter for no reason. He had excellent instincts about things.

There was sympathy in his face, though, and it made her eyes well up so she tried to pretend she'd gotten a speck of dust in one of them. She didn't think he bought it.

"I won't ask on the record. I wouldn't do it to you and I sure as hell wouldn't do it to Duff. But I still have to ask. Is everything all right with Duff?"

Scout nodded. "He's fine. Grumpy old man is all."

"Maybe it wouldn't be the worst idea for this to be his last season. He could take up fishing or something easy like that. Something without all the pressure."

"Jack McKeon was eighty when he managed for the Florida Marlins," Scout said defensively. It's what she said anytime someone asked about Duff and retiring.

"Yeah, he was. Take care of yourself, Scout. Call me if you need me."

Pete left without Scout having to say anything else. Which was good because now her lips were quivering and her throat was clogging.

Because Duff wasn't going to be eighty and managing the Minotaurs. And she didn't think he was going to retire, either.

CHAPTER TWELVE

"HEY, GUYS, COME on in," Pete said, opening the door wide.

Roy stepped inside and waited to be over-whelmed with stuff. After all, this was the home of Jocelyn Taft-Wright, who, before she'd given the bulk of her money to charity, had been considered the wealthiest woman on the planet. Before that, Roy imagined, there had to have been years of ac-cumulating priceless artifacts, art and furniture. What was the point of having all that money if you weren't going to spend it?

When Roy had money he hung around with peo-ple who had money. And it didn't take long to fig-ure out that the point of the cash was always about having stuff.

The rare thing, the priceless thing, the thing ev-eryone wanted but no one else had. Buying things was just about players separating themselves from the pack. Showing everyone who came into their world that they were somehow special on this earth because of this physical item.

Roy never much cared what people thought.

Other than the house for his father, Roy hadn't bought much. In hindsight, it was a shame because he'd had nothing to sell when his world collapsed. All his money had gone into the business. His awful failing business.

If he was able to get through a couple of seasons in the majors, he intended to kiss every dollar they paid him. Not out of greed, but out of a sad realization that he hadn't been made for anything other than baseball.

He thought of the tightness in his shoulder and tried not to let it mess with his head too much. Lane had done her thing after his last start, a game in which he gave up only one run in six innings of work. Definitely an improvement. Usually after one of her sessions he felt no pain by the second day. But three days removed from that start and still he could feel the pinch of fire just beneath his shoulder blade. Logically, he knew he should tell Lane and let her take a look, but something held him back.

No, not *something*. Fear. Plain old fear.

Focusing on the night ahead—his first real date with Lane—Roy pushed the fear deep down into this stomach and waited to be wowed and amazed with grandeur. Instead, the house was plain. And really ordinary. His jaw must have dropped because Pete laughed outright.

"I know, I know," Pete said, slapping Roy on the

back. "Everyone comes in expecting the place to be littered with Rembrandts and Picassos."

"My taste in art was always more pedestrian."

Roy took in the petite woman with the shoulder-length, dark blond hair. Nothing about her screamed *money*. Not her capri jeans and T-shirt, not her casual flip-flops. This was a woman who had made billions by being smarter than everyone else and yet she looked as normal as, well, any woman might.

"I'm Jo Wright," she said, holding out her hand.

Roy shook it and felt even more like a fool. Jocelyn had dedicated herself to the business of making money. She went to school to study it, got her masters. Worked at it until she was a success. Study, practice, work—much like what Roy had done with baseball.

What had made him think he could walk into the professional world like he had some right to be there? Just because he had some money in his pocket? He could see the arrogance in his thinking now. Could see how he'd assumed his success in baseball would translate into business success, even though he had little knowledge, little practice.

"It's very nice to meet you," he said somewhat awkwardly.

"I hear you're the best."

"*Was* the best," Roy said quickly, honestly. "Now I'm not sure what I am."

"Well, you had a good win for us a few days ago."

Jo smiled. "I'll take it. I'll also take you filling up my stadium with people. It might be only every seventh night, but that's good."

"Don't be fooled by the fact that she gave away most of her money. Jo still lives for the profit," Pete said good-naturedly as if this topic was one he'd teased his wife about often.

"It's the game," she said, rubbing her hands together with a gleeful expression on her face. "I have to win it. You understand, Roy, don't you?"

"Oh, Roy understands needing to win," Lane said behind him. "Hi, I'm Lane Baker, Duff's middle daughter. It's nice to meet you."

"Of course. You look very much like Scout only—"

Lane chuckled. "Softer," she said. "It's okay. Scout likes her hard edges. And I like my soft ones."

Roy bent to whisper in Lane's ear. "I would like to know your soft parts."

She wiggled and blushed a little and the thrilling satisfaction he got out of that was like nothing he'd ever felt before.

He got to do that now. He got to lean down and whisper seductive things in her ear to make her squirm. That's the level of relationship he now had with Lane Baker. It was a heady thing.

"You're so lame," she said in a way that sounded like she didn't mean it at all.

He was lame. He wasn't even really sure what

that meant, but that was fine as long as he was lame with Lanie.

They were being escorted through the house with its simple furniture and colorful throw rugs. Nothing fussy. Nothing that would make people feel uncomfortable. Just the home of a couple who enjoyed a normal life with some nice creature comforts. Like the fifty-inch television mounted to the wall and the surround-sound system. And the kitchen appliances, which seemed to be linked to some central computer network.

Had Jo talked to the oven?

"Grab a beer, then come outside," Pete said. "We'll be like men and grill."

Roy looked to Lane, who gave him the slight head nod indicating it was okay to leave her with Jocelyn. Another thing that astounded him—he and Lane had already fallen into that nonverbal communication that couples developed over time.

Roy had never gotten that far with Shannon. With her it had felt like he'd been dancing a very choreographed ballet in which everything he did was what a guy who was supposed to be in love did. When they went to parties he got her drinks and didn't leave her side. When they went out for dinner he opened her car door. When they had sex he made sure she had an orgasm before he let himself come.

He had behaved perfectly and yet none of it had been real. He wasn't even certain what had been the final trigger for the relationship. Something stupid, probably. Something as trivial as her not knowing that he preferred vanilla ice cream to chocolate. But once he had the awareness that they had nothing beyond the surface, he knew he had to end it.

Doing so six weeks before the wedding had been a blow she hadn't deserved. Roy consoled himself with the thought that even more pain would have resulted if, two years after their wedding, she had looked across the kitchen table at him and finally understood that she didn't know him.

That would never be the case with Lane. In part because by attempting to be the man she deserved he'd decided to be more open with people. And also because she already knew him. She knew him the very first night they met.

Roy grabbed two beers from the fridge and followed Pete. The grill was massive and high-tech since Roy was pretty sure Pete was talking to it as he threw down some hamburger patties. He handed Pete a beer and they stood together, listening to the sizzle.

There was something so right about men standing over fire—even if it was gas-powered—watching meat burn.

"Not a bad outing the other day," Pete said.

Roy cocked an eyebrow, his body tensing slightly. Hell, why had he relaxed in the first place? It wasn't like him to let his guard down around people. Especially around reporters. Yet, for some strange reason, he trusted Pete.

"Are you asking on or off the record?"

"Hey, I'm not on the job tonight. I promise. You don't want to talk sports, we can find something else to talk about. I mean, what do women talk about?"

"Men?"

"I don't want to talk about that. What about you and Lane? What's going on there?"

"I'm wooing her. Technically, this is our first date."

"Well, don't burp and screw that up."

Roy laughed. "Thanks. Got any other advice?"

"If she means anything to you, don't give up."

Roy could see the man was serious. "Your girl try to run away from you a few times?"

Pete turned toward the kitchen window. Roy could see the two women's heads were bent together in the task of shucking corn.

"Sometimes I think she still wants to run even though she knows I'll always chase her down."

"Why?"

Pete shook his head. "She's hung up about the age difference. About getting older. About the kid thing... Hell, I don't want to talk about this. Can we please talk about baseball?"

"Sure, because that's an easy subject, too. Let's talk about how I now ride the bus to Scranton with a bunch of kids, most of whom still have pimples on their faces. And let's discuss how a good outing these days is one in which I don't get shelled for nine runs."

"Oh? You think you've got a market on humility?" Pete said. "Try being married to one of the richest women in world. When she offers to buy your paper because she knows it's failing and plans to use the lost revenue as a tax write-off."

"Ouch."

"My life's work is a tax write-off."

"I lost eighty million dollars."

The two of them looked at each other, then burst out laughing. "Okay, man," Pete conceded. "I think you win."

Roy shook his head. "I have to say I never thought I would be able to laugh about it."

"It's only money. And trust me, when you're around someone who has so much of it, you start to understand how little it means. Jo spent years accumulating masses of it. None of it touched her. Not one damn penny. It's why she could give it all away. It's why I don't get mad at her when she pesters me about the paper, because I know, in her heart, she knows what matters. The material things don't mean anything in the end."

"If you're going to start to talk about love, I might want to go back to talking about baseball."

"The *L* word scares you, huh?"

Roy took a sip of his beer. Did it scare him? He

couldn't really say. He'd never been in love. He couldn't consider what he felt for Lane love—not even five years ago—because he'd always believed that love was more than one person's feelings. For it to be real it had to be shared. What his parents felt for each other was love. What he had with Shannon was pretend love. Maybe on both their parts. Was that because he was scared or because he kept comparing what he felt for her to what he'd felt for Lane? Roy wasn't sure.

The door opened and Lane walked out with a plate of corn on the cob.

"Jo says you want to grill these, too."

"Yep." Pete took the plate from her. "And I'll need—"

"Salt, butter and aluminum foil. I'll be back."

"You need a hand?" Roy asked.

Lane smiled easily. "Nope. Jo and I will be out in a few minutes so you better get all your man bonding in while you can."

She walked inside and Roy thought her leaving was fine because she was going to be back in a few minutes. Was that the beginning of love?

Lane had only recently admitted she didn't hate him. Love still seemed a far, faraway thing.

"Hey, while they're inside, can I talk to you about something serious?"

"Shoot."

"It's about Duff."

Roy must have made a face, because Pete waved the spatula in the air defensively.

"Hear me out. I tried to talk to Scout and she brushed me off. Says he's fine, but I've been around the team and him too long to know that's not the case. I'm not asking to get the dirt. I'm worried about Duff. He's been a part of this community for fifteen years. You're there every day. How do you think he's doing?"

"Duff's fine," Roy said instantly. He hated to lie to Pete. He really did, and he genuinely believed Pete was telling the truth about his concern. But being part of a team, really being part of a team, meant loyalty. Unconditional.

Roy had never felt that before, but he did now. His team was Team Baker and he wouldn't betray either Duff or Lane.

"Okay." Pete sighed. "If you say so."

"I say so."

The two men looked at each other and maybe Pete knew Roy was lying. Roy knew there wasn't anything he could control about that. All he knew was that Pete would never hear anything from Roy regarding Duff's health.

"You ever hear of a Jayson LaBec?"

Roy rolled the name around in his head. "Ballplayer, right? Why do I think there's some story there?"

"He *was* a ballplayer—an outfielder. Made it to

The Show for one game. He was chasing down a ball and ran face-first into a part of the wall where the padding had dropped away."

"I remember that story. Basically broke his entire face but somehow managed to hold on to the ball. Wasn't he in a coma for a while?"

"Induced to keep the brain swelling down. Anyway, he came out of it but was never going to play professionally again. Duff took him under his wing five years ago. Said the kid had the heart of a lion, which a baseball manager needs to have."

"Why are you telling me this?"

"The Rebels are bringing him up from Double-A to be an assistant coach. The word is they are grooming him for the top job."

"You think the Rebels are trying to push out Duff?"

Pete shrugged. "I'm saying I might not be the only one to notice the change in the old man in the past year. Just so you know. You want to get him through this season, someone on the inside needs to be covering for him."

Roy nodded. "No covering needed. I told you he's fine."

"Okay. I'm done talking about it, then. Hey, Jo!" he called inside. "Do we have cheese for these burgers?"

The two women came out with a truckload of supplies. They wrapped up corn and grilled it.

They loaded burgers with cheese and ate them. Roy watched the dynamic between Pete and his wife and he could see it between them. Love. A shared thing. No matter what obstacles got in their way, no matter what troubles they were having with the decisions that had to be made in life, the bond between them was a real and tangible thing.

Was he afraid of that? It was strange how quickly the answer came to him.

Hell, no.

"THAT WAS FUN," Lane said as Roy walked her to the door. It had been. The first real fun she'd had in a long time. When had she decided to stop doing that, to stop having fun? Probably five years ago, sometime during the divorce. A self-imposed punishment for failing in her marriage. For falling out of love with a man she was supposed to love forever.

For being attracted to another man who wasn't her husband.

"Yeah, I thought so, too. They're a cool couple. Did you know there was an age difference? I mean, I guess she might look a little older, but I didn't really notice it."

Lane nodded. "Yes, it's, like, ten years. I remember because there was all this trashy media around their engagement. Richest Woman in the World to Marry Boy Toy. That kind of thing."

"That couldn't be further from the truth of what they are."

Roy was right. She remembered Scout talking about them as a couple. About how they didn't look like they fit but they were the real thing. Except Lane didn't believe in the real thing anymore. How could she? She'd wanted to make her marriage work more than anyone, and yet she was responsible for it falling apart.

But after spending a night with Pete and Jo, it was hard to hold on to her cynicism. Or maybe not so hard.

"Jo wants to get a surrogate to have their child, but she doesn't think Pete is being as supportive as he needs to be, which makes her wonder if it's what he really wants."

Roy blinked a few times. "Wow. That's, like, a lot of information right there."

Lane shrugged. "We bonded. A few glasses of wine and it all spilled out of her. She loves him and she wants him to have the full experience of family life but she can't get pregnant so this is her only alternative."

"Why are you telling me this?"

Right. Because it wasn't cool to share someone else's secrets. Not that she was worried about Roy gossiping. It was a big deal to see him talking with the other guys about anything. She was fairly certain the team owner's infertility wasn't coming up as a topic.

"I'm just saying they are not a perfect couple. They have real issues they have to deal with and no one knows what that will do to their relationship."

"So what? They should just split up now and not even bother trying to work through it?"

"No, that's not what I'm saying. Of course you should fight for your relationship. Until you know you can't fight anymore."

Roy looked at her and she found herself squirming under his hard stare. "When are you going to forgive yourself, Lane?"

"What?"

"When are you going to accept the fact that you couldn't control how your feelings for Danny changed? You couldn't control your feelings for me, either. It just happened."

Lane shook her head. "See, I think that's bull. That's what everyone says when they get caught cheating. *I didn't mean for it to happen. I couldn't control my feelings.* A person can make decisions."

"Yeah. That's part of it, too. You could have made decisions. You could have said no when I asked you to come to my party. You could have said no to any of the dozens of times I asked you to have a hot dog with me. Why didn't you do that, Lane? Because you can't tell me you can control your feelings. Which means the only thing you could have done was make the decision to stay as far away from me as possible. But you didn't. You know why? Because you liked those feelings. Be honest about that."

Lane felt a jolt of bone-deep shame. He was right. She had liked spending time with him. She had started to anticipate when he would ask her to get a hot dog. Wondered what topic they would argue over as she filled her face with pork and mustard. When they traveled on road trips she scoured the areas for the best dog joints around and then would take him there so they could debate the merits of onions or relish.

She could have said no. But she hadn't. Maybe because part of her instinctively knew that Danny was cheating while he was away on his many golf and fishing trips. She suspected he was sleeping with other women when he stopped sleeping with her. But she couldn't let herself face it. Because once she accepted his infidelity, there was no marriage left worth fighting for.

Lane didn't think those outings with Roy were about revenge, though. It wasn't as if she ever considered any pain they might cause Danny, mostly because she knew he wouldn't have cared what she did or who she did it with. Even if she was doing it with Roy Walker.

No, she hadn't spent time with Roy to get even with Danny. She'd been lonely. Desperately lonely in the way only a wife could feel. A wife who was supposed to be loved but wasn't. A wife who was supposed to be part of a couple but wasn't. A wife who was supposed to love back but didn't.

She could have dealt with her loneliness some other way, though. She didn't have to be with Roy, but she wanted to be with him.

She dropped her face into her hands because she couldn't bear to look at him. "I'm a cheater. Just like my mother. If Duff knew, if he knew about that night, I think it would destroy him. Why do you want to have anything to do with me?"

She felt his hands pulling her hands away, then lifting her surely beet-red face to meet his.

"I kissed you, remember?"

"But I kissed you back. You said so. And all those times we went out for lunch…I liked it. Too much. I told myself it was innocent. I knew I'd never sleep with someone else while I was married. I called us frenemies. I joked to everyone about how much we fought and how maddening you were. But really, I knew we were getting closer. Real friends. The whole time…the whole time…and you were lying about liking hot dogs."

"Lanie, it happened. You're human. If I have to be a better man to deserve you, then you have to forgive yourself for me."

She tried to blink through the tears, could feel his hand wrapping around her neck. "How could you ever trust me? How could you ever be assured what I feel is lasting and real? I know I can't."

"Lanie, you are, and always have been, the realest thing in my life. Forgive yourself."

"I don't know if I can."

"Forgive yourself." This time he whispered the words as he pressed his lips against hers.

CHAPTER THIRTEEN

LANE WONDERED WHAT it would feel like. Since she'd admitted to Roy that she didn't hate him, she'd wondered if his kiss would be the same or different. She wondered if she could, in fact, forgive herself for what had been a sin.

To say she'd cheated on the same level Danny had was obviously a gross exaggeration. But she knew every time she'd gone to lunch with Roy, every time she reveled in their verbal battles, that she had been mentally, emotionally disloyal to her marriage.

All that time she'd told herself she needed to find ways to work on her marriage. Therapy. Marriage counselors. Trips away together instead of always apart. All that time she knew she hadn't really wanted any of that. She hadn't wanted to improve her marriage. She had just wanted out.

Only the thought of her pride and what her failure would do to Duff had kept her going for as long as she had.

Pride and failure. The two things that had brought her home after losing her patient.

She'd asked Roy to be a better man. A better

teammate, at least. He had asked her to forgive herself. Nice but, really, he should have demanded more. Because she needed to be a better person, too.

Lane wanted all of that. The forgiveness and the courage. And she wanted his kiss. Wanted to know what kissing Roy would feel like without the guilt. Without the self-recrimination. Without the sin.

She wasn't sure if she was there yet, but she did have one answer. His kiss certainly felt as good now as it had before. The way his firm lips owned hers. Not in some overbearing way as if he was trying to suck her dry or imprint himself on her. Just in a way that told her he was leading this dance. He was deciding when he would nibble and when he would suck. He was learning what she liked and giving her more of it.

His taste was as rich and dark and spicy as she remembered it. At the time she'd had the fleeting thought this was what it felt like to be a bad girl. This was what it felt like to kiss a bad boy.

That same feeling was still there. As if Roy was some kind of darkness she never thought she would embrace. Only she did embrace it—more than that, she craved it.

Yet underneath all that spice and darkness was the feeling of coming home, too.

She hadn't seen him in five years. Other than his final game, his no-no, the only mention of Roy Walker that had crossed her path was the news of his engagement. Though she hadn't admitted at the time, it had caused a sliver of pain in her body. Like a splinter she recognized was there but couldn't quite work out of her skin.

Then the news of his engagement ending. Six weeks before the wedding. One of the baseball wives Lane had remained friends with sent her an email with the subject heading Isn't This Typical.

Because everyone knew Roy was a bad guy. Everyone knew he was the villain of every story. Of course he would jilt his fiancée at the last minute. Of course he would leave a woman heartbroken nearly at the altar.

He'd done it for Lane. Or not precisely *for* her, but because of her.

Which meant she was part villain, too.

Lane couldn't lie to herself. There was something sexy about being the bad girl. Here she was with her tongue in Roy Walker's mouth. He was pulling her into his body and she was pressing up against his erection in a rhythm that made him groan. Her body was vibrating with the warm pleasure of feeling his hands on her hips, of feeling his wide, strong back under her hands.

She wanted desperately to touch his bare chest. She wanted to feel those dark swirls of hair under her fingers. Finally!

"Roy," she gasped, breaking away only to feel his mouth on the spot right beneath her ear. His teeth grazed her skin, then strengthened to nip, which had her knees melting.

Yes, there it was. That hint of sinful. The pressure of his teeth on her neck that said he was capable of biting. Five years. It had been five years since her last real kiss. Not some brush of lips after a blind date. Or the awkward feeling of having a tongue in her mouth that she didn't really want to be there.

No, it had been five years since her last real kiss and that kiss had been Roy's.

"Come home with me," he said into her ear before proceeding to suck on her earlobe.

Yes. The answer was there in her head. Yes, of course she would go home with him. Lie down beneath him. Let him inside.

"So are you two going to do it out here or what?"

Scout's voice cut like a knife between them. Instinctively, as if she was fifteen instead of thirty-one, Lane jumped away making sure there was at least three feet of space between her and Roy.

Duff's rule had always been three feet. As if that magic number would protect her virginity.

"Scout! What are you doing lurking by the front door?"

"What are you doing making out on the porch like a pair of high school sweethearts? This is a family-friendly, wholesome town, you know. Neighbors might not like the show you're putting on."

Lane belatedly remembered that Duff's house

faced the town's main street. Had cars passed them? They must have, but Lane hadn't heard a thing.

She was also familiar enough with the town—having lived here with Duff and Scout part of the time—that there wouldn't be a single soul in Minotaur Falls who didn't know that Duff Baker's daughter was seen making out with the infamous Roy Walker.

Roy Walker, who, with a six-inning, one-run outing, had just begun to turn the tide of the town's opinion following his first start.

"Go inside, Scout."

"Get a room, Lane."

The front door slammed shut behind her younger sister and Lane tried to see the bitterness for what it was and not as a personal insult. Scout was hurting, which meant seeing anyone else happy hurt even more.

Happy? Was Lane allowed to be happy? Her conscience didn't think so, which made feeling this way very strange.

"I don't suppose you've ever heard of Jayson LaBec?" Lane asked as a way of justifying her sister's actions to Roy.

"That's funny," Roy said, leaning against the porch rail, one leg crossed over the other, his arms crossed over his chest, looking entirely casual. Except his cock was still hard and outlined against his jeans. "You're the second person today to ask me that."

"The Rebels have brought him up to assist Duff. Not sure if they know something's up or not. Or they just think Duff might be done after this year. Jayson and Scout used to date. Jayson was the only guy Scout ever dated. They were really close, but then he got offered a job in Texas and she wouldn't go with him."

Roy nodded. "Not easy for her, then."

"You have to know Scout. She doesn't like change. I think it's why she likes baseball so much. Unlike other sports it's not always changing the rules. You should have seen her when they allowed instant replay. She wrote a six-page letter to Bud Selig detailing why it was an insult to the game, the country and God. Anyway, now everything is changing on her and she has to deal with Jayson coming back. Not just to the same town, but to the place she works, too."

"Did he break her heart? If he did and you want me to, I'll break his nose. With my right hand, of course."

"Of course." Lane smiled. "You know the funny thing is even though he was the one to leave, I think she broke his heart."

"Well, I imagine the next few months will get pretty interesting around here."

Lane didn't say anything. She knew what he was

really thinking, what he really wanted to ask. He stared at her for a beat. The porch was dark, the late spring moon giving just enough light for them to see each other. The fireflies buzzed around them, adding their strange glow to the mix. The tension was heavy like humidity hanging in the air.

"You're not coming home with me."

Of course he knew that already. He probably also knew her answer had been yes in her head when he first asked. But now it felt like Scout and her heartbreak stood between them. And their past heartbreak. And all the heartbreaks in the world.

Lane wasn't ready to get over all that and she definitely wasn't sure she was ready to start down that path that might lead to yet another heartbreak.

It was so hard to think about that when the kissing and the touching and the neck biting felt so good. Hard to remember that she didn't believe in happy endings anymore.

"I think I should be with her. Let her talk it out. A sister thing."

"You know we're doing this thing," Roy said, pointing to the space between them. "It's going to happen. I'm not losing this chance with you. Not a second time. No matter what I have to do."

Lane wasn't sure what to say to that.

"So you can run inside because you're obviously still freaking out and that's okay. Because I'm coming back tomorrow and the next day. I'm teaching

Billy how to throw a real curve. I'm taking you out again, only next time, it will be just us. And we are going to bed together."

Lane felt the hair on the back of her neck and her forearms stand as if called to attention. Her *hackles.* Roy always did manage to rile them.

"Oh, really? You think you can beat your chest, howl at the moon, swing some club like a baseball bat and that's going to do what? Make my girl parts quiver? I don't think so."

"A baseball bat is not the thing I'm going to be swinging, sweetheart, but it will be just as hard."

Lane wanted to laugh. She really did. She also wanted to jump a little and clap her hands because, for the first time since they had reunited, that sounded like the Roy Walker she used to know. She could be happy about that.

"Cliché much?" she said, her chin in the air. As a retort it was fairly lame, but snappy comebacks were challenging to think of when she was so giddy inside.

Roy pointed at her. "You want me."

"So you keep telling me," she drawled.

He smiled then and she smiled, too. This felt familiar.

"I'll be back, Lanie Baker."

"I'll count every waking second until you are." She said it with enough sarcasm that he couldn't possibly imagine she was telling the truth. Even though she might have been. A little.

She watched him walk off the porch, his shoulders back, his head high. His body moving in that fluid motion like he was getting ready to wind up, right before his release. An athlete who knew exactly what his physical being was capable of and what his mental strength could enhance.

Roy Walker was back. And Lane's girl parts were, in fact, quivering.

SCOUT KNEW HER bedroom ceiling had forty-two cracks in it. Small fissures that had spread out over time. There used to only be twenty-five, but then there had been that crazy earthquake with the epicenter in DC, but it had rippled through all of New York State. Just hard enough for people to know it was an earthquake.

Hard enough to put seventeen more cracks in the ceiling. Counting ceiling cracks had always been her thing. When her parents were shouting at each other downstairs, she could ignore it by counting the cracks.

When she'd had to live for months with her cheating mother, Scout would pretend Duff was on a long road trip. She would avoid speaking to her mother by locking herself in her bedroom. Since there was only so much time you could spend alone in your room without going mad, counting the ceiling cracks in the house they shared with her mother's new husband—because that's who Bob had always been to Scout—was simply a way to pass the time.

To keep her sanity until Duff called. Until finally she was able to convince everyone that she belonged with him.

Tonight Scout hadn't reached eighteen when she heard the knock on the door.

"Go away."

"I want to talk."

"I don't," Scout said. She didn't want to talk about how Lane and Roy had gone from mortal enemies to making out on the porch, even though Scout had known all along Lane had feelings for him. That whole "I hate Roy Walker" had always been such an obvious smoke screen. Barely hiding what she really felt for him.

But what was a sister supposed to say?

You're not in love with your husband anymore. You haven't been for years, but you're too stubborn and won't let go. You've got the hots for this other guy if you would only admit it.

Lane would have never done that five years ago. The mere suggestion she hadn't been actively fighting to keep her marriage together would have infuriated her. It definitely would have driven a wedge between them.

Sometimes sisters did what they had to and kept

their mouths shut. Because Lane had needed Scout five years ago.

Now Lane wanted to return the favor, but Scout wasn't up for some sisterly sympathy.

"Look, I'm sorry I interrupted you and Roy, okay? I will acknowledge there was a level of immaturity there. But seriously, I want to be alone."

The door opened. Freaking family. They always thought they knew better.

"If you really wanted to be alone, you wouldn't have interrupted us," Lane said so logically Scout wanted to slap her.

Instead she inched over on the bed to allow Lane to lie down alongside her. They stared at the ceiling.

"Talk to me," Lane said.

"Why? What does talking accomplish?"

"It helps to get your feelings out. It allows other people to offer things like sympathy and empathy. It also helps you to sort out your own thoughts and, most importantly, it prevents the development of ulcers."

Scout shook her head. "Do you know there are times when I absolutely hate you?"

"Yep. It's the beauty about being sisters. We can love each other, hate each other, like each other or not. At the end of the day it doesn't matter, though, because we're sisters and that's not going to change. Ever. No matter what happens."

No matter what happens. It was code for Duff

being really sick, but Scout couldn't go there now. She was keeping that locked in a room inside her mind. With no key around to open it. Because as Lane had said, there was no point in borrowing trouble until she knew what the trouble was. Probably the same reason Duff had held off seeing a damn doctor for so long. If he wasn't diagnosed, then technically, there was nothing wrong with him.

No, the reason she'd clenched her teeth as she watched Roy and Lane practically inhale each other wasn't because of Duff. It was because *he* was coming back and she knew she wasn't at a place where she could handle it yet. Four years and she wasn't over him.

She couldn't go to the stadium, walk into Duff's office and see Jayson there and keep her manner as casual and mature as she wanted it to be.

Hey, Jayson, long time no see. Heard you were coming up to Triple-A. You must have really impressed them in Texas. So how is everything? Your mom? Doby. How old is that big hound now? Fourteen? Fifteen? Well, good to have you on the team. Looking forward to working with you.

The speech sounded great in her head. It sounded like someone who hadn't spent the past four years thinking about him. It sounded like she could keep her job and work with him on a daily basis and everything would be all right.

But when she thought of the actual moment, the

seeing-him-again moment, she knew she wouldn't be able to get those words out. Instead, she would want to hold him, or hit him. She would want to ask why she hadn't been enough for him to stay. She would want to know if there had been someone else. Someone better for him than her.

Lane hated Roy because Roy had screwed her over big-time, yet they managed to find their way to a place where they were kissing. Scout had loved Jayson and yet all she could imagine was this stiff formality between them as though they had meant nothing to each other.

When, truly, he had meant everything to her.

"I can't do it. I can't work with him," Scout said. Since Lane wasn't leaving, there was no point in holding this all in. It was just so damn humiliating.

"Then don't. There isn't a team in the league who doesn't know your scouting talent. You could have your pick of any job you wanted."

Scout huffed. "Right, because with all this going down, now is the time to leave Duff and start heading off to every high school in every small town in America. You remember what scouting is, right? You go to see the players, they don't come to you."

Lane turned on her side, but Scout didn't want to face her. Instead she kept her gaze pinned to the ceiling. Almost willing it to form another crack so she could count that.

"I don't mean right now. I just meant you don't

have to think about it long-term. He'll show up. It will be awkward. Maybe you get over that, maybe you don't. In a couple of months if things still haven't changed, you can find another job. It's not the end of the world, that's all I'm saying."

Leaving the Minotaurs. Leaving Duff—or maybe Duff leaving her, because that's what she thought Lane was implying—would, in fact, be the end of her world.

"I'm not strong like you. I can't just pick my life up and rebuild it somewhere else. This is the home I know. The place I know. I don't want to leave it. I get why that's messed up. I mean, look at me. I'm pathetic. I should have been over him—it's been four years. No sane person can't let go after four years. Damn it! Why did he have to come back?"

Scout felt Lane's hand on her arm. "I don't know why he's coming back. If he's as talented as everyone says, I'm not sure why this job in particular holds so much appeal. But you won't have any of those answers until he gets here and you see how he reacts to you. And how you react to him."

"You're being logical again," Scout warned her.

"Well, how about this for some nonlogic. You make it sound like a courageous thing that I left my husband, baseball and everything else behind. You know what I figured out recently? I just ran away. I did it again after losing my patient. I couldn't deal with the fact that maybe I had missed signs I should have seen. So what did I do? Run away from work to come back here. I'm not courageous at all. I'm this secret coward. And you want to talk about insanity? You just caught me with Roy's tongue in my mouth. Roy Walker! I hate Roy Walker. Or at least, I thought I did. Until I realized I didn't."

"Good thing you didn't get that tattoo I mentioned." Scout rolled on her side to face her sister. "Why can't I be over Jayson? I want to be over him."

"Maybe his coming back will do the trick. Maybe you'll take one look at him and wonder what you ever saw in him."

Lane said the words to bolster her, but Scout knew she really didn't mean them. Jayson had been the most beautiful man she'd ever seen. Beautiful to her, with his broken face that had been put back together. She doubted four years would have changed him that much.

"Maybe. Now you tell me what the kiss was about. Is it official? Are you guys, like, a thing now?"

Rolling onto her back, Lane sighed and put her arm across her head. "I can't think about that. It's too much all at once."

"But you want to be."

"I don't know. I'm thinking with Roy I might not have much choice. He can be pretty persistent when he wants to be."

"All the players know he's teaching Billy Madden how to throw a curve so he can win your heart and get into your pants."

"Yep. Consider it my duty to the Minotaurs. You guys get another lightning thrower who can change it up with a curve and I get an orgasm."

This time Scout was the one to pat Lane's arm. "That's the way you do it, Lanie. Duff would applaud that attitude. Like taking a hit to get on base. Team first and all that. It's good to have you back in baseball, sis."

Lane smiled. "You know what? It's good to be back."

CHAPTER FOURTEEN

"No, WATCH OUT," Roy said, moving Billy off the mound. The season was in full swing and he'd been working with Billy for weeks with only incremental progress. "You're showcasing the pitch with your hand position. A batter in the bigs sees you on the mound, he's going to know what's coming. He knows what's coming, he's taking it yard."

Billy stepped back to make room for Roy. Roy showed the kid what he was talking about and he could see the kid paying attention.

It was crazy. All those years of protecting his secrets, protecting his talents, and suddenly Roy had all this stuff to give. People to give it to. It was a hell of a revelation. When he'd left baseball he thought he wanted nothing to do with the game. After spending so much of his life committed to throwing a ball at the exclusion of almost everything else, it seemed normal that he would want to try something new and different.

Now he understood the hubris in that decision. The idea that he could handle *new and different* as if it was the same as baseball, as if he'd simply had a talent for it, was laughable.

So what came next after his comeback? Could he do something that allowed him to be involved with the game? Stay connected to it this time instead of turning his back on it. Maybe take all the knowledge he'd gained over the years and find a way to distribute it.

Wouldn't that be some kind of irony? The most closemouthed, hated pitcher in the sport…a pitching coach.

But that option wasn't for right now. That was some day down the road after he'd made it back to the majors. Right now his focus had to be on securing the future he'd lost. The present was about one contract and only one contract. What came after that, who knew?

"Show me your curve," Billy said. "I want to see how it bends from up close."

Roy hesitated. After his last bullpen session he noticed that his shoulder wasn't feeling right. He had a therapy session scheduled with Lane later today. He hoped her fingers would ease the tightness down his left side. That with some anti-inflammatory medication should put him in good shape for his next outing.

An outing where he knew some Rebels scouts would be attending. Word had gotten out that his last few starts had been infinitely stronger than his first. Little did they know part of his motivation for better pitching was to get Lane Baker in bed. Something that still hadn't happened after he'd kissed her on the porch a few weeks ago, much to his great disappointment.

But the curve, that pitch seemed to aggravate the shoulder more than the others. So he hesitated before looking down at his left arm.

"Don't give me any shit."

Billy held up his hands. "What are you talking about? I didn't say anything."

Roy growled. "I'm not talking to you, okay?"

"Then who are you talking to."

"My arm," Roy admitted.

"Dude, that's messed up."

"Listen to me, all great starting pitchers have a thing."

"A thing?"

"Yeah. A thing that's theirs. A thing that keeps the noise away. A thing that keeps them on the mound when they just threw a high fastball in the zone and gave up a grand slam. A thing. My thing is I talk to my arm."

Clearly Billy was confused by the concept. Roy almost smiled as he watched the kid try to form a serious question.

"Like what do you say to it?"

"I say, 'Don't give me any shit.'"

"Does it listen?"

"Not very often. Let's see if it did today. Javier, you ready?"

The catcher, who had been patiently waiting for them to discuss Roy's relationship with his arm, got into his familiar crouch. Roy wound up and threw, letting the ball go and watching as it headed straight, straight, straight, then curved and trailed downward just at the end. He felt the tug of muscle in his shoulder, a burn that ran down his arm and back, and he grimaced in pain.

It had been worth it, though. The pitch had been a thing of beauty. No hitter, he didn't care how good, would have made contact with that ball.

"Dude, you should thank your arm."

Roy laughed. "I don't like to give him too big an ego."

"Says the man with the giant-size ego," Lane said as she walked across the field. She wore a pair of short shorts, flip-flops and some breezy summer top that draped around her and ended near her thighs. She looked like everything that was good on a late spring day and he wanted to eat her like soft ice cream.

"Right," Roy said, unable to prevent the smile from his lips even though Lane Baker had proven to be quite a challenge over the past few weeks. A few lunch dates between his practices. Dinner when he wasn't on the road with the team. All of it ending with a kiss on the porch and nothing else.

He wasn't quite sure if she was playing hard to get, or was just too scared to think about what a relationship between them would look like. Either way, she was making him work for it. The sick part was that he liked it. He liked that he had to fight for her. It fueled his competitiveness. Made him want to win.

Made him feel like the man he used to be.

"Okay, Billy, this is it. Show me your curve," Lane said. "I want to see something actually bend this time besides your elbow."

Roy held his mitt up as a signal for Javier to toss him back the ball. Even catching it had hurt.

"Hey, was that a wince?" Lane asked him.

"Huh?" He played dumb to her concern. "No, I'm fine."

She looked at him suspiciously for a second but then must have decided to let it drop. "We've got a session after this and we'll see what's up."

"I'm telling you I'm fine. Normal soreness, nothing more."

"Yep. You're fine, and Duff's fine, so he tells me. All the men in my life are fine. I'm sort of getting sick of hearing it."

Roy beamed. "I'm a man in your life?"

Lane cocked her head. "Maybe. After I see Billy's curveball."

"Kid, you blow this for me and I will kill you."

"Come on, man," Billy groaned. "You're putting me under too much pressure."

"You want pressure, imagine this. Game seven of the World Series, bottom of the ninth inning, your team is up one to nothing. You're pitching a complete game shutout so the manager isn't taking you off the mound. But now you've loaded the bases with two outs. The count is three balls, two strikes—"

Billy nearly shuddered. "I'm getting chills just thinking about it."

Roy got in his face. "That's pressure. That's when you talk to your arm and you say you're going to throw a strike he can't hit because I demand it. That's when you're in control and the arm is just there to do your bidding."

"Got it. Got it."

"It's all a mental game then. A chess match between you and the batter. If you throw a fastball and leave it a little high, home run. Game over. You throw your changeup, which he probably thinks is coming, and maybe he gets a hit and runners score. Game over. You throw your curve and you're off by a few inches, you'll walk in the tying run and still leave the bases loaded."

"Stop, man," Billy whispered. "I think I'm going to throw up."

"But you stand up there on that mound and you throw that pitch I just threw, that batter will be still swinging at it when you're shaking champagne in your teammates' faces. Now go throw that pitch."

Billy solemnly took the mound. As if the stadium was filled with people, as if he could hear the shouts of the fans. He checked the bases as if he was trying to keep the runners on. Then he fired up and threw his ball.

Roy looked at the kid's face when he straightened up. They both turned to Lane to get her reaction.

"It's better." She nodded. "Still not great. Keep working on it, Billy. Roy, come find me when you're done."

They watched as she made her way toward the dugout.

"Wow," Billy said. "That was sort of anticlimactic."

Roy beamed. "Yes, it was, but that, my friend, was probably enough to do the trick. You just threw a strike."

Billy snickered. "You're getting laid today."

"That's right," Roy said, holding up his fist to give the kid a knuckle bump.

"You know I can still hear you," she called over her shoulder as she descended the steps.

The two men laughed and then Roy jogged to catch up with her. "Keep working on it, Billy," Roy called to the kid. "See you tonight at the game."

"Yeah, Roy. Good luck."

Neither of them were pitching tonight, but they would sit in the dugout and watch.

Roy caught up with Lane as she was making her way through the empty lockers. "Hey, do you ever worry you're going to come across a bunch of guys wearing nothing but their jockstraps?"

"I always call out before I come into the lockers. No one is here yet. Besides, do you know how many guys I've seen in their jockstraps?"

"I don't think I want to know that number," Roy mumbled.

"Do you think Billy knows that little scene you described out there actually happened?"

Roy had wondered if she would remember. She didn't know him then, but before she turned her back on baseball, she'd been the game's biggest fan. She could probably name the starting pitcher of every Game Seven ever played.

That had been his third year in the league. His first World Series. Duff was managing what would be his last year with the Founders.

Roy had thrown his curve.

He would never forget it. The look on the batter's face when he realized he'd swung and missed. The sight of that ball nestled in his catcher's glove. So completely sneaky and devious that pitch was, it was practically unhittable. Then came that rush of accomplishment followed quickly by the satisfaction of knowing he'd been born to do something and he'd actually done it.

He'd promised himself he wouldn't go back to relive those moments. He wouldn't revel in the accomplishments he'd achieved on the field. Instead he'd focus only on the future.

He didn't want to be one of *those guys* who talked about the glory of years passed and games won. The guys who wanted nothing more than to go back and the only way they had to do that was to talk about it over and over.

Remember that time when...

"I don't know. It was a long time ago."

"Almost fifteen years ago, but I still remember every moment of that game. What's even crazier was that you were pitching on a three-day rotation."

"It was the only way to pitch three games in the series." Roy remembered how numb his arm was for what felt like months after that game. He barely had enough strength to lift a spoon to his mouth and he drove with only his right hand on the wheel for weeks. All of it totally worth it.

"Duff should have brought in the closer after you walked the first batter."

Roy's eyebrows shot up. "What? You didn't have faith I could do it?"

"It's not a matter of faith. It's a matter of averages. That's the manager's job and you know it. You

were a lefty with a righty coming to the plate. You
had thrown over a hundred pitches on a three-day
rotation. He should have brought in the closer. A
few days later, I asked him why he didn't."

"What did he say?"

"'Did you see that pitch, Lanie? I left him out
there because I knew he had that pitch in him. I had
to let him throw it just to see what would happen.'"

"Yeah," Roy said, trying not to feel sad. These
past few weeks hadn't gotten any better for Duff. If
anything, the days had gotten harder for him. Only
Roy didn't know how to tell Lane without betraying Duff. "That sounds like him."

"God, Duff loves baseball."

Lane's eyes welled up and Roy could feel the
emotion pouring off her. The sadness they both
shared. He didn't want to think about what it would
mean to not have Duff sitting in the dugout encouraging him as Roy slogged his way through his
comeback. He didn't want to think about the game
of baseball, period, without Duff Baker being part
of it.

"You said he went to see the doctor."

"Yep. That's what he said. I even called to make
sure he kept the appointment and he did. But, of
course, the doctor can't tell me anything directly
unless Duff gives his permission, which he didn't
and Duff said everything is fine."

"But you don't believe him?"

Lane looked at him and Roy could see there was no point in covering for Duff.

"Do you think he's fine?"

Roy didn't, but he still didn't want to say it out loud.

"Hey, I'm hungry. Let's eat."

Food was always a great distracter, Roy thought. It was either that or more hugging, but he sensed Lane would break down with more hugging and he knew he didn't want to make her cry again.

"I was going to work on your arm," she reminded him, taking a deep breath as if she was pulling herself together.

"You can do that after food. What are you up for?"

Then he saw it. The entirely evil grin on her face. "You know what I really want?"

Roy groaned. "Oh, don't say it."

"I'm just saying, you helped Billy with his curveball and that's great. But if you really want to impress a girl, you have to give her what she wants to eat."

"You would be that cruel when you now know the truth?"

Lane shrugged.

Apparently she would. "Fine." He sighed. "Let's go get some hot dogs."

"Look, Roy, you know you want a bite." Lane waved the hot dog in his face. "Onions, spicy mustard."

"I will have my revenge."

Lane laughed, then with even more evil intent she wrapped her mouth around the dog perhaps a little suggestively and took a bite, groaning in pleasure as the salty pork product smothered in oniony goodness filled her mouth.

"Mmm," she mumbled around the mouthful. "So round and firm… It just explodes in my mouth… with flavor."

"Keep it coming, Baker. Keep it coming."

Lane put the dog down and wiped her hands with paper napkins. They were sitting outside at Lane's all-time favorite eating establishment, The Dog Shack.

A place that, much to Roy's chagrin, served hot dogs and nothing else.

"Don't you just want to try it? See if you still really hate it? I mean, how long has it been since you've eaten one?"

"When was the last time we had lunch together before the party?"

Lane didn't tell him that she knew when that was. It was the Opening Day Fair here in Minotaur Falls. She had bribed him with a few therapy sessions if he would be part of the fair's activities to raise money for the Youth Athletic League.

He'd sat in a dunk tank for hours then she'd brought him here to get a dog before they headed back to watch the game. That day she'd also learned he'd arranged for a year's supply of baseball equipment for the Little League program without telling anyone. And he'd eaten two hot dogs, smiling the whole time.

She tried to think of one thing Danny had ever done for her that came even close to that level of… what? *Sweetness* wasn't the word. Nothing about Roy could be considered sweet. But there was a self-sacrificing aspect to his nature that she couldn't help but be moved by.

"You used to love them as a kid," she reminded him.

Roy looked at the hot dog she'd ordered for him. A straight-up chili cheese dog. Messy but delicious.

"They used to be this symbol to me," he said. "Of my single-mindedness. Like all I could play was baseball and all I could eat was hot dogs and anything else was sacrilegious."

"Maybe it's time to let that go. Maybe you can stop thinking that it has to be all or nothing. All baseball or no baseball. All hot dogs or no hot dogs."

Lane knew they were talking about more than fast food. Roy did, too, for that matter.

"What about you? Married to a baseball player, then no baseball at all."

"I think I'm ready to be over that. Since being

here, being around the stadium, listening to Duff and Scout talk about the game, I realize the only person I hurt by giving up something I loved was me. I thought I was doing it to forget Danny. Forget you. Now I'm wondering if I wasn't trying to punish myself. I guess the first step in forgiving myself is letting me have baseball back. Definitely my ban on hot dogs is over."

She sank her teeth into another bite and made a sound that was nearly orgasmic. Partly because, damn, she had missed hot dogs and mostly because she wanted to tease Roy to point of pain.

"You're having fun getting me hard, aren't you?"

"Hard? Really? With just a couple of moans? Aren't you a little old for that?"

"I'm a little desperate for that."

He had been patient, Lane thought. Patient when they went on dates on his off nights. Happy to kiss her good-night at the door because he seemed to sense she wasn't ready to make that next step.

"You know my decision to wait hasn't been about Billy and his damn curveball."

"I know."

"You scare me," Lane admitted. Scared her because she still didn't know if she could trust herself, let alone trust Roy.

"I know."

"Don't I scare you back?" Lane asked. "I mean, are you ready for a real relationship? You just ended an engagement not that long ago. You lost your company. You've got the stress of trying to make a comeback, not to mention the pain of it."

"Are you worried I won't be able to hold myself up when I'm sliding deep inside you? I promise you, Lane, the shoulder will hold for that."

She knew he was being deliberately provocative again, but still she couldn't dislodge the image from her head. Given that she was battling her flight-or-fight mechanism, he didn't make it easier when he said things that had her wanting to flop on her back on a bed somewhere and let him prove he was in fine physical condition.

"I'm being serious, Roy. You have all this stuff happening in your life. What does the other side of us having sex look like to you?"

"You're asking me what my postorgasm face looks like? A lot like this," he said, pointing to his face, "only a lot happier and with much less tension."

"I'm serious."

"What are you really asking?" His eyes narrowed as if something had just occurred to him. "Are you ready to go back to Virginia? Is that what this conversation is about? You know I'll support whatever decision you make regarding that, Lanie."

Which, honestly, was so nice to hear. Had Danny ever supported her in anything? The problem with each question like that was she felt more foolish when she admitted the answer. No, Danny had never sacrificed anything for her. He'd cared about her career only so long as he got the treatment he needed. She'd been so stupid with her choices back then that it was almost embarrassing. She'd been young, but was that really her only excuse?

Or maybe it was because she never really had a chance to see what a solid marriage, a happy marriage, was supposed to look like. Certainly her parents hadn't been happy. And even though she lived part-time with her mother and Bob, she had never wanted to look too closely at that relationship. It felt like too much of a betrayal to Duff even though she acknowledged that her mother was happy.

Regardless, what she really needed to do was to forgive herself for those mistakes. Roy was right about that. Forgive herself and move on. If only it was that easy. If only she didn't keep making mistakes.

"I don't know if I will ever be ready to go back," she said, answering his question honestly. "I don't know if I can trust myself again."

"It was important work, Lane. You made a difference in people's lives."

"I know that. And I'm not saying I wouldn't try to find some other work just as meaningful. I don't know if I can get past what happened."

"Like I said. Whatever you decide to do. I'm there."

"That's my point. Where is *there*? I mean, if

everything goes according to plan, you'll be playing for the Rebels sometime after the all-star break. Where does that leave us?"

"Lane, not to bring up a sore subject but, you have had a relationship with a professional baseball player. You know what the schedule is like. I find ways to come see you during the season. You find ways to make it to a few of my games. Then during the off-season, I go where you go. It's simple."

Except it wasn't simple at all. Because all that time during the season when Danny had been bouncing around the country he had also been banging every baseball bunny in sight.

Roy isn't Danny.

The thought surfaced, but Lane quickly suppressed it. Because it was so easy to think that was the case. To think that Roy would never hurt her the way Danny had, that Roy would never cheat. That Roy would never deface the institution of marriage and everything it represented so completely.

How could she not remember the pain he'd caused her by setting her up the way he had? And how could she not wonder if he might hurt her again? Just one more reason the idea of a relationship was so frightening.

"So you're going to follow me wherever I go and we're going to be together?" Lane tossed those words out like they were the most ridiculous things ever. Even though there was this crazy rush of happiness at the thought.

Am I really ready for this? Ready to be happy?

"I imagine we will be here in the Falls for the foreseeable future. And yes, we're going to be together. If losing all of my money has taught me anything, it's that you can't take anything for granted in life. Not eighty million dollars and not this."

"This?"

"Us."

"See, that's just it. You're already thinking there is an *us* and I'm still working on maybe. My father might be sick. My sister might be headed for an emotional breakdown. I might never work with amputees again and, oh, just a reminder, I don't believe in happily-ever-after anymore. That's the person you want to be an *us* with?"

"Yep. Don't forget about the cheater and the coward, too. I like it all rolled up in one big Lanie package."

Lane wanted to scream with frustration. "Roy, think about where our lives are right now, forgetting the past, forgetting our history. If we were two strangers who met, I would say now is the worst time for either of us to think about starting a relationship."

"But there is a past and part of that past is us. We're not starting anything. The way I look at it we're already halfway there. We've been on this collision course since the moment you laughed at me for making a pass at you and called me on my shit. And yes, my life is shit. You told me to make it better. And yes, you've got issues and I've told you what you need to do about them. Why can't we do those things together...in bed?"

It seemed so easy for him and maybe it was. Maybe losing everything had made him unafraid. That hadn't been the case with Lane. Losing everything had made her never want to try again.

"What if I'm using you as some kind of emotional crutch?" she offered.

"I'll risk it, as long as you're doing so on top of my cock."

"Roy!"

"Lane." He rebutted with his eyebrow-raising trick. "Trust me. I'm on the verge of fixing all your issues. I just need to get you into bed."

She could have slapped him, but you really couldn't slap Roy Walker for being Roy Walker. Then she'd be slapping him every damn day of his life.

"Fine. You think everything is going to be better with sex—"

Roy laughed. "I *know* everything is going to be better during sex. Because sex feels really good. Going out on a limb here, I think it's going to feel extra good with you."

Trust him. That's what he wanted from her. She

wasn't sure she had that much to give. But if she was being honest with herself, she knew this part, the part with them together in a bed, had been inevitable. Maybe from the start.

"Roy?"

"Yes, Lanie?"

"Eat your hot dog and let's get out of here."

"Yes, ma'am." Without hesitation, he picked up his chili dog and started devouring it. Devouring it like a man who had been hungry for a very long time.

CHAPTER FIFTEEN

Roy drove them to his place at record speed.

"What about your arm?" Lane asked.

"What about it?"

"I was supposed to give you a therapy session."

"You can do that after…while you're naked." Roy immediately went to every fantasy he'd ever had that involved Lane working on his neck, back or shoulder, then stripping and climbing on top of him. That those fantasies might become a reality was making his erection throb in anticipation.

"I'm not working on you naked. I'm not some kind of happy-ending therapist. I take my work very seriously."

"I do, too. I'll take it even more seriously when you're naked. But if you insist on wearing panties or something like that, then that's okay, too."

"What did you mean earlier when you said the shoulder would hold for sex?"

Roy nearly cursed under his breath. She was too damn perceptive. He didn't want to talk about his shoulder or the burning sensation he'd felt when he'd thrown that curveball. He definitely didn't want to talk about it with Lane. She would start asking questions and pester him to see a doctor. All he had to do was get through his next start with a good outing. Let the Rebels know he was back to form. Then he'd see a doctor, make sure he could pass a physical in anticipation of either playing for the Rebels or being traded to another team.

No, he definitely didn't want to talk about his arm. He'd rather say sexy things that would make Lane shiver with anticipation when he finally got her into bed.

Roy moved his right hand off the wheel and on to Lane's thigh, which was exposed by the white shorts she wore. He ran his hand down to her knee then up as high as the shorts would allow. He felt her toned muscles tense and he considered what that thigh would feel like wrapped around his hip.

"Honey, I need you to focus. It's almost one o'clock now. The game starts at eight, but I have to be at the clubhouse by six. That gives me only three hours to make you come about a half dozen times before I have to shower and drink enough fluids so I don't pass out by the sixth inning."

"You're not even pitching tonight."

"Did you not hear me say I was going to make you come six times? That kind of focused effort takes a lot of energy."

"You're all talk and don't think I don't know what

you're doing by avoiding the conversation regarding your shoulder."

"All talk, huh? I'm sensing a bet in there somewhere."

"Roy, as fun as it is to see you've got your old swagger back, don't think for a second I will not call you on your bullshit."

This time his hand moved from her thigh straight to the heart of her. His hand, bigger than a normal man's hand thereby better able to grip the ball, cupped her fully and with just a shift of his fingers he knew he was hitting buttons that were making her squirm in her seat belt.

"Roy, someone might see."

His middle finger circled where he knew her opening would be, giving her a hint of what this might feel like without her shorts. Then he thought, why wait?

"Unbutton your shorts and push them and your panties down your thighs."

"Yeah, that's not going to happen."

However, Roy noticed she didn't move to push his hand away. In fact, she might have been arching her hips ever so slightly to deepen the contact.

He glanced at her top, some loose, summery thing that ballooned down to her thighs making the shorts mostly peekaboo anyway.

"No one will see, and we're going to start with one orgasm right now."

"Roy, you can't do that and drive."

"I'm a very safe driver. And I love the way you're not saying no so much as refuting my skills as both lover and driver. You've already decided to trust me with your body if nothing else. You might as well go big or go home."

He cupped her again more firmly, then slid his hand to where the button of her shorts was. In two quick seconds the shorts were unbuttoned and the zipper was down.

"Come on, babe, I'm going to need a little help here. Just slide those shorts right off your hips. Enough so I can get to the good stuff."

"Good stuff? You sound like a sixteen-year-old boy."

"Nah, I was definitely not as talented a *driver* at sixteen as I am now, so be grateful you're here with me. Again, I notice you're deflecting. You know you want to," he said seductively.

Then just when he was about to laugh and tell her what a prude she was for not buying into car sex, she did the most amazing sexual thing any woman had ever done for him.

She actually did what he asked.

Just a slight hitch of her hips, the soft push of her hands against the shorts. When he ran his hand over the exposed thigh and up, this time there was no restriction, no barrier, just the slick heat of her.

"That's it, baby," he said. It was maddening. All

he wanted to do was stare at the sweet patch of her body she'd exposed. Instead he had to keep his eyes on the road. He made careful turns to avoid the main street, weaving his way through back roads that were virtually deserted at midafternoon, during the work week.

It was when he reached the first stop sign that he took a moment to get his fingers right where he wanted them on her body. Like applying the perfect grip on a baseball to make the ball go in the direction he commanded.

His thrust his middle finger just inside her and felt a rush of wetness, proving that the entire time she'd been protesting she'd been getting turned on by his words.

With tiny little thrusts he coaxed that heat from her body and used it to make it easier for his other fingers to slide through her slick lips. When he pushed on the gas pedal, that little forward thrust of the car's momentum was enough to jolt her and push his finger deeper inside her body.

"Jeezus, I can't wait to be inside you."

"Roy…"

That was it, nothing else. Just his name. A whisper that let him know he was doing it, he was making Lanie Baker feel good. He angled his thumb up over her clit with a firm stroking motion.

"Come to me, baby. Move those hips right up to the edge. Let me get a little deeper."

Lane dropped her head against the headrest and pushed her hips as close to the edge of the seat as her seat belt would allow. She shifted her thighs a little wider and then Roy was able to do shallow little plunges with first one finger, then two. Then go even deeper until he could hear her breathing start to grow uneven. A few intense circles from his callous thumb, right where she was most sensitive, and he knew he was close to making her scream.

He really wanted to hear Lane scream.

"Talk to me, baby. Tell me where you are."

They were only a couple of blocks away from his house but Roy had no intention of exiting the car without delivering to Lane the first of many orgasms to come with him.

Rather than answer she pushed her hand down on his and turned her head toward him. "Right there, just right there."

Roy could feel her fingers sliding through his, joining them together as he pushed her a little harder, slipped inside her a little deeper.

"Roy," she squeaked, then squeezed around his fingers in a way that told him she'd come for him. It wasn't a full-on scream, but it was his name and it sounded really, really good.

Number one.

He pulled into his driveway and parked the car. Watched as she slid her shorts up and mentally created the image of him sliding them down her legs again. Only the next time she would be standing in the middle of his bedroom.

"I can't believe I did that," she breathed. Then she opened the car door but paused when she saw Roy wasn't moving. "Aren't you coming inside?"

"I seriously think if I attempt to stand right now, I might break my boner in half."

She chuckled and Roy watched in fascination as she reciprocated the act of placing her hand over his jean-clad thigh, then moving it up and up until she was cupping him as firmly as he had cupped her.

He, too, allowed his head to fall against the headrest and just let himself feel the pleasure in his groin.

Then the even bigger pleasure of the moment hit him. This was Lane Baker. The princess of baseball. And they were together and touching each other intimately.

A few months ago he thought he'd lost everything. His fiancée, his money, certainly his pride. If there really were such a thing as fate and all those events led to this moment, then he would gladly lose it all over again.

"I had everything five years ago," he said, the words tumbling out of his mouth unchecked. He couldn't stop them. "Money, fame, the glory of knowing I was the best in the game. But I didn't have you. Now I have nothing. Not a freaking dime to my name, but I just made you come and I feel like a king."

She brushed her hand gently across his cheek with her knuckles. "For being such an ass sometimes you do say the nicest things."

"You love the ass in me, admit it."

"I admit nothing so as not to encourage your assedness. Come inside, Roy Walker. It's my turn to make you come."

He pulled her hand to his lips and kissed her knuckles. He remembered talking with Pete about being afraid of the *L* word and Roy not knowing if that was a thing for him because he hadn't ever been in love before.

They were going to bed together now and somehow he knew it would change everything.

"Are you ready?" she asked.

"Yes. I'm ready."

And he wasn't scared at all.

HOLDING HER HAND, which seemed odd to Lane because she didn't take Roy for the type of guy who displayed his affection, Roy led her inside his home. Not stopping in any room, he took her all the way upstairs to his bedroom, which was situated at the front of the house. The furniture was boring and nondescript. The comforter a bland cream color. Not his, of course.

Oddly, Lane flashed on a memory of his apartment on the night of his party. He'd taken her to his bedroom then, too. She recalled sophisticated prints on the wall. Silver silk throws on the bed.

None of that seemed like him, either. It seemed to achieve a particular look the decorator had put together. Lane couldn't help wonder if there was a place in the world that reflected who Roy was. His town house in Philadelphia maybe, but that was for sale.

Not that she was any different. Her apartment in Virginia had been nothing more than a place to stay before she left for work and a place to return to when she finished work.

It reminded her of where they both were in their lives—a little lost. However, in this place and in this time, they could be lost together.

They didn't speak. None of his sexy commands, none of her righteous indignation, which was nothing more than an attempt to get him to utter more of those sexy commands. Because Roy Walker telling her to slide out of her shorts for him was about the hottest thing anyone had ever asked her to do.

Instead they listened to the buzz of the air-conditioning unit that was in the bedroom window. The whisper of her flowing green top as she whisked it over her head. The zip of his jeans coming undone. Soon they were naked and he was heading to the bathroom to grab a condom from the medicine cabinet.

For an anxious moment Lane stood in the center of the room with her arms wrapped around her waist. Roy had wanted her for a long time. He'd told her how many fantasies he'd had about her. Ones in which she worked on his body while naked.

That was a lot of pressure to live up to for a woman who hadn't had sex in a very long time. When he returned with a strip of three condoms and placed them on the nightstand next to the bed, she almost found herself gulping.

"Uh, Roy, you should know it's been a while for me. I mean, I know you've been thinking about this…or at least you used to think about this with me, but I'm just saying that—"

He put his fingers against her lips, the same fingers he put inside her body. That stopped her rambling and she had this crazy urge to shock him. To make him see her as the most erotic creature in the universe by sucking those same fingers into her mouth and letting him know how much pleasure he had given her.

"Lane, this isn't some fantasy to play out. This is you and me and our first time together. I'm not thinking about anything other than how lucky I am to be here, in this moment, with you."

She felt her heart tug a little. This was Roy Walker, at one time the biggest badass pitcher in baseball. And for some inexplicable reason, of all the women in the world he could pick from, he wanted her.

He'd wanted her then and he wanted her now.

"Okay, but I really wish you would go back to saying the dirty things. Sometimes they are easier to hear than the really sweet things."

"How about your nipples are already tight for me and I haven't even sucked on them yet.

"That's better."

And it was. It was raw and simple and uncomplicated. She couldn't say her feelings weren't involved in this moment. She knew herself too well for that to be the case. But if she could think about the sex and only the sex, then she wouldn't have to deal with the other, messier feelings she wasn't ready to put a name to.

Sex, Lane thought. Sex was good. She missed sex. This was Roy and she wasn't married and nothing that happened in this bedroom would leave her with any lingering feelings of guilt.

She put her hands on his chest. The chest that she had touched before but never allowed herself to gaze at too long while working on his shoulder or back. The pattern and swirls of dark hair, like some kind of sexy van Gogh painting. This is what she had waited for. This was what she most thought about when she thought about touching him.

Running her fingers through those fine hairs, she nearly moaned at the pure physical joy of touching him. The way those swirls caressed her fingers, clinging to them even as she tried to tug free. Deliberately tugging hard enough to make him smile because he knew she was being a little mischievous.

"Lane, not that I'm not thoroughly enjoying this, but I do have other body parts covered in the same hair you seem to love so much."

She lifted her face to him and smiled. "You mean your head?"

"One of them definitely has a head."

She laughed even as she reached one hand down to caress him. No surprise that he was heavy and thick and completely comfortable in his body. The Roy Walker of old walked like a man who knew what his body could do. What his arm could do on the mound, what his cock could do in a bed.

Flashes of that Roy Walker were coming back and she imagined she was in for a rather impressive show. Suddenly Lane was done with the playing, the teasing, even the talking. She wanted to have him inside her, she wanted to feel what that would be like. She wanted to know the power and the strength of him over her and under her and behind her.

Would three condoms be enough?

"Take me to bed, Roy."

"Yes, ma'am."

He backed her against the bed and toppled her with a gentle push. Her legs dangled over the edge of the mattress and he stepped between them. He touched her cheek so gently with his ever-powerful left hand and then used it to run over her breasts, his thumb tweaking one nipple, then sliding over to tweak the other.

"Lucky bastard," Roy mumbled.

"What?" Lane asked, not really able to hear him with the hum of pleasure vibrating through her body.

"Nothing," he said. "Just enjoying the view."

His hand continued to roam while his other one came between her legs again. Teasing and tempting, slipping inside only to slip out again so quickly it was like he hadn't even been there. Like he wanted to get her to the point of asking for more and longer.

Lane was not above begging.

"Please, Roy. I need you inside me. Now."

Reaching for the condom, he used his teeth to tear it open then slid it over his cock. He gripped her thighs and wrapped them around his hips until she locked her ankles together. He still stood so she had to tilt her hips to him to give him an angle. Then, with his right arm braced on the bed near her head, he pushed inside her in a heavy thrust.

At first, her body resisted him, which he seemed to sense as he stilled above her. But he didn't pull out or ask if she was okay. He simply waited for her to accept him. Embrace him. Reach for him.

Lane considered what a perfect metaphor that

was for their relationship. Roy was always pushing against her resistance, but rather than retreat, he seemed to wait in front of her until she realized he wasn't going anywhere. So there was nothing else to do but accept him. It was how they became friends. It was how they became lovers.

She felt full of his body. Tight and stretched but not in a painful way. She had this irrational thought that she was being branded by him so fundamentally that no one would ever touch her so closely, or come so deeply inside of her, again.

"Lanie, you ready? Tell me you're ready, babe."

She knew what he was asking. He wanted to move and demand and take. Only he wouldn't do any of that until she was ready for him. Until he knew she'd accepted him fully.

"Yes. Please. Now, now."

It was the only encouragement he needed. With a hard thrust he was moving into her steadily, his left hand gripping her ass and pulling her closer to him while his right arm braced his body above hers.

There wasn't any finesse in this and it was delicious. Lane just lay back on the bed, her hands on his chest because that's where she most wanted them. Sliding through his hairy swirls, brushing his nipples with her thumbs as he moved over her in a steady pounding rhythm. When a particularly hard thrust rocked her on the bed, she tugged at his hair in retaliation. Until he grunted.

She looked up at him and could see him smiling and it seemed like the oddest thing in the world to be feeling her whole body coming undone but smiling at the same time. But that's how it was with his hips snapping against her and his smile making her chuckle. Then he hit a spot deep inside that made her body tighten and her mouth open in a soundless scream of ecstasy.

He pushed deep and held her to him and she heard his groans of pleasure. Delighted at the fact that she could give him that same pleasure. Like she was the most seductive woman on the planet for having made Roy come.

Finally he collapsed on top of her and the feel of those swirls now damp with this sweat teasing her nipples made the aftershocks of her orgasm go on and on. He kissed her neck, her lips and they laughed as the realization of what they had finally, *finally* done hit them.

It was as he was nuzzling her neck and whispering sweet words about how soft she was and how beautiful she was, that something else occurred to Lane.

"Roy?"

"Yes, baby?"

"You braced yourself over me with your right

hand. You really didn't think the other one was going to hold."

"Shit," he muttered into her neck.

"What aren't you telling me about your left shoulder?"

CHAPTER SIXTEEN

"I MEAN IT, ROY. You made that comment about it holding up and then you didn't put any weight on it. I can put two and two together."

Roy came out of the bathroom having disposed of the condom and stood by the bed literally and figuratively naked. "Okay, clearly we're going to need another round of sex because that obviously didn't blow your mind. You should not be able to put one and one together after having sex with me."

"You blew my mind during. It came back after we were done."

"That shouldn't happen for at least an hour. I'm losing my touch."

Lane rose onto her knees and Roy was distracted by her beautiful naked body. He hadn't come close to loving every part of her. The need to be inside her had overwhelmed him. Now he was cataloging what he'd skipped over.

He hadn't spent any time on her breasts. He hadn't used his mouth on her clit. He hadn't kissed the inside of her elbow or the back of her knee or the small of her back.

He needed to do that. Because he wanted every part of her. He wanted every part of Lane Baker.

With Shannon, he always had this protocol to follow. Her pleasure first, then his. With Lane, he hadn't been able to plan. All he'd wanted was to be inside her, driving her hard. And there was this weird sense that it was okay. That sex between them shouldn't follow some predictable pattern. Like getting her off with his fingers while driving.

He cupped her breast and bent down to kiss her still firm nipple. Brown and pert. Delicious.

"Roy, stop distracting me and tell me about your shoulder."

She was too stubborn by far.

"It's a little stiff, nothing to worry about. When I threw that curve this morning it hurt so I didn't want to put any more pressure on it. Like I said, no big deal."

"I'm trying to think of a good surface I could put you on to work it. Do you have a long, flat table?"

"Sweetheart, the only surface I want you to work with me on is this one."

Roy flopped on the bed and took her with him so that, after a bit of shifting limbs, he was on his back and she was laid out on top of him. The soft brush of hair between her legs teasing his still semi-hard penis was making him certain of his decision.

"Roy, what if it's serious?"

"Look, the arm isn't going to fall off, okay? We'll

leave a little early to head to the stadium and you can work on me there in one of the therapy rooms. I've got two days before I have to pitch again and by tomorrow, I'm sure I'll be fine."

"You know your next outing is in front of the Rebels scouts. Duff said he's splitting you and Billy so they can see you both."

Roy nodded. That's how it worked at this level. It wasn't always so much about winning the game—although to the players that was a natural desire—as it was about development and standing out.

Standing out so you could move up.

"I can't believe I taught that kid a third pitch," Roy muttered, although not really all that upset about it. Billy was a good kid and if he could harness a little more mental focus to go along with his physical talent, he might have a shot in the majors.

"You know it doesn't have to be either-or—the Rebels might take both of you."

"Yeah," he said, running his hand down her back, giving her butt a playful slap. "But if it is him and not me, then I get to blame you. That could be fun. Delivering your punishment."

She wiggled after another playful slap. "Stop that. Roy, what if it is one or the other and what if it is Billy?"

Roy cocked an eyebrow. "Your continued lack of faith in me is truly stunning. I think I might be hurt if I wasn't so blissfully satisfied."

"It's not that. I know you've put everything into this plan, but I'm sitting here thinking there are a lot of things that can go wrong and I don't know if you have a backup plan."

Roy reached up to touch her face. Looking into her eyes he saw the concern there. He teased her about not having any faith but truthfully, her worry for him felt even better. She cared. She might still be freaked out about where they were going. He had no doubt that she'd put away that fear only temporarily in order to have sex. But she had feelings for him that went beyond casual. That was an amazing thing.

After wanting her for so long and having her be this missing piece he thought he would never have a chance to get back, she was now lying on top of him naked, worried about his pain, his future.

Life could be awfully strange and wonderful.

"My plan? Let's see. I can live off you."

"I'm currently unemployed, remember?"

"Yeah, but you have to have all that money from the divorce." Roy laughed. "Now that would be ironic if we lived on Danny Worthless's alimony check. I'm not going to lie, I would take a perverse thrill in doing so."

"I don't have much money and he doesn't give me alimony."

"What? That doesn't make sense. You had Samantha representing you. She's a ruthless, maniacal shark and everybody knows it. Plus, she's your sister. Danny's lawyer wouldn't have been so much as a snack for her."

Lane smiled. "She did rough him up pretty good. I wanted everything in a lump sum. The last thing I needed was some monthly check reminding me year in and year out what a mistake I'd made. I took a lot of that money and gave it to various different charities, some colleges to offer tuitions for baseball players. A lot of it to inner-city high schools for equipment and improving the field conditions. There's actually one school in DC that named the field after me when I gave them enough money to build a baseball diamond."

Roy kissed her sweetly. "Here I thought you hated baseball after the divorce."

"I told myself giving away the money was me making my break with the game final. Don't get me wrong, I didn't give it all away. I put some in an IRA for retirement, but I wasn't going to be one of those ex-wives enjoying spending their husband's money. And there was the guilt factor, too. I knew I didn't really deserve it."

"You have to stop that, Lanie. Stop punishing yourself. Not that I could see you as the type to gleefully spend someone else's money."

"Which means using me as your sugar mama is not exactly a viable plan. I need to figure out where I go from here, Roy, and if the comeback doesn't work out the way you have it planned, you will, too."

"I have to say postcoital chats with you are a real downer."

"It's just that I'm worried—"

"For me. I know," Roy said. "I like it. A lot. But trust me when I tell you, I got this. It's going to work out. Then you'll get your stuff sorted out and we'll do that together. A few more innings of Roy Walker pitching, one more contract and you. It's all I need."

He could feel her squirming on top of him. Like a worm trying to get off a hook, but he wasn't having it. Reaching over to the nightstand he ripped off another condom.

"Roy, we should get showered and head to the stadium so I can take a look at that arm. See if I can feel anything going on with the muscles."

"Oh, you want to do this in the shower?"

"Roy!"

With little effort, because she really wasn't in any hurry to get off him, he was able to hold her pressed against him. With one hand he deftly rolled on the condom. Her squirming had the dual effect of making him hard and making him feel like he needed to bind her to him again in a fundamental physical way.

With a shift of his hips and her hips they were connected again. Even though she was still squirming, the soft sigh in his ear told him it wasn't about trying to get away anymore. She braced herself above him, with her neck arched back. She moved her hips in slow circles that were driving him insane with the need to plunge deeper, but she was so lost in her pleasure, he didn't want to disturb that. He wanted her to relish every moment of them together.

The sight of her bending over so she could rub her breasts against his chest nearly undid him.

"Say my name, Lanie. Say it with me inside you"

"Roy," she quickly answered, then bent to kiss him. Her tongue pushed into his mouth even as his dick pushed into her body. This was heaven. This was the thing he'd never even known he was missing with a woman. This was the thing he'd always thought he might have had with Lane until he lost it.

This was love.

Too bad she wasn't ready to hear it yet.

"OH, YEAH, RIGHT THERE. Oh, baby, that's *soooo* good!"

Lane looked at Roy, who was finally stretched out on her therapy table in one of the rooms outside of the lockers. She had the door shut, but as loud as he was, there was no doubt every Minotaurs player getting ready for the game that started soon could hear him.

"Are you serious?"

She had her finger pressed deep into a muscle

she was trying to convince to loosen its death grip on the surrounding nerves. The inflammation was considerable under his armpit. She was concerned the problem might be with his rotator cuff. Any kind of tear might require surgery to fix and that certainly would put an end to his comeback plan for this year.

At his age, another year gone, it might put an end to the plan indefinitely.

Which meant Lane was panicking about that, panicking about the fact he seemed so certain they could make a relationship between them work. She hadn't even told him the part about her never marrying again. Because, somehow, she knew that wouldn't sit well with him.

This was on top of all her other life worries and still, he was making sex noises in a deliberate attempt to embarrass her with the team. He probably thought he was being extremely funny.

"Hey, I warned you what would happen."

"Roy, no threat you could make was going to convince me to work on you topless. I'm a professional. Would I make you go out to the mound in your jockstrap and nothing else?"

He turned his head in her direction. "Do you fantasize about that? Because, I mean, maybe later when everyone is gone…"

"You're impossible."

"You love it."

The fact that she did a little made it difficult to refute that claim. The fact that the word *love* was used in any capacity around her made her want to squirm. Since not moving was part of her job, she controlled herself.

"Besides it's not like they don't all know you're my girl now."

Right, because when they'd pulled up to the stadium and gotten out of the Jeep, Roy had made a big show of kissing her as the other players were arriving. If there were any doubts as to what Lane and Roy had been doing all afternoon, he'd squashed them. His teammates hooted and howled until finally Billy shouted, "You're welcome."

"Was that really necessary?" Lane asked.

"Yes."

"To humiliate me?"

"No, for you to get it through your head that we are, in fact, a couple. Granted, I gave you only four orgasms instead of the six that were promised, but there is no backing out now. You came a lot."

"Sex doesn't make a relationship."

It was hard to say that like she meant it. What she and Roy had shared that afternoon hadn't felt like just sex. It hadn't even felt like crazy good, first-time sex. It had felt like they had done it a million times before and would do it a million more times before they were old and gray.

Like they had always been connected that way,

which, of course, was ridiculous and nonsensical. Fairy tales and happy endings were things that happened only in books and movies, and no one was more cynical about love than Lane.

Yet she couldn't shake the thought that there was some kind of weird destiny thing happening here. And that idea instantly made her consider running for the hills because she didn't know if she was capable of succeeding in a relationship.

That train of thought made her angry at herself. She'd failed at her marriage so she left baseball. She'd failed at her job, so she came home. She had just had the most amazing sex of her life with a man who was quickly becoming important to her and, rather than wearing a goofy grin on her face, she was riddled with self-doubt.

"Roy, I don't want to be a coward," Lane whispered. She felt compelled to tell him. To let him know that her instincts were working against him and what he wanted.

"You're not."

"What if you want things I can't give you?"

"Not going to happen, either."

That annoyed her. Like he thought by the power of being Roy Walker, he could overcome all her natural fears. Still she kept her finger steady on the pulse of his artery, waiting for the muscle to give up the fight.

"I'm never getting married again," she blurted out. "Just so you know."

"Wow. Talk about lightning fast. You go from hating me to having sex with me to marriage. Lane, honey, you need to slow that train down."

Her face flamed red and she knew he was teasing her again. She knew she hadn't been wrong to tell him of her decision never to marry again. Because she absolutely meant it.

He called them an *us*. An *us* got married eventually, but she never would.

"Fine, be that way, I'm just telling you the truth."

"Got it. No proposing today. Check."

"You're such an ass."

She watched Roy close his eyes and smile like all was right in his world. So different than the man who had stood in Duff's office all those weeks ago. That man had been broken. This man on her table might have something physically wrong with him, but he was fully the man she knew before.

Maybe even better. Because the Roy she knew back then hadn't smiled a lot. He'd been intense, he'd been focused, he'd driven her crazy with his banter and sarcasm.

But he hadn't smiled.

"Roy, are you happy?"

He turned to face her, his eyes level with hers as she sat on the stool. And she knew that he was happy without him having to say it.

"Ridiculously happy right now."

"Because you got laid," she said, trying to deflect the seriousness of what she felt from him. Like, because of her, he was happy and that was such a profound feeling. Especially when happiness seemed so elusive to her.

Aren't you happy now?

She'd never really had that with Danny. In the beginning they were just two kids and they loved each other. She thought she made him happy, but she never had a sense that he was altered because she loved him.

Danny was perpetually upbeat. Never down. Danny made her happy for a while and then he made her horribly depressed. She'd seen him only once after that party, at the divorce settlement. He hadn't worn a scowl, just the resigned expression of a man who was about to give away a lot of money he didn't want to. Even in divorcing Danny, she hadn't made a significant impact on his emotions.

Roy, she had made happy. She had put that smile on his face.

He grazed his knuckles along her cheek. "Not because I got laid, Lanie. Because I got laid by *you.*"

Slowly she slid her hand out from underneath him. She thought about finding another pressure point to attack, but she was too rattled by everything going on in her head. Besides she didn't think it would make a difference. The inflammation in his shoulder was way more pronounced than she'd expected.

Yes, she'd made him happy. And now she was going to make him supremely unhappy. The reciprocating pain she felt in her chest was a real and physical thing. It was like looking at Duff asleep in the passenger seat of the car and knowing something was wrong. Just knowing it in her gut. She worked on arms and shoulders all the time.

What she felt in Roy didn't feel like average stiffness.

"Roy, I know you're not going to want to hear this, but I think you need to see a doctor and you need to do it before you throw again."

He sat up slowly, as she instructed after each session to let the blood rush surging through his body settle down.

His smile had disappeared. "That's not going to happen."

"Roy, it has to. There is a lot of swelling here and here," she said, putting her hand on his back where the skin was still hot from her efforts. "I can't be certain without an MRI, but I'm worried there's some kind of tear in the rotator cuff."

"There is no tear. There is a little soreness. I'm pitching in front of the scouts in two days. I have to. You know everything depends on this."

"See, that's what I mean. You need another backup plan."

"Lanie, this is the backup plan. And the backup plan's backup plan. One contract, one year and, if I do it smarter this time, I'm set for life."

"There are other options. There is TV, there is radio."

"No, there isn't!" he shouted. "You don't think I considered all of those ideas before I even thought of putting a uniform on? You think that signing up for this kind of humiliation wasn't my absolute last idea? I went down this road with my accountant. I considered all of my options and, in the end, there was only one. Lanie, this is all I am. It's all I do. It cost me eighty million dollars to figure that out. My name is Roy Walker and I pitch lightning. That's it."

"It's not everything you are. Look at what you did with Billy—"

"Yeah, look at what I did with Billy. What a great idea, Lane. Now we're splitting the innings and my chance of getting that contract went down because they've got an option with a kid who now has a little more depth to his game."

"So you resent me for that? Because I asked you to do that?"

"No," he said, lowering his voice. "No. I helped the kid and it felt good. I'm not regretting that. But the reality doesn't change. He's my competition. We don't know what the Rebels' GM's plan is, but I have to go into the next game thinking I need to be better than Billy. That's a fact."

"If you see a doctor and nothing's wrong, then you lose nothing."

"Not true. The scouts hear about me even walking past a doctor's office door and it will sound the alarm. The only way this works if they believe I'm a hundred percent healthy."

"And if you're not?"

He hopped off the table and reached for his jersey. "Tomorrow all I have to do is guarantee myself one more year. Nothing is going to stop that. Not even you."

"You're being stubborn."

"And you're being naive. You know players play through pain all the time."

"Pain, yes, not a tear in the rotator cuff. If it's a small tear, you could have surgery—"

Roy laughed as if she'd told some hilarious joke.

"We've gone from seeing a doctor to surgery? Teams might buy into me coming back. They might sign off on using me out of the bullpen or as a potential closer. I have surgery and they won't even buy me a ticket to the game."

"You can't wish away what is likely a real problem."

"Watch me." He opened the door—with his right hand—and didn't look back as he headed to the lockers.

She stared at the empty table and cursed under her breath.

Damn it, she didn't want this. She didn't want any of this. She'd come home to evaluate her job situation and suddenly she was dealing with two stubborn men who wouldn't face what was right in front of their faces. Her father, who she loved desperately, and Roy, who she...

Who made her so damn mad!

Lane kicked the table and cursed even louder as the pain ricocheted through her foot.

"Seems a little unfair taking your anger out on the table." Duff leaned against the doorframe. He looked even thinner than he had when she first came home. Still he was smiling and there was a twinkle in his eye so she knew he'd overheard much, if not all, of their fight.

"He's being a stubborn jackass," she said. "Gee, I wonder where he gets his hatred of doctors?"

Duff laughed. "Couldn't say. Why, I just saw a doctor a while ago." His expression sobered. "Roy's a little desperate right now and desperate men will do foolish things. I'll tell you this, though. The man who stormed out of his room with his chin three feet ahead of his body was the Roy Walker I remember. Good to see him back. I knew you would be the one to do it, too."

"I think there is something wrong with his arm," she confessed. Roy would be furious with her for saying anything, but she couldn't not tell Duff. He had to know the condition of his players. Remaining silent was close to being unethical. "I have no proof, of course. There is no MRI. But if you see something on the mound…"

"I'll keep my eye on him."

"Will you?" she asked maybe more sharply than she should have. "Will you be able to? After all, it's an eight o'clock start and we know how you like to be in bed by then."

Duff didn't even flinch. "Yeah, well, I'll take a nap first and that should get me through the game."

"I don't get it! You know there's something wrong. Who was this doctor you saw? What did he really say? Because the word *fine* doesn't cut it anymore, Duff. Everyone knows there is something wrong! They're bringing up Jayson LaBec because something is wrong. Why won't you let us help you?"

Duff scowled. "I am letting you help me. Driving me to the away games so I don't have to bounce around on the bus, that's a help. Scout doing the office stuff, that's a help. I'm a little worn down and my girls are here doing what they can do. What's so wrong about that?"

When he put it that way it sounded so simple.

"Now go upstairs and watch the game. You can work off your mad with a few hot dogs and a beer. Then you and Roy can make up like couples do."

"I already had a hot dog today."

"When was the last time Lane Baker stopped at one dog? You know it's dollar-dog night tonight?"

Dollar-dog night. Or as Lane referred to it, hot-dog heaven. Her ceiling, at one point, had been nine dogs in nine innings. As ornery as she felt right now she bet she could top that.

Eating her worries away wasn't an adult solution, but it might be the only one in her arsenal right now.

"A few hot dogs aren't going to fix everything, Duff."

"Nope, but they sure aren't going to hurt anything, either."

Truer words, Lane thought, had never been said.

CHAPTER SEVENTEEN

"WHAT ARE YOU doing here?"

That was a hell of a greeting. Lane had just come down the stairs after getting out of bed. She stared at Scout, sitting at the kitchen table already freshly showered and ready for the day, and was envious at how put-together her sister looked. A cup of coffee on her right and the *Minotaur Falls Gazette* opened on her left—this was how she started every day.

Like any crabby sister in a thoroughly bad mood, Lane had this awful urge to grab the newspaper and crumple it into a ball just so they could get into a fight about it.

"Don't even think about it," Scout said, eyeing Lane and correctly identifying her motivation.

Probably just as well they weren't going to fight. Lane's head felt stuffed with cotton balls and her eyelids felt three sizes too big. She'd been crying, which was always a bad idea for her. One, it never accomplished anything, and two, it made her look like some weird sea creature from hell.

"What do you mean what am I doing here? I live

here." She could still snap at her sister. Snapping was a perfectly acceptable way to vent her frustration.

"Everyone knows you and Roy are together. Figured you would be spending nights at his place."

"Figured wrong," Lane said, dully, her anger seeping out of her. After their blowout, she'd stayed to watch a few innings but then left. Roy didn't call or text her. She didn't call or text him.

Then she'd cried until she fell asleep. Her first day as part of an official couple was not off to a great start.

Lane slumped in one of the chairs and Scout had the decency to get her a cup of coffee. Scout put the mug in front of Lane and waited for an explanation.

There was no point in not telling Scout. She would probably hear it from Duff anyway. "He's mad at me."

"Jeez, after one day. What did you do to piss him off?"

"I think there might be something wrong with his arm."

"Oh, no."

"Yeah. He doesn't want to hear about it, of course."

"Lane, his next start—"

"I know!" Lane shouted. "I know it's important. I know it's his one chance to make this comeback. But if there is something seriously wrong—and I think there is—he's won't be able to pitch through it. I don't care if he thinks he's some kind of super-hero pitcher."

"You know him, Lanie. He won't back down. He's too close."

"As the daughter of a former player and current manager, I understand. As a therapist, I can't stand to watch him potentially do structural damage to his arm. As his—who knows what we are now—it just sucks. He's in pain and I'm hurting for him and—"

"You were rooting for him. For his comeback."

"I was rooting for him." Lane sighed.

Scout shrugged. "You're going to have to let it play out."

Lane sipped her coffee and felt the cotton balls recede. Although when she touched her eyes she could feel how puffy they were. Damn, when was the last time she'd cried over a guy? At the end of her marriage she'd cried buckets, but that had more to do with her failure than any grief or other emotion about Danny.

No, she hadn't really cried over a guy since high school. Roy was different because, beyond all the drama, they were friends.

Lane's tears weren't because he hadn't called or texted—it was reasonable to assume he was pissed. It was reasonable to assume he was furious if Duff said anything to him about the arm—Roy would know where the information came from. No, Lane had spent most of the night crying because she was sad for her friend. She didn't want to see him go on that mound and not do well.

"Yeah, I know."

"So it's true. You guys are, like, a couple now."

Lane leaned back in her chair, thinking how if she didn't have to get out of her pajamas all day, it would be a good thing. "I don't know what we are. I don't know what happens after his next start. I don't know anything."

"You going back to Virginia, then?"

Lane straightened and looked at her sister. "Why would you say that?"

Scout tilted her head, her did-you-really-ask-me-that-question? expression on her face. "Lane, it's what you do."

"It isn't." The denial came instantly, even though Lane felt some shame because the thoughts of how easy it would be to return to Virginia had crossed her mind. "Okay, maybe it's what I used to do."

"Don't get so upset about it. Everyone has their thing. You run. I hide. None of it is particularly healthy, but everyone has to deal with shit in their own way. You know who I blame?"

"Let me guess," Lane said, knowing she didn't need to bother.

"Mom."

"You really need to get over it."

"Why, when she's such a convenient scapegoat?"

"Because that's not any way to live. Hiding. Running. When I saw the pattern in my life, I was horrified. It's cowardice and that's not who I thought I was. Which means I'm changing it. Starting now."

"Oh, for crying out loud, Lanie, that is so like you. You discovered a weakness and you're horrified? The great and almighty Lane Baker. The perfect daughter to both her mother and her father even after a bitter divorce. The perfect sister to both her older and her younger sister, even though each of them basically can't stand the other. The perfect therapist. The perfect everything. Except not the perfect wife to Danny Worthless, which is why, rather than accept the fact you picked the wrong guy, you had to give up on every guy and turn your back on a game you love as some kind of self-inflicted punishment. You're not perfect, Lane."

The accusations stung—possibly because they came close to the truth.

"I never said I was perfect, Scout. Forget my tendency to run. You want another harsh fact? I was basically seeing Roy while I was still married to Danny. I mean, it wasn't sexual or anything like that, but we went out for lunch. We would hang out after his therapy sessions. We spent that day together at the charity fair here in the Falls. I mean, what was that if it wasn't a date? So I'm a runner and a cheat."

"So what? You spent the day with him. You were friends."

"It was more than friends."

"Fine. You liked him. I knew it," Scout said. "I knew it by how much you hated him after that party."

"I'm giving you examples how not perfect I am. Stop letting me off the hook."

"That's my point, Lane, no one is. Only you beat yourself up for not being perfect more than anyone I have ever met. You think you can control everything and you can't. Case in point—your own feelings."

"So what am I supposed to do? Stop trying? Sue me, I want to be a better person. I don't want to make mistakes and I don't want to fail at anything. Because failing blows. So, no, I'm not going back to Virginia, because Duff needs me. No, I don't know what Roy and I are, but I'm trying not to run from it, either, even though it makes me crazy scared inside."

"And your work?"

"I suppose there have to be veterans somewhere in New York State who need my help."

Scout smiled. "I like that plan."

"Was this some kind psychiatry session?" Lane felt as if she'd been tricked into both confessing her feelings and committing to staying in Minotaur Falls indefinitely.

"No," Scout said. "But I'm glad you're staying. And I'm glad I was right about you and Roy."

"What if this is the end for him, Scout? He thinks being a pitcher is all he is."

"What do you think?"

Lane thought about the story he'd told Billy yesterday. The way Billy's eyes widened and his voice dropped to this soft whisper as if he was in awe of the man standing before him. Then Billy threw a legitimate curveball, something he'd never been able to do before.

"I think Roy has a lot to offer the game. I'm hoping he sees he can still belong to it, even if he's not pitching anymore."

"He'll need a strong woman to help him see that, because if his next start doesn't go well, then he'll be one tough son of a bitch to live with."

Lane finished her coffee. "Guess I better go do my making up now, then. In preparation of managing the beast I might have on my hands tomorrow night."

"You got a plan?"

Lane gave her sister the same expression Scout had used earlier. "Please, I'm going to get naked."

"That should work."

Lane stood and put her mug in the sink, then turned to Scout. "You know, we talked about my running problem but not about your hiding problem."

"See, that's where we're different. I don't think hiding is a problem."

Lane didn't necessarily agree, but there were only so many battles she could fight in one day. Still, she had to ask. "Where are you going to hide when the person you're hiding from lives in the same town?"

"This house. I mean he wouldn't come here, right? The stadium, sure. But it's not like he's going to walk up the front steps and ring the doorbell. Right?"

Lane shook her head. "I don't know. You knew him better than I did."

Scout nodded confidently. "I'm right. I'm sure I'm right."

THE DOORBELL RANG at an unusual hour of the day and the irony wasn't lost on Scout. Hadn't she tempted fate this morning? Shaking her head at the sudden onslaught of crazy thoughts, she used some sound logic and realized the mailman was probably dropping off a package or something. Refusing to believe it could be anyone else, she didn't bother to look out the window near the door.

It wasn't the mailman.

"Hey, Scout."

It was strange because she'd been practicing her greeting ever since she heard he was coming back. Over and over. She had prepared speeches about them being able to work together. She had practiced scenarios in which she pretended she barely remembered him. Her favorite was the completely friendly greeting when she seemed so carefree and untouched that he never for a second suspected he'd taken her heart with him when he left for Texas.

"You going to say something?"

Damn, she'd already lost her window of opportunity for the carefree and untouched approach. The longer her silence dragged out the more dramatic the moment was becoming and she definitely didn't want drama. Not with Jayson.

"Hi."

There. That was something. A noise. It sounded a little breathy and squeaky, but it was considered a general greeting.

"Can I come in?"

In? In! No, he couldn't come in. If he came in, then there would definitely be nowhere to hide. No place to take shelter from the Jayson LaBec storm. But if she said something like "I would rather you didn't. If we have to speak, let's do it on the porch," then that would mark them as hostile enemies. Then he would know how raw her emotions about him still were and she didn't want to give him that satisfaction.

"Sure."

More sound. This time with a little more breath. She opened the door wider and watched as he stepped into the living room. He wasn't tall, maybe only a few inches taller than her five-foot-five. He wasn't handsome—probably not to anyone but her.

His broken face, which had been put back together by plastic surgeons, still didn't look exactly right.

The famous play, when the rookie gave everything he had, including running into the wall to catch the ball, had cost Jayson a broken nose, two broken cheekbones and two weeks in an induced coma so the swelling could subside enough for the damage to be repaired.

Scout hadn't known him back then, but she had certainly known about his feat. Some called his actions ridiculous. After all, who would sacrifice life and limb for a game? But some fans thought he was a hero.

Stupidly, Scout was one of those fans. He'd held on to the ball, even after the collision.

He didn't look much different now than when he had left. Maybe a little tanner. He was originally from New Orleans so it was possible he had preferred the heat of Texas to the mostly cool springs and harsh winters in the Northeast. He'd never really said.

Funny. There was a time Scout had thought she knew everything there was to know about Jayson. But whether he liked the weather here wasn't one of those things.

It made her sad.

"Where is Duff?"

Good, she thought, he's got questions. Questions she could answer. "At the stadium."

So Jayson hadn't gone there first. Instead he'd come here. To her home. A thousand crazy thoughts about what that meant raced through her head.

"Good, because I was hoping we could talk alone."

"Why?" Scout winced. That came out too sharply. She'd been taken off guard by his statement. He had come to the house first. He asked to come inside. He was happy that Duff wasn't here because he wanted them to talk.

Alone.

Maybe he felt the impact of this reunion, too. Maybe this wasn't easy for him, either. He certainly hadn't led with the "Hey, Scout. Good to see you again. Long time no talk" approach.

No, he looked very serious and very somber.

Wait...*somber*? This wasn't about her then. This wasn't about their past or their failed relationship. Or why he left her and why he'd decided to come back.

This was about Duff.

"It's about Duff," Jayson said.

Damn, she hated when she was right all the time.

"What about him?" Scout asked, crossing her arms over her chest.

Jayson dropped his gaze to her arms and, suddenly, she felt ridiculous. She uncrossed them and stuck her hands into her back pockets.

"Are we going to do this the easy way or the hard way?"

Scout blinked. That was Jayson's thing, what he always said. The easy way or the hard way. He'd said it the first time they made love. She remembered the goofy smile on his face, the tenderness in his eyes. She'd been so crazy for him. So absolutely over-her-head in love with him that the sex had freaked her out. Like she couldn't possibly be good enough for him, or sexy enough for him. He'd taken her hands in his and kissed them, looked right into her eyes and asked, "Are we going to do this the easy way or the hard way? Because this first time I think I would prefer the easy way. Don't get me wrong, the hard way's fun, too."

"Scout?"

She blinked again and wondered if there was some small dark place where she could get to quicker than he could find her. She doubted it. She was fast but so was he.

"I'm not sure what you mean."

There, that sounded reasonable. Not like some heartbroken woman who couldn't imagine that the person standing across from her would ever use that expression in any other context with her ever again.

"Scout, I've been hearing rumors and I want to hear the truth. From you. Is there something wrong with Duff? Something I need to know about?"

"He's seventy-five years old. He takes naps sometimes. Is that what you're asking?"

Jayson sighed. "I want to know why I was called up after the start of the season to be his assistant."

"Shouldn't you be asking the Rebels' GM that question?"

"Scout, I don't want to do this."

"Do what?"

"Play this game. Not with you. I decided to come here because I got the sense Duff was in trouble. And no matter how hard it is for me to be standing here right now, there is nothing I wouldn't do for that man. He practically gave me my life back."

"It's hard for you to be standing here?"

His jaw dropped and Scout was reminded of how easily she could drive him crazy. Because when it came to him, she never assumed anything. She never tried to guess what he was thinking. Because she never wanted to think something wonderful was going to happen, only to be disappointed.

For instance, maybe it was only hard for him to stand here because he'd thought when they finally called him up, it would be for a bigger role than assistant manager. Maybe it was hard to stand here because his girlfriend was waiting in the car and he thought that might be awkward for Scout.

"Yes, it's hard!"

She remembered that when he yelled, his Southern accent became a little more pronounced.

"I mean, jeezus on crutches, Scout. You think there is any way I would take this job if it wasn't about helping Duff? You think I like this? Standing here in front of you, looking at you. You think this is fun for me?"

Scout winced at that. He'd been mad when he left. She remembered that vividly. So mad at her. She had been mad, too, because she hadn't wanted him to leave. She never understood why it was so obvious to him that she was wrong to not follow him, while he was right to leave.

"You're still mad at me," she whispered. Of all the scenarios she imagined, the ones where he'd moved on, the ones where he said they could be friends, the ones where they treated each other with casual indifference, Scout didn't think she had ever imagined this one.

"Yes, I'm still mad at you," he said, his hands now on his hips. "Four flippin' years and I walk in here and you've got your arms crossed and spout your one-word answers and yes, I realize I am still just as mad at you. However, I'm stuck here because this is where the Rebels say I need to be. You understand I'm on a path, right? You know where I'm going?"

Scout nodded. She knew where he was going. She wanted to tell him how proud she was of him. She wanted to hear him say "thank you" in person.

"I cannot mess this up."

"You won't," she said confidently. "You'll be great. Duff's just tired a lot. You'll see. He could really use the help. I'm sure he's probably thinking this is his last season."

"Do you know that?"

No. Scout didn't know anything. She thought about telling Jayson. Just opening her mouth and spilling all her fears and all her heartache on his shoulders. Then maybe he'd pull her into his arms and everything that had been wrong in the past four years would be right again.

But she didn't. Because he said it wasn't easy to look at her and he was still mad and that meant there was no magical fix. He'd come because he thought Duff was in trouble. He was loyal and good like that.

Scout couldn't pretend this reunion was anything more than that.

"He hasn't said it absolutely, but I know it's getting harder to keep up with the young guys. Everyone on the team now is 'kid' because he can't remember their names. I think he's ready to walk away."

Jayson nodded thoughtfully. "Okay. I mean, I guess if they want me to help him finish out the season, it might make the transition next season easier. I was just surprised they pulled me up so early. Then I heard some rumors..."

"GMs." Scout shrugged. "Who knows what they're thinking? And sometimes rumors are just rumors."

She wondered what he would think when he saw Duff. It had been four years since Jayson had seen him, although Scout knew they had talked on the phone during that time. When Jayson had left for Texas he made one thing clear—his departure meant the end of his relationship with her, but not his relationship with Duff. She would have to accept that.

And she had. Grudgingly. After all, Duff was *her* father. As long as he never mentioned Jayson's name or said what they had talked about, she could pretend it wasn't happening.

She could also pretend she wasn't sometimes listening outside Duff's office door when they were talking just to hear one side of a conversation Jayson was having. Even if she couldn't hear him.

"Okay. I'm heading over to the stadium now, get reacquainted with everyone." He paused. Scout could see it in his face, his put-together-again face, that this hadn't been easy for him. Anger had seemed to fade into awkwardness and that made her even sadder.

She and Jayson had never been awkward around each other. Except for that first time they had made love. She'd been such a ninny. A real girly-girl ninny.

In hindsight it might have been easier if she had told him it was her first time.

"How are Pete and Jocelyn?"

"Good. Real good." Since thinking about them made Scout think about their wedding, which made her think about that night with Jayson, she found there really wasn't anything more she wanted to say about them.

Jayson nodded. "Okay, then, I'll be on my way."

"Wait," Scout said, reaching out to grab his arm. He wore a short-sleeve polo shirt and she could feel the faint blond hairs on his arm. She pulled her hand back as if the contact was too much to bear.

"Now there's a word I've waited a long time for you to say."

Scout wasn't sure how to respond to that and Jayson was clearly annoyed for having said anything.

"What, Scout?"

"It's about my job. I've basically been running a lot of the operations for Duff. While he's been focused on the players and game-day management."

"Well, I imagine that will become my responsibility now."

Scout bit her lip. She would not cry in front of him. She'd bite through her lip before she did that. "So, I'm guessing that means you want me gone."

"Gone?"

"Fired. You're firing me."

"Oh, hell, Scout. I'm not firing you. You're the

best damn judgment of talent on the East Coast. You think I don't know that? You think I don't realize I got to where I am because of everything you taught me?"

Nope, she thought. She would not cry. No matter what, she couldn't do that in front him, because she was sure if she started, she wouldn't stop.

"You'll go back to doing what you do best."

Breathing deeply through her nose, she nodded. "Okay."

He leaned toward her. "I wouldn't do that to you. I wouldn't come here and take this away from you. You know that, right?"

She did. Jayson would never be so cruel no matter how angry he was with her.

It wasn't a question of him taking it from her, she thought. It was more a question of her being able to handle working for him. She still wasn't sure.

"You go to the stadium. Duff will be excited to see you."

Then I can go hide in my bedroom and cry in private.

"I'll see you around, Scout."

"Yep." Not unless he planned to crawl into her closet because, the way she felt right now, hiding in her bedroom wasn't going to be enough. This level of anxiety called for a closet.

Nope, she didn't have a problem. Not at all.

CHAPTER EIGHTEEN

"Roy, LET ME IN," Lane called through the door as she continued to knock.

"Go away."

"Seriously? You're going to stay mad at me just because you're in denial about your arm."

Suddenly the door opened and he stepped onto the porch looking around as if to check that no one had heard her.

"I don't think there are any Rebels scouts hiding in the bushes."

Roy cocked his eyebrow. "You're calling me out for being in denial? You've been in denial about us for years."

"You're right. In the end, look where it got us— five years older and still fighting about the wrong stuff. See, this is me standing on your porch, knocking on your door. This is me not running in the opposite direction. So the least you can do is meet me halfway."

He went back inside, leaving the door open for her. She shut the door behind her and followed Roy to the living room, where he sat on the couch with his head in his hands.

"Look, Lane, I get this is you trying. And part of me is crazy excited by that because I know how hard this for you."

"Do you, Roy?" Lane asked as she stood in front of him. "Do you know I stopped believing in things like happily-ever-after? Do you know I've gone into every first date for the past five years thinking that I wouldn't let it get beyond three or four dates? Right out of the gate I put this ending on it so I knew it would never get that far."

"Because Danny hurt you."

"Because you hurt me! Because you made me realize that I picked the wrong guy. Because you made me see what an idiot I had been. But, of course, I could never be with you. Because that would make it official. Like I had left Danny for you. Thank God, you set me up at that party and gave me a reason to hate you, otherwise everyone might have known how I felt about you. So yes, this is hard. Five-years-of-denial hard. But I'm here and I'm doing it and it's for you. You can't push me away the first time I say something you don't like."

He lifted his head and she could see in his eyes the fear that was eating him up inside. She kneeled between his legs.

He cupped her cheek in that way of his she liked.

Liked the idea that he could see his left hand was good for something other than holding a ball.

"I didn't mean to push you away. I need you to understand I have to do this. I need to know you believe I can do it. I want you to have faith in me. Believe in me. You have to know it makes a difference when I'm out there."

"Okay." She wanted to tell him that belief and faith couldn't fix a messed-up shoulder, but she could acknowledge that her doubt wouldn't change anything. If he wanted her to be on his side, then she would be on his side.

"Okay?"

"I get that I can't stop you," she admitted. "I realize you need to see this out and I'll be there for you while you do. But I need to know what happens after tomorrow."

"After tomorrow I get a one-year deal to pitch for a team making a run at the playoffs. After tomorrow I go back to doing what I'm supposed to do and I get control of my life."

"If that doesn't happen? Not that I don't have faith in you. I do. This is just a what-if."

His whole body tensed. She could practically feel the muscles in his legs tighten around her.

"It will happen. There can't be any other outcome."

"You're more than a pitcher, Roy. I know you

don't believe that, but I see in you all the things you are. I guess that's all I wanted you to know."

She looked at him and knew he doubted her. Duff had said she would be the one to give Roy his swagger back. Now Lane knew it was more than that. It wasn't about his confidence in himself as a ballplayer. It was about his confidence in himself as a man.

Lane figured there was one sure way to boost a man's confidence in himself. She stood and started to unfasten the buttons of her sleeveless blouse.

"What are you doing?"

"I'm getting naked." Lane shucked the blouse then reached for the button and zipper on her cutoff jean shorts.

"Don't get me wrong, I applaud the idea. But if this is some kind of pity f—"

"Don't say that," she said, cutting off his words with her finger on his lips. "You said we're doing this thing. You said we're an *us*. So this is me getting naked after a fight as a way to make up with you. As a way for me to say no matter what happens tomorrow, I'm not running."

She undid the front clasp of her bra and then shimmied quickly out of her panties. A seductive stripper she was not. But standing naked in his living room while he was still fully clothed was probably the most vulnerable she'd allowed herself to be since the day she got married.

Roy stood and wrapped his right arm around her back, pressing her against his fully clothed body. Like he, too, recognized the power imbalance and wanted to savor it for a moment. The feel of his jeans rubbing against her thighs, and his T-shirt brushing her breasts were strangely erotic. As though she was here only for his pleasure. To make him happy.

To make him hard.

Oddly enough, that made her feel like the powerful one instead of the vulnerable one.

Looking up at Roy, she could see his gaze was fixed on her breasts. Then he stepped back and his gaze dropped lower to the place between her legs.

"Now that you have me where you want me," he said drily, "whatever are you going to do with me?"

Right, Lane thought. Because she did have the power. It was so exhilarating, she was greedy for more of it.

"Well, you do have to pitch tomorrow, so we don't want you exerting a lot of energy. I mean, we have to factor in your age."

She pushed on his chest hard enough that he got the idea. He dropped onto the sofa and she, once more, got between his knees.

"Absolutely," Roy agreed with a devilish smile on his face. "If I have to lie back and take it, then that's what I have to do."

"Of course, we don't want any pressure on your

arms so make sure you keep those at your side out of the way."

Roy threw each of them on the top of the sofa. With his arms stretched out, his legs falling open, he might have looked like a man who was about to be drawn and quartered if his smile hadn't grown exponentially larger.

Which wasn't the only thing getting bigger.

"Be gentle with me," he muttered as Lane reached for the button at his waist.

It took a little work between the two of them until his boxer briefs and jeans were tossed over Lane's shoulder and Roy had taken off his T-shirt so that Lane could see her favorite piece of sculpture—a living, breathing, naked Roy Walker.

It was like she couldn't control her hands. They needed to touch him everywhere. His chest, his stomach, the inside of his thighs, the back of his calves. And the whole time, he kept his hands gripping the cushions, purposefully turning control over to her.

She loved it. Loved the freedom she had to do anything that might make him groan in pleasure. A gentle bite on the inside of his thigh. A quick lick of the top of his ridiculously hard cock. It jutted out from his body like this fierce thing that demanded to be served, but since Lane was in control it would have to wait until she was ready.

"Lane, you're killing me."

"Really, is it bad?" she asked, knowing it wasn't when she brushed his balls with her knuckles making his whole body shift and strain.

"So bad. So, so, so bad. Please don't stop."

Lane cupped his heavy sac in her hand, his poor erection straining for some equal attention. Now Roy truly did look like a man being tortured on the rack—in the most delicious way.

"Lane, please."

It was almost cruel to make a man as proud as Roy beg. Really, Lane shouldn't be having anywhere near as much fun as she was. Finally, she gave him what she knew he needed, taking the head of his cock inside her mouth as deep as she could.

The sound of his low deep groan echoed in his living room and gave Lane her own thrill of excitement. She was completely and thoroughly aroused and had this urge to touch herself between her legs even as she continued to work Roy's hard penis in and out of her mouth. She didn't want the distraction of her pleasure to ruin this, not when she was completely confident that he would make sure she had her own turn.

This was for him. She curled one hand on top of his thigh, her nails digging in just enough for that hint of pain to add to his frenzy. While her other hand stroked the base of his erection as she used her tongue to play with him until he was thrusting his hips. Pressing deeper into her mouth, unable to stop the driving urgency of his body.

"Lane, go get a condom. Get on top of me."

Sit on Roy's lap. Ride him. Yes, that would be fun, but not this time. This was her making up to him.

She sucked him harder and he nearly whimpered until he must have understood that she intended to finish him this way. It was as if his body gave up the struggle. She felt his hand in her hair tugging. Not to pull her away, but to let her know he was there. She could sense the heat of him, the tension in him, the need in him.

Then the pleasure. He cried out and she stayed with him taking him in, enjoying his release almost as much as he was.

Then all that tension and heat faded and he sprawled on the couch, limp and sedate. Lane kissed his stomach, then his chest and then crawled up his body until she was in his lap, her head resting on his shoulder.

Like some innocent kitten who didn't even realize what she'd done to wreck a man as thoroughly as Roy Walker.

"Am I forgiven, then?" she asked sweetly even as she nibbled his earlobe.

"For, like, ever."

Lane chuckled.

"But, Lane, you know it wasn't all your fault. I purposefully didn't call you last night."

"I know."

"As your boyfriend—yes, I said the word *boyfriend*, which feels ridiculous but I'll go with it for now—that was really poor behavior on my part."

Lane smiled and kissed his neck, knowing exactly where he was taking this.

"It was. Whatever will you do to make it up to me?"

She could feel Roy shift, moving her so that she was on the couch and he was on his knees in front of her. The sight alone was enough to overcome her with anticipation.

"Be gentle with me," she said, repeating his words.

As he lifted her thighs over his broad shoulders so that her feet dangled down his back, she could see his devilish smile return.

"Sorry, sweetheart, that's not going to happen. You better hold on for the ride."

No, it wasn't gentle. Instead it was a monsoon of feeling and quite possibly the best ride of Lane's life.

SCOUT LOOKED AT the paperwork on the desk and struggled to summon any enthusiasm to tackle it. She was still rattled by her meeting with Jayson earlier that afternoon. None of the work was super important, just the everyday tasks of running a minor-league team.

Player evaluation forms, spreadsheet updates that tracked all the guys' statistics, employer applications that had to be filled out for the foreign players with green cards. Of course, the hardest part of the job was determining which players were washing out—who weren't making it to The Show, who needed to move on so the guys from Single-A and Double-A could move up and have their chance.

All of the work that typically fell into the hands of the manager, but Scout had been handling it for over a year now.

Now it would be Jayson's job. Jayson, who she would have to see every day. Or maybe not. If he meant what he'd said about putting her back in the role she was best at, that meant she would start scouting again. Scouting meant traveling.

Something she couldn't do with Duff in the shape he was in. Jayson would have to realize that. Maybe he wouldn't see how bad Duff's condition was, but he would certainly see that a man Duff's age needed to have someone look out for him. Scout couldn't do that if she was scouring every high school up and down the East Coast looking for talent.

Unless, of course, Lane truly intended to stick it out in Minotaur Falls.

Suddenly, Scout was seized by an irrational burst of anger. She had always taken care of Duff. She had stayed with him after the divorce, not dividing her time between her traitorous mother and father the way Lane had.

It wasn't fair that Lane got to come back now and take over everything.

Scout grimaced as she remembered that she had purposefully asked Lane to come home. Scout wanted her to stay home, too. As much as they squawked at each other, having her sister close while she dealt with Duff and then Jayson's return had been nice. Like having a support system where before the weight of everything had fallen on her shoulders. No, she didn't want Lane to leave. But Scout didn't want to start traveling, either.

Would Jayson fire her, then? Would she be handing him the excuse he needed to get rid of her so his days weren't filled with her awkward presence?

Sorry, Scout, I just don't see any other place for you in this organization. Unless you'd consider an administrative role?

Translation: glorified secretary. A position that had nothing to do with the actual game of baseball. Nothing to do with the decision-making process about who was advancing and who wasn't, evaluating talent and knowing she was dead-on right when she did it.

Those were her real skills. Not booking hotels or arranging buses for the team. All that stuff was important, too. Forget that they already had people in those positions, for Scout it would be taking a major step backward in her career.

That meant her only option would be to find a new job. A new life. Something not connected to baseball.

Would there be any reason left to exist?

"Hey, kiddo. What are you doing?"

Scout lifted her head at her father's voice. The sound seemed to instantly break through the hysterical drama happening in her head.

"Worrying for nothing."

Duff smiled. He loved to tease her about that. All his girls loved to worry for nothing. A trait he never specifically blamed on their mother but would declare adamantly they hadn't gotten from him.

"Well, stop that. It causes wrinkles."

"I'll try."

"Saw your boy just now. We had a good meeting of the minds."

"He's not my boy, Duff," Scout said tightly. "We broke up, remember?"

Because he left. Not because she wouldn't go. Scout was certain that had been the case. She had been wronged.

Then why does he still seem so angry with me?

"I remember. Like it was yesterday. Hadn't seen so many tears from your eyes since the day you left your mother's womb. My goodness you were shook up."

"Thanks for the reminder. But we saw each other earlier today. He came to the house. It's fine. It will be fine."

Duff nodded, his hands tucked into the pockets of his uniform pants. There was a game tonight, but Scout knew that Duff sometimes chose to wear his uniform from the start of the workday regardless of the game time. He joked that when he died he wanted to be buried in a uniform.

Suddenly the joke didn't seem so funny. Just like the one about dying at the stadium was no longer amusing.

"Well, that's good. I told him how important you are to the team. Wouldn't want to let hard feelings get in the way of that. On either side."

"What did he say?" Scout asked, then bit the inside of her lip, waiting for that answer.

"Agreed with me completely. He's no dummy. He knows what you can do. Hell, if you hadn't been born a girl, you and I both know it would be you in that chair getting ready to take over for me."

"Do you ever regret that, Duff? That one of us hadn't been born a boy and could have followed in your footsteps. Helped continue your legacy."

He frowned and Scout knew she'd upset him. It wasn't the first time she asked the question. She was ten when Duff had found her hiding behind a tree crying. She'd gone to the baseball diamond where all the Little League players who had been drafted by the different coaches were gathering together to see their teams for the first time.

At first she hadn't understood why no one had drafted her. She was one of the best pitchers for her age and everyone knew it. Her mother had to tell her the hard truth that she wasn't allowed to move up to the next level because she was a girl. Because her mother wouldn't let her continue to play with the older boys.

Girls play softball because girls are soft.

Matty Warner had informed her when he'd seen her standing on the sidelines looking longingly at the teams. Still reeling from the idea that her baseball career was over, she might have punched him in the nose if she hadn't been so terribly heartbroken.

I don't want to play softball! I want to play baseball! Why couldn't I have been a boy?

Scout remembered so clearly how angry Duff had been.

Because you're my Scout! My perfect baby girl and I wouldn't have you any other way. Don't ever say something like that. That you wish you were someone else or something else. Because I love you the most just the way you are.

He had taken her to get ice cream, but, of course, he had a game to manage that night. That was when he'd been in the majors. Scout had sat in the special family booth upstairs with her binoculars watching every moment of every play. Sometimes she liked the distance to get a broad view of the game. Some-times she liked to sit behind home plate. It didn't matter. As long as she was at the game. As long as Duff was somewhere in the stadium with her, then it seemed like everything was okay in the world, even if she was a girl.

"Now why would you say a thing like that?" Duff asked. "You know I wouldn't have you any other way. You're my baby girl."

Were his eyes red? Did she hear a slight hitch in his breath?

"I know, Dad. I know. It just sucks that I'll never be a manager."

"You don't know that," he said gruffly. "World is changing every day. I mean, they've got instant replay in baseball for Pete's sake. If that's possible, then anything is possible."

Scout laughed.

"I'm going to go lie down a bit before the game."

"Sounds like a plan," Scout said.

"Then we should talk about how we're going to work everything out with you and Jayson and what each of you should be responsible for."

"Jayson and I can handle that. You don't need to worry about any of it."

Duff nodded and Scout could see the relief in his eyes. Probably happy he wouldn't have to be in a room with the two of them together. His beloved daughter and his groomed successor.

Who hated each other.

Or, if not hated each other, just didn't love each other anymore.

At least she was sure Jayson didn't love her. No, he was angry with her, which was wrong considering he'd been the one to leave her. She was supposed to be the angry one.

"You'll wake me thirty minutes before the game?"

He'd been doing that lately. Power napping until the last possible minute. Then he'd splash water on his face and make his way to the field in time for the National Anthem.

"Sure, Duff. Go check those eyelids out."

He chuckled, then headed to his office.

He said the doctor had told him everything was fine. Scout didn't believe it, but it wasn't like she could keep nagging when he'd done what she'd asked. So the future was unknown. Given everything that had happened in the past few weeks, Scout decided that was about as good as she could hope for.

After all, there really was no point in worrying for nothing.

CHAPTER NINETEEN

ROY REMEMBERED THINKING that his arm felt great when he woke up the next morning. Days of rest, hours of therapy from Lane and anti-inflammation medication were a perfect combination to cure what ailed him. Not to mention a sexual marathon with Lane that had left his body feeling loose and good all over.

He remembered being excited to put on his uniform. This was a big game for him. Maybe not a Game Seven of the World Series, but in terms of the impact on his life, this could be the most important game he'd ever pitched.

He remembered throwing to Javier during warmup thinking his fastball was zinging, which meant his changeup would be devastating. He was Roy Walker. He'd pitched to the best, had beaten the best. These were Triple-A hitters and he was going to crush them.

"You own them. Every last one of them," he said to his arm. "Go out there and remind them who you are."

He'd jogged to the mound. Kicked around the

dirt a little to let it all settle in and didn't once think about the scouts in the stands, or Lane, or anything other than what he had to do that day.

He remembered thinking as he threw that first pitch that today was going to be a great day.

He stopped thinking that after the first inning.

"How you feeling, Roy," Harry asked him.

"Fine."

"You're pace is a little slow. You sure everything is okay?"

"Did anyone get a hit that inning?" he asked, snapping at his pitching coach. He could see Duff, who was farther down the bench, lift his head to look at him, but Duff didn't say anything.

"Nope."

"Then there is your answer." Roy had a towel wrapped around his left arm, as was his habit to keep it warm between innings. He sat on the top of the bench and sipped Gatorade until the nausea in his stomach subsided.

Nausea caused by the piercing pain that rippled through his body after every pitch he threw.

Lane was right. Something was wrong. He thought about telling Duff. Billy would need to get warmed up sooner than planned. Right now he was slated to pitch the second half so he wouldn't start to throw until the third inning.

Plus the kid had been nervous as hell in the locker room before the game. Roy had this crazy idea of sitting with him, maybe distracting him a bit. Then he remembered the two of them were auditioning tonight and no one knew how many parts were available to hand out.

He could have told the kid that his adrenaline rush would cause him to overpower the ball. That he should start with firing heat because his fastball would be unhittable. Only that was Harry's job.

Harry, who probably didn't remember what that adrenaline rush could do to a body.

Instead, Roy said nothing. Just sat in front of his locker, going through his normal routine until the kid finally approached.

"Hey, man, good luck."

"You never wish the competition luck, kid. It shows weakness."

"You're not the competition. You're a teammate."

Roy shook his head and gave him a hard stare that probably threw the kid for a loop after the weeks of camaraderie between them. "Tonight, I'm the competition."

"Yeah. Whatever."

Now the kid was out in the bullpen probably wasting all his energy crossing and uncrossing his legs a thousand times. A nervous habit Roy had noticed. Or maybe Billy was talking shit about Roy. Reminding the other guys what an asshole he really was. How, now that he'd hooked up with Lane, he'd reverted to his old ways of going it alone.

At least his anger toward Roy would take his mind off what was coming up for him.

Coming up for him sooner than he expected.

"No, you will do this," Roy muttered to his arm. "This is our last chance."

He could play through pain. He'd done it before and he'd finished that inning without giving up a hit. Three more innings and that's all the scouts would need to see. Then Duff would bring in the kid.

Roy watched the Minotaurs' third batter strike out. A three-up, three-down inning. It was time to go back to work. He threw off the towel and picked up his glove. In seconds he was on the mound and looking at the next batter. Some big whale of a guy the Trenton, New Jersey, team had just called up.

Javier called for a curveball.

Roy shook him off.

A changeup. Fine, Roy thought, the batter would probably be expecting speed. He wound up, threw the ball and tried not to wince as the pain shot down his arm, his back and his neck.

Strike.

"Do not do this to me," he told the arm. "We need this. This is all we are and they are watching right now."

Javier called for the curveball again. No doubt he'd done some scouting on the batter and knew he couldn't handle a major-league curveball.

Roy shook him off. The curveball was how this had started. The way he had to release the ball put pressure on his shoulder. He couldn't chance throwing it and being able to control his reaction to the pain.

Javier changed the signal to a cutter. Roy threw it, but bounced it over the plate.

One ball, one strike.

A fastball. This he could throw. He fired away and while the pain was intense he could manage it.

One ball, two strikes.

The key was to get out of these innings quickly. The fewer pitches he threw, the less damage he could do to the arm. Then he would take Lane's advice and see a doctor. Even if the scouts liked what they saw, he would have to have a physical. If he could get into a doctor before that, maybe fix whatever was broken without anyone knowing, then he still had a chance. The plan was still in play. He just needed to get through these next three outs. Then six more after that.

Then he could claim he had the flu or some other ailment to skip his next few starts.

"You got this," he muttered to his arm, letting the pain recede before he got into position.

Javier called for the curveball. It made sense. He needed only one more strike. Deciding to risk it for the out, Roy wound up and let it rip. The pain was sharp, so mind-numbing he almost fell to his knees.

Instinctively he tried to grip his left shoulder with his right hand as if assuring himself that the arm was still attached.

The batter had swung and missed. Strike three. He was out. But so was Roy.

Not realizing there was a problem, Javier tossed the ball to Roy. He caught it in his mitt, and transferred the ball to his left hand. He could grip it, but he couldn't lift his arm to throw it.

He looked at the useless appendage. He wanted to rail at it, wanted to curse it, wanted to explain in graphic detail how thoroughly it had just hosed them both. Only he couldn't. Looking at it now, it was like some sad, old dog, who had done everything his master had asked but had finally broken down.

Every pitcher knew there were only so many bullets in the gun. Roy had just thrown his last one. At least it had been for a strike.

He turned and saw Duff, not Harry, coming to the mound. Duff must have seen something in the delivery or known based on Roy's body language.

"Looks like you're in a bit of pain out here, Roy."

"I can't lift my arm. It's completely numb."

Duff nodded. He made the signal to the bullpen to get Billy warming up. For an injury situation Billy would have all the time he needed.

"Well, you gave it your best shot," Duff said with

an easy shrug. As if the end of someone's second chance was an everyday occurrence.

"Tell the kid, I said...good luck."

"Will do."

"Duff, thanks for giving me a chance at this. Playing ball again. Maybe a shot being what I was again. But more than that, thanks for reminding me what I loved about the game. I know you didn't have to do any of that. I appreciate it."

Duff tilted his head back and laughed. Roy thought this wasn't the most inspiring manager-pitcher meeting on the mound.

"Roy Walker, I didn't give you a second chance at baseball. Hell, I knew the odds of you coming back were a million to one. My God, son, you're thirty-seven years old. What did you think was going to happen to your arm when you started throwing again?"

If Roy hadn't loved the man so much, he might have decked him. With his right arm, of course, because he couldn't lift his left. "Then what the hell was this all about? Were you setting me up to fail?"

"No, son, like I said, there was that million-to-one shot. Bringing you back wasn't really for a second chance at baseball. It was for a second chance at her." Duff turned and pointed to the seats just over the first baseline. Lane was standing near the rail over the dugout. He could see from here how worried she was.

For him.

"Without baseball, without a future, am I good enough for her?" Roy didn't see how he could be.

"See, just because you ask that question, makes me think you are. Don't screw up. Now, let the ball go, son, it's time to move on with your life."

Roy opened his hand and the ball dropped and rolled into the grass.

He turned and walked toward the dugout and when he got close, he saw she was crying. Once again he made Lane Baker cry.

"You were right," he called up to her.

"I'm sorry I was."

He nodded, then headed to the lockers. As long as he didn't move his arm, the pain wasn't so bad. He wanted to take a quick shower then spend the rest of the game on the dugout bench watching Billy.

Because that's what a good teammate did.

Then he would probably have to head to the hospital since he was pretty sure his arm was only hanging on by a thread.

THE NEXT DAY Lane sat in a chair near Roy's hospital bed and listened as the orthopedic surgeon broke down the details of Roy's injury. A severe tear in the rotator cuff would require surgery to repair. Also, the pain he'd been feeling was mostly coming from an inflamed bursa that would need to be removed. Not to mention the bone spurs that had formed that the doctor would shave down. Then with enough time for healing and physical therapy he should get back his full range of motion. There would most likely always be some weakness in the arm, but the numbness he was experiencing now would improve.

Of course, he would never pitch professionally again, but he'd be able to pitch a Little League game in about a year.

"Swell," Roy said.

"It could have been worse," the doctor said.

"No, Doc, it couldn't have been."

The surgery could be scheduled as early as the next morning. Since Roy knew any chance he had of pitching again was over, there was no point in getting a second opinion or finding some top-flight specialist to operate on him.

The word was already out that he was having rotator cuff surgery. He'd listened to Mike and Mike talk about it all morning. Next year Roy would be thirty-eight, and no team would take a chance on a pitcher coming back from that.

"Your dad called," Lane told him once they were alone. She held up his cell as if to suggest she had no problem answering it.

"Devastated, I'm sure." They would have to talk about it. Roy would have to tell his father that this time his career was well and truly over. No second chances. No comebacks. He hoped his old man didn't cry. That would be uncomfortable.

"More worried, I think. He's coming to see you and I told him I thought that was a good idea. He'll be here in a few days."

"You really think you can fix us, don't you?"

Lane smiled. "I think I should try. That's what a good girlfriend—and yes, I said the word *girlfriend*—would do."

Roy leaned his head against the pillow. "I think we need to talk."

All night and all day, laying in the hospital bed, he'd been thinking about what their future might look like and he couldn't see it. He'd joked about living off her money, but he sure as hell wasn't going to do that. He thought about his idea of becoming a coach, but that seemed like such a far-out scenario that it didn't touch the here and now.

They were two unemployed people in their thirties and one of them was a flat-out failure.

Lane Baker deserved more.

"Don't you do it, Roy. Don't you say what I know you're going to say."

He could hear the hurt and anger in her voice, but he was trying to be reasonable. Logical. Sensible. "I have nothing to offer you."

"Except yourself."

"A has-been baseball player with no money and no prospects. With no skill set to make him suitable

for any other job besides maybe being a car salesman."

"So? Then you'll be a damn good car salesman."

"Lanie, you're not seeing the big picture."

She rose and folded her arms across her body,
leaning over him so he could see her eyes were
practically on fire with her rage.

"Oh, no, I'm seeing the big picture. I'm seeing the Roy Walker who forced me to acknowledge my feelings for him, who then immediately
backed away because we were too messed-up for
each other. But you went on to show me what kind
of person you could be. Which scared me, Roy. Because I really like that person and I didn't think that
would ever happen again for me. I am so scared of
what I feel for you that I put on my running shoes
every damn day. But then I take them off. For you.
I asked you what the plan was after yesterday."

"I told you, there is no plan."

"Then make one."

With that she stormed out of the room and Roy
couldn't help but worry that he was going to disap-
point Duff and screw up this second chance, too.

LANE STORMED DOWN the hallway with this urge to
keep on walking. Go home, get in her car and drive.
Drive until she didn't remember where she came
from anymore.

"Damn it," she cursed under her breath. She

knew this might happen. This was why she had wanted him to think about what might happen if his arm let him down. She wanted some security for his future so he could still see them together. Security because, if she was taking this risk of giving her heart to someone again, something she promised herself five years ago she would never do, then she damn sure wanted to give her heart to someone who would take good care of it.

"We need to talk," she muttered. The words of doom for any relationship. Did he honestly think she would let him get away with that?

It made no sense. How could it be clear as day to him with a contract in his hand, but murky as dishwater without that contract?

Because he only sees himself as a pitcher.

Lane wanted to shake him, she was so angry. How could a man have so much confidence in one area of his life and so little in any other?

It's why he needs me.

The truth of that thought resonated throughout her body. Roy Walker needed her and she knew it. What he needed most from her was the ability to see himself for the man he was. Not the baseball player.

Lane stopped at the end of the hallway. Left or right? Or back the way she came? She didn't think she was ready for that yet. To the right was the nurses' station. The elevator across from it opened and she saw Duff coming out with a man wearing a white coat.

The two of them were talking and, for a second, Lane wondered if the doctor was Roy's surgeon, but the hair color was wrong—it was darker, where Roy's doctor had blond hair. Was this the doctor Duff had seen? It occurred to her this might be the perfect opportunity to ambush Duff. She could ask the doctor her questions directly. What tests he'd run, what actions he'd taken? She would force Duff's hand and make him agree to give her access to his medical records.

Then, finally, she would have some real answers.

"You'll let me know, Duff."

"Will do, Doc. Not quite there yet."

"I just don't want to see you in any pain. There's no reason for it."

"Yep."

"Why are you in pain?" Lane asked. Her plan had been abandoned the moment she'd heard the word *pain*. Pain. A frightening word sinking into her head like a foreign object.

"Has he been to see you?" Lane asked the doctor—Dr. J. Mason according to the badge on his lab coat. When he said nothing, Lane turned back to Duff. "Duff, is this the doctor you saw a few weeks ago? The one you told me said everything was fine?"

"One of my daughters," Duff said to the doctor in lieu of answering Lane's question.

"I'll let you two talk."

The doctor left and Lane watched him go with this sick feeling inside her chest. What did she and Duff need to talk about? Why had he sounded so serious?

Without realizing it was happening, Duff had taken her hand and led her to a couch just inside a lounge area. Where families waited for information about their loved ones. Instinctively, Lane knew she didn't want to be in this room.

That urge to get up and keep walking was powerful, but Duff sat next to her holding her hand and there was no way she could leave him. Not now.

"You didn't see this doctor a few weeks ago," she said because she could see he was having a hard time starting the conversation. "You saw him long before that."

Duff nodded. "A couple of months ago. I just couldn't keep my damn eyes open. Felt weak as a kitten all the time and it was annoying as all heck."

Lane didn't want to ask this next question, didn't want to hear this next answer.

"It's cancer, baby."

Lane nodded. She let the word crash against her like a wave at the beach, then let it recede so she could see it for what it was. *Cancer*. Her father had cancer.

"Okay, Duff. Well, at least we know, right? So we have to start treatment. Chemotherapy and radiation and they've got all these new experimental drugs—"

"No, baby. It's basically filled me up. Liver, pancreas, stomach. All that stuff you're talking about isn't going to cure me. It's just going to make me sick as a dog on the way out. I've decided not to go down that path."

"Duff, there is no other path…"

Lane stopped herself. What he was saying, what he was thinking was unimaginable. He was sick. Of course he was sick. Anyone could look at him and see that he was sick. But he wasn't dying.

Duff couldn't die.

He patted her knee. "I'm seventy-six next month. I've had an amazing life with three beautiful daughters. I don't want to spend my last days puking into some toilet. I just want to relax in my own home and let nature do its thing."

"Duff, you have to fight." The words were soft and broken because even as she said them, she could see that he didn't have strength to fight.

He shook his head. "Lanie, life is a game and every game has to end sometime. The way I look at it, I won. Now it's time to leave the field."

"You're really okay with this decision?"

"*Okay* probably isn't the right word. I'm scared about what's coming. The doctor laid it out for me pretty good. Hospice will be called in to help you girls with the messy stuff and that put my mind at ease a little. Plus I've got some time left. Time to put things right. I'll want Samantha to come home, too."

Yes, Samantha needed to come. She, more than anyone, needed to make sure that she and Duff had made peace before the end. Also, Scout, for as much as she pretended to hate Samantha, would need her. Samantha had a way of keeping Scout from spiraling out of control...

Scout.

"Does Scout know?"

Lane watched her father break. Tears filled his eyes and his lip shook. It took a few minutes, but finally he seemed to be able to get control of himself again.

"Didn't know how to do it. Wanted to wait as long as I could. Sorry I had to lie to you, but a lie seemed easier than the truth," he said gruffly. "Just didn't know how to tell my baby girl. But I guess it has to be done."

Lane nodded as she fought her own tears and, for a time, the two of them sat there, holding hands, saying nothing.

"Hey, guys, there you are. I've been all over the hospital looking for you. I heard about Roy— Jeez," Scout said as she approached. "You both look like hell. Is it that bad? I mean, his arm didn't actually fall off, did it?"

Lane looked at her sister and tried to remember this moment. This moment before Scout learned the truth and knew for certain what the future would bring. Not a vague notion of some day. But finite months until they lost their father.

"He tore the rotator cuff. He needs surgery," Lane told them both. "They're doing it tomorrow morning."

"Look, I get it's a bummer he's not going to have his big comeback, but it's not like he's going to die."

"No," Lane said. "He's not."

Lane looked at her father, who was looking at her. He nodded and she nodded back. It was time.

"What?" Scout asked. "What am I missing?"

Duff stood then, slowly, cautiously, always waiting that extra beat to make sure his legs would support him. His weakness a visceral thing now that Lane knew the truth.

He took his youngest daughter by the hand and started to lead Scout away. He would want to find a private spot. Scout didn't like to cry in front of people. Not even her family.

"Come on, baby girl, I need to tell you something."

Lane watched the two of them walk down the hall and had this urge—no, *need*—to go see Roy. She wanted to lie next to him and have him tell her that everything would be all right even though she knew it wouldn't.

Only Roy wanted them to *talk* and, frankly, Lane didn't think her heart could handle any more pain today. Duff had already broken it.

So instead she went home and waited for her sister and father to join her. Scout would need her there. Roy and their talk would have to wait another day.

CHAPTER TWENTY

ROY WAS WATCHING a baseball game, not entirely sure why he subjected himself to this level of torture, when he heard a knock on the door. Whoever was there wasn't hospital personnel, because they didn't knock.

He had this irrational hope Lane had come back. Mostly because he hated hospitals and preferred her to be sitting with him. She made him feel not so alone. He still hadn't come up with a plan for them so any talking they did probably wouldn't end well.

If he could think of something, just one thing he could do to make him worthy of her... But there was nothing. His left arm hung lifelessly at his side. The one thing that made him special. He'd never been more honest than when he'd told her he had nothing to offer her.

Except you.

Was that enough?

From his earliest memory, his father had been throwing a ball to him, asking Roy to throw it back. He remembered that feeling he got in his stomach every time his dad told his mom about what kind of arm their son had.

You should see this kid throw, Ruthie. I really think he's got something.

Roy had beamed with pride in those early days. Lapped up all the love and attention like a puppy who had just found a home. Then his father told him his new name was Roy. Because Roy was a great baseball name and he was going to be a great baseball player.

And he had been.

Now he wasn't.

"Come in," Roy called out. If it was Lane, she wouldn't have waited for him to respond, she would have come in ready for round two. Whoever it was, Roy decided, he would rather have the company than be stuck with his own thoughts, which sucked right now.

A man who looked vaguely familiar walked into the room. He was average height, maybe a few years younger than Roy and looked like he'd had his nose broken a time or two.

"Roy Walker? I'm Jayson LaBec."

"Oh, right. Duff's new assistant. I'd stand, but the arm has put me out of commission."

"So I heard. Sorry to hear about that."

Roy couldn't shrug without pain, so he did nothing. There were no platitudes in the world to brush over a career-ending injury.

"You know, the reason I left baseball when I did the first time was to avoid this exact scenario," Roy said. "That expression people get on their faces when they are looking at an athlete who they know is done. Half sad, half pity. I never wanted to see that look on anyone's face."

Jayson nodded. "I remember that look, too. Only for me, it didn't come after a long and great career. I have no pity for you, my friend."

"Oh, right, you're the face guy. Sorry."

Jayson pulled up a seat and chuckled. "My claim to fame—being known as the face guy."

"How come you couldn't come back after that? I mean, once the bones healed, what stopped you?"

"It was more than bones healing. My vision was messed up for a while, then the brain, which took a pretty big pop, needed to heal. To this day I get dizzy spells if I run too fast. Not a great thing for an outfielder to play with."

"No. Kind of like a pitcher with no shoulder."

"Kind of like that."

"So, if you're not here to feel sorry for me, then why are you here?"

"I was at the game yesterday. I talked to the two scouts the Rebels sent to watch the game and they were impressed with Billy Madden's progression. Really impressed. Said last time they saw him he didn't have the curveball in his arsenal. I talked to Billy about it and he said you taught him."

"He needed another pitch," Roy said, "if he was going to make it to the majors. I had my reasons for helping him out."

"Both scouts said the same thing. They don't think he's ready yet, but maybe another season in Triple-A and he'll get there. Billy told me to say hi, by the way. Hopes you're feeling better."

"Did he have the sad, pitiful look on his face when he said it?"

"Yep."

Right. Because for him the excitement was just starting. Roy waited for a surge of jealousy or maybe resentment, but neither came. The truth was he was happy for the kid. If he made it, then there was a certain satisfaction in knowing Roy had played a part.

"Well, he needs to sharpen the angle of it a little. He also needs a little more control over his fastball. I told Harry that."

"That's why I'm here. I would like to offer you a job as a pitching coach."

Roy blinked a few times in astonishment. "Jayson, I'm not going to lie, I was thinking maybe I could do something like that in the future. But I don't know if I'm ready to coach at this level. Hell, I've never even coached a Little League team."

Jayson laughed. "Roy, it's not like coming up through the ranks as a player. You don't have to coach Little League, then high school, then Single-A and Double-A. You know more about pitching than most kids at this level will ever know. More importantly, you can explain what you know to someone so that the knowledge transfers. Not all great players can do that. Either they can't teach it or they can't handle the fact that the person they're trying to teach will never do it as well as they did. In a few weeks you turned Billy Madden into a better player. That's a guy I want on my coaching staff."

"Your coaching staff?" The word annoyed Roy. "Last time I checked it was still Duff's team. Duff's staff."

Jayson's face changed, as if a dark cloud passed over it. "You don't know then. I didn't realize. I figured since you were seeing Lane—"

"What don't I know?"

Jayson looked a way for a moment. Then he took a breath. "Duff's retiring. In a couple of weeks. He's giving me time to settle in before I take over as the club's manager." He seemed a little too remorseful at the thought of taking over the top job.

"There's something else. What aren't you telling me?"

"Not my place to tell it. You'll have to talk to Duff."

And Roy would. Suddenly he had this urgent need to call Lane. To hear her voice and know she was okay. It was like some weird, sixth sense. Thinking that she needed him but he was stuck in a hospital bed without the use of an arm. An arm he could be using to hold her.

"Anyway, are you interested? I imagine when Duff steps down, Harry will, too. I think he was just hanging on to support Duff."

A coaching position. Roy Walker. The biggest protector of all his trade secrets and now he would open up and spill the beans about everything. His dad might go apoplectic when he heard. Or maybe not. Maybe he'd be proud to know that Roy was carrying on the family tradition.

The irony was not lost on Roy. "I'm definitely interested."

Jayson smiled then. "Good. You get that arm fixed and we'll talk specifics once you're back on your feet."

Jayson stood as if to leave.

"Hey, can you do me a favor?" Roy asked. "My cell phone is on that table. Can you grab it for me?"

Jayson handed him the phone. Roy waited until the door closed—no need for his future boss to see how pathetic he was over a woman. Or maybe it wouldn't have mattered. Maybe this was what love looked like and people wouldn't think it was pathetic at all.

He fumbled using his right hand but eventually hit Lane's name on his contact list. His disappointment was extreme when it went to voice mail.

After the beep, he paused. He should tell her he was worried about her. He should ask about Duff.

Hell, he should tell her he loved her. Because he did and the knowledge didn't scare him at all. Suddenly it made sense to him. Loving her, being loved by her, had nothing to do with being a baseball player. It had everything to do with being a man. That's why it had always been Lane for him. Why she was different than any other woman he'd known. She had always seen through him. The facade of his badass image. The lone wolf. The stud pitcher.

She had always looked at him and seen him for who he was—Roy Walker the man. The only other person who had ever done that was his mother.

He loved Lane and, because he loved her, that made him worthy of her.

What an idiot he'd been.

"Lanie, please come back. I have a plan."

LANE SAT BESIDE Roy's bed and listened to him snore gently. The doctor had told her the surgery went well and had handed her a list of physical therapists he would need to work with in the next six to eight weeks. Lane smiled politely and tossed the list out.

No one besides her was touching Roy Walker's shoulder. Or the rest of his body, either.

She hadn't gotten his voice mail until this morning as she was driving to the hospital to see him.

That was probably just as well given the emotional toll Duff's news had taken on everybody. Everybody but Duff that is, as he was able to go to sleep and let his daughters deal with the fallout.

Lane had called Samantha and told her the news. She'd said she needed to tie up a few loose ends but would be here as soon as possible. Her lack of emotional response was a nice contrast to the zombie that was now her sister Scout.

Scout hadn't eaten, said anything, or even so much as blinked since learning about their father's terminal cancer. At one point Lane tried to talk to her, to start making plans about how they might best care for Duff in these final months. Scout had gotten up from the table and gone to her room and Lane hadn't seen her since.

Scout was officially in hiding.

Knowing Roy's surgery was scheduled for early in the morning, Lane left the house soon after waking, wanting to be there for Roy when he came out of the anesthesia. By the time she got here, the surgery had already been completed and he'd been moved from post-op to his room.

Eventually his eyes blinked open and he shifted then groaned as if the motion had caused him pain. She stood and put her hand on his right arm. "Hey. Easy there. Try to be as still as you can."

"My arm hurts like a son of a bitch," he mumbled.

She held up a cup filled with water and ice and he took a few sips.

"That's what happens when someone with a knife cuts into it."

"I think I like the numbness better." Roy sighed. "Did the doctor say how it went? They asked me a bunch of questions coming out of the anesthetic, but I wasn't really with it enough to ask about the arm."

"The surgeon said it went well. Nothing out of the ordinary."

"I needed you," Roy said suddenly as if he had just remembered something important.

Lane shrugged. "I'm here."

"No, I needed to tell you something, but there was something else…Duff. What's the matter with Duff?"

"How did you know?"

"Jayson LaBec stopped by. Actually he offered me a job. Said he wanted someone like me on *his* staff."

Lane nodded. Now it made sense. It wasn't some coincidence that Jayson had been called here now. Duff must have told the Rebels' GM about his condition. Setting up all of his little ducks in a row as it were. A good manager making sure all of the necessary pieces were in place for his team to succeed once he was gone.

"He said Duff was retiring. Just giving Jayson a

few weeks to settle in, but I could see something in his face…"

"Duff's not retiring, Roy." Lane braced herself and then just said it. Because it had to be said. There was no hiding from it anymore. "He's dying. He told us last night. It's cancer and he's chosen not to undergo any treatment."

She watched Roy close his eyes and she knew he felt the pain of the news keenly. Especially given what Duff had done for him by giving him a second chance at his career.

"Is he sure? I mean, not even chemo?"

Lane shook her head. "It's too far spread and he doesn't want spend his last days like that. Said he won the game and now it's time to leave the field."

Roy snorted. "Sounds like something he'd say. Damn it, Lane."

"I know."

"How are you holding up?"

Lane shrugged. She wasn't as calm as Samantha apparently was. She wasn't as lost as Scout definitely was. She was just sad. Sad and scared about what came next.

Roy scooched over a few inches and patted the empty space on his right side.

"Roy, I can't. Your arm." Though even as he made the gesture, she knew it was right where she wanted to be.

"Lane, please just this once, do as I ask. I need you and you need me."

Yes, she thought. He was right. She scrambled up on the bed ever so careful of not moving him until she settled against his right side.

"That's better." He sighed.

He was right. It was.

"So what's this plan of yours?" she asked, wondering if he remembered leaving the message on her phone.

"The plan is we're going to be together."

Lane lifted her head. Surprised by his sudden change of mind. She'd figured she would have to pound on his thick skull way longer than that. "But, Roy, you're not a pitcher anymore. Why would I possibly want you?"

He scowled. "You know it makes me sound ridiculous when you say it like that."

"Good. Because you were being ridiculous when you said it. Did you really think you have to be something to be worthy of me? When who you are now is all I ever wanted or needed."

"You know it's not the craziest thing for a man to want to have a little pride," Roy grumbled. "Still, I can concede I was a little bit of an idiot in that regard. I get it now."

"Get what?"

"Why I love you."

Lane gasped. He said it so easily. Like he'd been

saying it for years. It was strange, too, because Lane had thought she would never want to hear those words again. Or if she did hear them, she would never believe in them. Danny had said he loved her all the time when he hadn't. She'd told Danny she loved him, even after she stopped.

She thought love was just a word and really nothing more.

But it didn't sound like just a word when Roy said it. It sounded different to her ears, to her head and to her heart. It sounded like the truest thing anyone had ever said to her.

"Because I do love you, Lane Baker. I love that you know me. I figure if you know the real me and you still like me, well then, that makes me worthy enough for you."

"I do like you," she whispered, settling her head on his chest again.

"I think you more than like me."

Well, if she never thought she would hear the word again from a man, she certainly never thought she would say it to another man. For five years she'd dodged it, ran from it, avoided it at any costs. It was supposed to be the biggest, scariest thing in the world to her. The thought of committing to someone again, of failing someone again? Impossible. Never going to happen.

Only sitting here now in this room with Roy, her ear pressed against his chest, listening to the steady beat of his heart, knowing what was in store for them in the coming months, it felt like the least scariest thing. A kitten instead of a monster. A bunny instead of a rattlesnake.

After all, who was afraid of kittens and bunnies?

"I love you, Roy."

"Yeah, I know. I feel it. I know it scares you, too, so you don't have to say it if you don't want to."

"I don't know. I'm not as scared as I thought I would be." She lifted her head again and looked into his eyes, because she wanted him to know this came from the depth of her soul. "I'm going to try harder than I ever have to not fail you, Roy Walker. I'm not as cocky as I was in the past. I know I can't control everything the future brings, but I promise I'll try as hard as I can."

"Lane, that's part of your problem. You think this is all on you. You think you're the one who fails when something doesn't work out. But we're in this together. We're going to try together."

Lane nodded. *Together*. Okay, she thought. That might work.

"I'm never getting married again," she said. The words popped out of her mouth like some pledge she had learned to recite every morning upon waking up. She'd said it before, but she hoped he understood how serious she was about that.

He cocked his eyebrow and she knew she was

done for. "Sorry, babe. Yeah, you are. In, like, a few weeks."

"A few weeks?"

"We'll both want Duff there. A simple ceremony in the backyard...or even better we'll do it at the stadium. Duff would love that. A wedding in the outfield. I'll still have the sling, but it should make for an interesting story to tell our kids. Wait until they find out they could have been millionaires but I blew it all on video games."

"Kids!" Lane squeaked. There was going to be a wedding. Duff was going to see her marry Roy. There were going to be kids. It seemed like too much happiness in the face of all this sadness that surrounded them.

"Kids. A marriage. A family. That's life, Lanie, and now I can see we wasted five years of it being stubborn. Duff gets it. He knows you only get one shot at it, and that it doesn't last forever. We're not wasting one more minute messing around."

"Roy, I can't get married while my father is dying. It just seems so wrong."

"We'll ask him what he wants. Scout and Samantha, too. Their opinions matter. But I'm pretty sure Duff will tell us he'd rather be there in person."

Lane thought so, too.

"I can't protect you from what's coming," Roy said. "I can't make it any easier. But, if you'll pardon the pun, I can shoulder the burden with you. We'll get through this, Lanie, together."

Lane believed him.

She rested her head on his chest and the two of them shared the silence and the sense of belonging to one another. She was loved and she loved. That love made her stronger not weaker. Like she was capable of anything. Even surviving her father's death.

There was just one thing she had to set straight.

"Roy?"

"Hmm," he said, and she knew he was dozing off again, content that his future was settled.

"I am not getting married on a baseball diamond."

"Come on, it will be fun."

"Not going to happen."

"I'll make Billy the ring bearer. We can sew our wedding rings on to a baseball and he can throw the ball to the pastor when it's time."

"Again, no."

"We'll do it right before a game and then all the fans will be chanting, 'Run, run, run.'"

"Nope."

"Instead of pronouncing us man and wife we can make the pastor say, 'Play ball!'"

"You think you're being funny when you're so not."

Roy chuckled and squeezed her a little closer.

"Our first dance can be to the National Anthem.

We'll serve everyone hot dogs at the reception. You would like that."

"Keep it coming, Walker."

"I plan to, Lanie. I plan to keep it coming for the rest of our lives."

And that, Lane thought, definitely didn't sound scary at all.

* * * * *

Look for the next
THE BAKERS OF BASEBALL *story*
by Stephanie Doyle!
Coming later in 2015
from Harlequin Superromance.

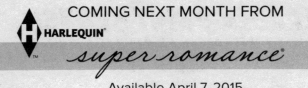

COMING NEXT MONTH FROM

HARLEQUIN®

super romance®

Available April 7, 2015

#1980 TO LOVE A COP
by Janice Kay Johnson

After what Laura Vennetti and her son have been through, she's avoided all contact with the police. Then her son brings detective Ethan Winter into their lives. Immediately Laura can see how different he is from her late husband. And the irresistible attraction she feels toward Ethan tempts her to try again.

#1981 MY WAY BACK TO YOU
by Pamela Hearon

Married too young, divorced too soon? Maggie Russell and Jeff Wells haven't seen each other in years, but as they reunite to move their son into his college dorm, they discover the attraction between them is still present—and very strong. Yet so are the reasons they shouldn't be together...

#1982 THOSE CASSABAW DAYS
The Malone Brothers
by Cindy Homberger

Emily Quinn and Matt Malone were inseparable until tragedy struck. Fifteen years later, Emily returns to Cassabaw to open a café. Matt, too, is back—quiet, sullen and angry after a stint in the marines. Emily's determined to bring out the old Matt. Dare she hope for even more?

#1983 NIGHTS UNDER THE TENNESSEE STARS
by Joanne Rock

Erin Finley is wary of TV producer Remy Weldon. She can't deny his appeal, but Remy's Cajun charm seems to hide a dark pain—one that no amount of love could ever heal. And her biggest fear is that he'll be around only as long as the lights are on...

LARGER-PRINT BOOKS!

GET 2 FREE LARGER-PRINT NOVELS PLUS

2 FREE GIFTS!

◆HARLEQUIN®

Romance

From the Heart, For the Heart

YES! Please send me 2 FREE LARGER-PRINT Harlequin® Romance novels and my 2 FREE gifts (gifts are worth about $10). After receiving them, if I don't wish to receive any more books, I can return the shipping statement marked "cancel." If I don't cancel, I will receive 4 brand-new novels every month and be billed just $4.84 per book in the U.S. or $5.24 per book in Canada. That's a savings of at least 19% off the cover price! It's quite a bargain! Shipping and handling is just 50¢ per book in the U.S. and 75¢ per book in Canada.* I understand that accepting the 2 free books and gifts places me under no obligation to buy anything. I can always return a shipment and cancel at any time. Even if I never buy another book, the two free books and gifts are mine to keep forever.

119/319 HDN F43Y

Name _____ (PLEASE PRINT) _____

Address _____ Apt. #

City _____ State/Prov. _____ Zip/Postal Code

Signature (if under 18, a parent or guardian must sign)

Mail to the **Harlequin® Reader Service:**
IN U.S.A.: P.O. Box 1867, Buffalo, NY 14240-1867
IN CANADA: P.O. Box 609, Fort Erie, Ontario L2A 5X3

Want to try two free books from another line?
Call 1-800-873-8635 or visit www.ReaderService.com.

* Terms and prices subject to change without notice. Prices do not include applicable taxes. Sales tax applicable in N.Y. Canadian residents will be charged applicable taxes. Offer not valid in Quebec. This offer is limited to one order per household. Not valid for current subscribers to Harlequin Romance Larger-Print books. All orders subject to credit approval. Credit or debit balances in a customer's account(s) may be offset by any other outstanding balance owed by or to the customer. Please allow 4 to 6 weeks for delivery. Offer available while quantities last.

Your Privacy—The Harlequin® Reader Service is committed to protecting your privacy. Our Privacy Policy is available online at www.ReaderService.com or upon request from the Harlequin Reader Service.

We make a portion of our mailing list available to reputable third parties that offer products we believe may interest you. If you prefer that we not exchange your name with third parties, or if you wish to clarify or modify your communication preferences, please visit us at www.ReaderService.com/consumerschoice or write to us at Harlequin Reader Service Preference Service, P.O. Box 9062, Buffalo, NY 14269. Include your complete name and address.

HRLP13R

LARGER-PRINT BOOKS!

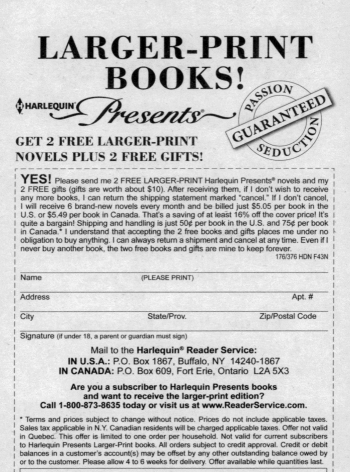

HARLEQUIN *Presents*

PASSION
GUARANTEED
SEDUCTION

GET 2 FREE LARGER-PRINT NOVELS PLUS 2 FREE GIFTS!

YES! Please send me 2 FREE LARGER-PRINT Harlequin Presents® novels and my 2 FREE gifts (gifts are worth about $10). After receiving them, if I don't wish to receive any more books, I can return the shipping statement marked "cancel." If I don't cancel, I will receive 6 brand-new novels every month and be billed just $5.05 per book in the U.S. or $5.49 per book in Canada. That's a saving of at least 16% off the cover price! It's quite a bargain! Shipping and handling is just 50¢ per book in the U.S. and 75¢ per book in Canada.* I understand that accepting the 2 free books and gifts places me under no obligation to buy anything. I can always return a shipment and cancel at any time. Even if I never buy another book, the two free books and gifts are mine to keep forever.

176/376 HDN F43N

Name	(PLEASE PRINT)	
Address		Apt. #
City	State/Prov.	Zip/Postal Code

Signature (if under 18, a parent or guardian must sign)

Mail to the Harlequin® Reader Service:
IN U.S.A.: P.O. Box 1867, Buffalo, NY 14240-1867
IN CANADA: P.O. Box 609, Fort Erie, Ontario L2A 5X3

Are you a subscriber to Harlequin Presents books and want to receive the larger-print edition?
Call 1-800-873-8635 today or visit us at www.ReaderService.com.

* Terms and prices subject to change without notice. Prices do not include applicable taxes. Sales tax applicable in N.Y. Canadian residents will be charged applicable taxes. Offer not valid in Quebec. This offer is limited to one order per household. Not valid for current subscribers to Harlequin Presents Larger-Print books. All orders subject to credit approval. Credit or debit balances in a customer's account(s) may be offset by any other outstanding balance owed by or to the customer. Please allow 4 to 6 weeks for delivery. Offer available while quantities last.

Your Privacy—The Harlequin® Reader Service is committed to protecting your privacy. Our Privacy Policy is available online at www.ReaderService.com or upon request from the Harlequin Reader Service.

We make a portion of our mailing list available to reputable third parties that offer products we believe may interest you. If you prefer that we not exchange your name with third parties, or if you wish to clarify or modify your communication preferences, please visit us at www.ReaderService.com/consumerchoice or write to us at Harlequin Reader Service Preference Service, P.O. Box 9062, Buffalo, NY 14269. Include your complete name and address.

Reader Service.com

Manage your account online!

- Review your order history
- Manage your payments
- Update your address

> ### We've designed
> ### the Harlequin® Reader Service
> ### website just for you.

Enjoy all the features!

- Reader excerpts from any series
- Respond to mailings and special monthly offers
- Discover new series available to you
- Browse the Bonus Bucks catalog
- Share your feedback

Visit us at:
ReaderService.com

RS13